A ROGUE IN ROME

THE GRAND TOURS OF THE ARISTOCRACY
BOOK 4

LINDA RAE SANDE

Twisted Teacup
PUBLISHING

ALSO BY LINDA RAE SANDE

The Daughters of the Aristocracy

The Kiss of a Viscount

The Grace of a Duke

The Seduction of an Earl

The Sons of the Aristocracy

Tuesday Nights

The Widowed Countess

My Fair Groom

The Sisters of the Aristocracy

The Story of a Baron

The Passion of a Marquess

The Desire of a Lady

The Brothers of the Aristocracy

The Love of a Rake

The Caress of a Commander

The Epiphany of an Explorer

The Widows of the Aristocracy

The Gossip of an Earl

The Enigma of a Widow

The Secrets of a Viscount

The Widowers of the Aristocracy

The Dream of a Duchess

The Vision of a Viscountess

The Conundrum of a Clerk

The Charity of a Viscount

The Cousins of the Aristocracy

The Promise of a Gentleman

The Pride of a Gentleman

The Holidays of the Aristocracy

The Christmas of a Countess

The Knot of a Knight

The Holiday of a Marquess

The Snow Angel of a Duke

The Ivy of an Earl

The Heirs of the Aristocracy

The Angel of an Astronomer

The Puzzle of a Bastard

The Choice of a Cavalier

The Bargain of a Baroness

The Jewel of an Earl's Heir

The Vixen of a Viscount

The Honor of an Heir

The Rose of a Sultan's Son

The Ladies of the Aristocracy

The Lady of a Grump

The Lady of a Sultan

The Pursuit of a Duchess

The Loyalty of a Lyon

Note: Translations of select titles are available in German, Italian, Spanish and Portuguese.

CHARACTER LIST
AND FAMILY TREE

William Slater, Earl of Bellingham (1792), heir to the Devonville marquessate

Barbara Higgins Slater, Countess of Bellingham

Donald Slater (1811), true father of the Marchese Montblanc and cousin to Randolph and Thomas Forster

Nicoletta D'Avalos Slater, Marchesa Montblanc

Antony, Marchese Montblanc, son of Donald and Nicoletta

Amalia, daughter of Donald and Nicoletta

Ricardo Malgeri, the late Marchese Montblanc and Nicoletta's real father

Edoardo D'Avalos, current Conte D'Avalos and older brother to Nicoletta

Armenia D'Avalos, aunt to Nicoletta and Edoardo, spinster

Patrick McAdams, McAdams Textiles, widower

Vittoria D'Avalos, daughter of Conte Eduardo D'Avalos

David Slater, Viscount Penton (1819), son of Will and Barbara and cousin to Randolph and Thomas Forster

Randolph Forster (1817), heir to the Gisborn earldom and cousin to Donald and David

Diana Henley Forster (1820), wife to Randy and second cousin to Randy, Tom, and David

Thomas Forster (1819), younger brother to Randolph

Helen Tennison Forster (1821), wife of Thomas

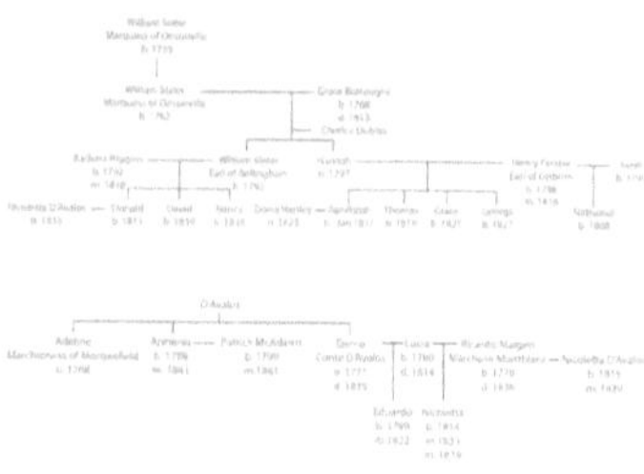

CHAPTER 1
THE START IS NOT
ALWAYS THE BEGINNING

September 1841, Palazzo D'Avalos, Rome, Kingdom of the Two Sicilies

Although Vittoria D'Avalos was possessed of an active imagination, the very last thing she expected to happen at her come-out ball was actually happening. The very event her late mother had warned could happen to any unsuspecting young lady.

Ruination.

Being caught in the clutches of a young buck well known for his antics at such fêtes might well mean she would no longer be allowed out in Society. She might even be forced to marry the rogue.

The one who seemed intent on ruining her? None other than the self-proclaimed Lothario, *Don* Luciano Nicholas Michael Tucci, heir to a *contea* located near Naples. He was far too handsome for his own good, his dark hair, brown eyes, and height causing young girls to blush and their mothers to hope he might one day pay a call when their husbands weren't at home.

Unfortunately, he knew it.

Widows adored him for his bed sport. Husbands cursed him for his audacity when it came to flirting with their wives. Young ladies were both attracted and repulsed by him, for even if any one of them managed to secure a promise of marriage, none of them wanted an unfaithful husband.

How could this be happening?

Vittoria had only managed to make her way down the stairs and into the ballroom a few minutes ago! Most of the guests were still arriving.

Did *Don* Luciano Tucci, better known as *Don* Diavala, not know she would defend her own honor?

Of course not. He didn't know her from Eve.

But she knew him.

At least, she knew *of* him. Even if she hadn't truly been out in Society before this evening, she had overheard gossip whilst shopping. Listened intently as her modiste shared scandalous news of *Don* Diavala as she hemmed her gowns.

Then there was her great aunt Armenia, who seemed to know of every aristocrat's various bed partners, probably because she had at one time participated—although apparently not because it was her choice to do so.

Vittoria hadn't learned his name by way of a formal introduction, for no names had been exchanged that evening. Surrounded by a number of aristocrats, her father was otherwise engaged in his hosting duties and unavailable to do the honors.

When the rake grabbed her hand, led her out to a corridor, and pulled her into an alcove barely hidden by a marble statue of Apollo, the Roman copy a perfect replica of the Greek original, she was already imagining what she might do to him.

If he lifted her skirts, she would pull the knife from her garter and hold it to his throat.

If he attempted a kiss, she would bite his lip until it bled.

If he thought for one second he was going to capture one of her breasts and give it a squeeze, she would do the same to the bulge at the top of his thighs, the one he had proudly displayed upon capturing her hand.

Lorenzo, the footman who saw to the second floor of Palazzo D'Avalos, had explained she could either squeeze his arousal hard or jam her knee into it, effectively forcing her attacker to bend over so she could use the same knee to good effect upon his face, possibly breaking his nose. A hard chop with the heel of her hand to the back of his neck would send him to the floor in a world of hurt.

She couldn't consider the other scenarios she had imagined when they were suddenly behind a dark curtain. The image of Apollo's pose came to her mind's eye, and she thought of one more way she might defend herself.

"What *are* you doing?" she asked in a hoarse whisper.

"Stealing a kiss, of course. Maybe filling my hand with one of your gorgeous tits? What else would I be doing?" Luciano asked in a hoarse whisper, his rich brown eyes growing darker as his pupils dilated in the dimness.

Her eyes widened with a combination of shock and excitement. This was some of what her mother had warned her could happen, and now she had to decide for certain if she was of a mind to participate or send him to the floor in pain. "Oh, I thought perhaps you intended to take my virtue."

His brows arched as a smirk lifted the corner of one lip, and Vittoria immediately regretted her words. For a moment, the sounds from the ballroom—the music, the murmur of conversations, and the baritone voice of the butler announcing the latest arrival to the ball—faded into the background. All she could hear was his inhalation of breath followed by a chuckle that sounded positively devilish.

Not that she had any idea what a devil's chuckle would sound like, but if she did, this was it.

Don Luciano Tucci apparently wished to live up to his reputation.

"Is that what *you* want, my pet?" he asked, one of his dark brows arching in a manner that made him appear positively demonic.

"Are you... are you the *diavolo*?" she asked, her voice quavering.

She almost believed she was fearful.

Almost.

"They don't call me *Don* Diavala because I'm an angel," he countered, a guttural sound accompanying his words.

"I don't suppose they do," she replied in a breathy voice, sliding a silk-gloved hand down his hip and then to where the bulge of his engorged manhood rested at the top of his thighs.

He inhaled sharply when her hand cupped his sac through his tight pantaloons and gently lifted it. "Anxious, are we?" he asked, his gloved hand sliding up her arm to her elbow. When he moved it to cover one of her breasts, she, too, inhaled, not intending for her move to cause the mound to fit perfectly into his palm.

She lifted her knee almost in reflex, but given the layers of petticoats beneath her ballgown, the limb proved ineffectual.

Her hand did not, though, her thumb jabbing into soft tissue as her fingers squeezed as hard as they could.

Luciano let out a yowl at the very moment the drape

disappeared from in front of them, revealing another young man.

"*Mia donna*, are you in need of assistance?" the intruder asked in perhaps the worst Italian she had ever heard.

Reacting to her squeeze with a breathless curse, Luciano bent over. At the same moment Vittoria chopped the back of his neck, the interloper shoved a knee up and into the heir's face.

The unmistakeable sound of cartilage being rearranged was a precursor to a howl of pain that sounded more animalistic than human.

"Come with me," the other man said, taking her hand in his.

"What?" Before she could decide which fate would be better—being discovered in an alcove with *Don* Diavala or on the arm of the tall Englishman in the adjacent corridor—it was too late.

She was suddenly out from behind the curtain and walking with her arm on his, their steps measured as Luciano's moans of pain and curses continued from inside the alcove.

A footman and the butler had already come from around a corner, and in their rush to determine the source of the animalistic yowling, they bumped the caryatid supporting the marble statue of Apollo.

Vittoria almost felt sorry for the Roman god. Surely Apollo didn't deserve his fate when he toppled from his caryatid and fell on the heir, one of his arrows impaling the very region that had suffered so much indignity only a moment ago.

The servants fared better, but barely, offering expressions of sympathy and the promise of a physician.

Beyond that, Vittoria knew not what fate awaited *Don*

Diavala. The Englishman had already steered her into the library and quickly shut the door.

A phrase her grandmother had said when she was young—something along the lines of 'from out of the pan and into the fire'—came to mind before she squared her shoulders and planted her hands on her hips.

If this man intended to continue what *Don* Luciano had started, he would find himself in the same world of hurt.

CHAPTER 2
THIS IS THE ALMOST
THE BEGINNING

Two hours earlier, in Vittoria's bedchamber

"Is it too tight? I think it's too tight," Nicoletta D'Avalos Slater, Marquesa Montblanc, said in Italian as she regarded her reflection in a cheval mirror.

"It's fine, Aunt Nikky," Vittoria assured her, waving away the lady's maid who had seen to her hair. "It shows off your rising moons to good effect." The younger woman dipped her head and glanced down the front of her own bodice. "I wish Papa would have allowed me to wear such a gown."

Nicoletta glanced at her only niece and allowed a long sigh. "Oh, but your gown is gorgeous. My brother must have dropped a good deal of coin with your modiste," she murmured, fingering the silver-on-silver moiré silk. Underneath the yards and yards of draped fabric making up the bell skirt of the otherwise fitted gown was a series of puffy petticoats and every last bit of the tulle the modiste could claim she possessed. Set aside on the dressing table was a pair of dove gray gloves, the closest match to the silver. A diamond encrusted comb, a prized possession of Vittoria's late mother, was already gracing her hair.

"Which is why I only have *two* gowns this Season," Vittoria complained, her fingers nervously pinching one of the bows holding up the drape on the right side. There were a number of rosebud bows sewn onto the skirt as well as at the edges of her square-cut bodice and along the seams of the long sleeves, their tails appearing as if they were connected to the next one in the row. She feared if someone dared pull one of them, they might all come undone and the gown would drop to her feet.

"Is the other just as beautiful?" Nicoletta asked, her critical gaze still on her own red satin and black lace gown. In her past, she had worn the gown at one of the balls of her first and only Season. Back then, the gown had been perfectly respectable for a young lady. The bodice hadn't been nearly as tight.

She hadn't been married back then, though. Nor had she given birth to two babes.

"More so, I think. It's blue, but not light blue. More vivid," she said, pulling Nicoletta from her reverie. Vittoria opened the door to a wardrobe and pinched the skirt of the other ballgown.

"Oh, it will be perfect with your black hair," Nicoletta breathed. She reached out with a red-gloved hand and fingered the fine silk deNaples fabric. "I may have to borrow it," she teased.

Her niece grinned, knowing there was no way the gown would fit her aunt. "I do appreciate you and *Zia* Armenia seeing to my come-out," Vittoria said, sadness settling over her features. Color had been applied to the high cheekbones of her heart-shaped face and to her full lips. Above her upturned nose was a pair of eyes that seemed to change their hue from brown to sapphire blue depending on what she wore. Dark brows matched her black hair, currently swept up into a coiffure that was already threatening to escape its pins and the diamond comb.

"Oh, I wouldn't miss this," Nicoletta replied. "I am only sorry your mother could not see you looking so radiant," she added. "She would be so proud of you."

Vittoria dipped her head. "She is watching from heaven, as Papa would say." The loss of the contessa the year prior from a terrible fever had forced the delay of Vittoria's come-out and had left her father, Edoardo Enrico Vincenzo D'Avalos, heartbroken.

Knowing he required a new wife, Vittoria had encouraged him to use her come-out ball as a means of meeting a potential contessa. Although Edoardo had visibly winced, she knew he had been considering the possibility when she managed a peek at the guest list earlier that afternoon. A number of young widows and unmarried daughters of aristocrats were included. Those names had been preceded by other names unfamiliar to her, such as one her father claimed belonged to a wealthy American. "Probably too old for you, but I may wish to do business with him," her father had said when she asked about Patrick McAdams.

Nicoletta resisted the urge to wince. The entire time she had grown up with her brother, Edoardo, she had never thought him capable of empathy. To have concern for others. To think of someone besides himself. He had been the epitome of a spoiled Italian aristocrat.

Edoardo had left Catania for Rome years before her own come-out, managing to regain some of the influence their father had lost with his poor investments and incessant social climbing.

Marriage and family had changed Edoardo, though. Inheriting an earldom had sobered him, but it was family that had made him a responsible aristocrat. He had married the daughter of a duca and used the funds from her generous dowry to make the renovations necessary to restore Palazzo D'Avalos in Roma so it was more glorious than when their father had inherited the title the century prior.

Even now, she knew Edoardo was downstairs seeing to the last-minute details of the ball he was to host on his daughter's behalf. The guests would begin arriving in only a few minutes.

"Please know that the special guests we have invited will not detract from your come-out," Nicoletta said.

Vittoria whirled around to stare at her aunt. "Special guests?" she repeated.

"Donald's family," Nicoletta replied, keeping her voice low. "They arrived in Roma only yesterday and have taken up residence in the Villa Montblanc."

Her dark brows furrowing in confusion, Vittoria asked, "Is that why you're staying with *Zia* Armenia at Villa D'Avalos?" Her eyes rounded. "To avoid them?"

"No, of course not," Nicoletta replied on a chuckle. "To *surprise* them. They think we are on Sicily, in the Villa Montblanc near Catania," she explained. "And Donald believes they aren't arriving here until next week."

Vittoria scoffed, obviously not agreeing with the subterfuge. "How did you manage to convince Donald to stay at Armenia's instead of at your villa?"

Nicoletta's grin widened. "I told him I was having the parlor repainted and couldn't abide the awful odor."

Shaking her head as she tittered at hearing her aunt's machinations, Vittoria asked, "Are these the people who have been touring Egypt of late?"

"They are."

"Didn't one of the young men get married whilst there?"

Nicoletta didn't try to hide her surprise her niece would remember the details of her cousin-by-marriage, Thomas, ending up in a marriage of his own. She was looking forward to meeting the young lady, Helen, and Cousin Randy's new bride as well.

"Indeed. So now both the Gisborn heirs are off the marriage mart, as they would say in England," Nicoletta responded. "Which is too bad for you."

Her mother-in-law, Barbara, had written to say that Randy had been "quite vexed" by his second cousin, Diana Henley, so she was relieved to learn they had married whilst the family was in Athens. Nicoletta thought perhaps she had misunderstood the meaning of the word "vexed", for she couldn't sort why that would be grounds for a man to marry.

What impressed Nicoletta the most, though, was learning the young lady was not only the daughter of an archaeologist, but that she was one as well. Nicoletta had never heard of a female working in the field of archaeology. "Roma is to be their last stop on their Grand Tour," she explained, closing the door to the ornately-carved wardrobe. "So I saw to it they had invitations to this ball."

"Well, I am honored, I suppose," Vittoria said, turning her attention to the cheval mirror and standing where Nicoletta had been doing so only moments ago.

"I am glad to hear it. Besides, it means more young men with whom to dance."

Vittoria blinked before her eyes widened in delight. She fussed with a couple of hairpins when another lock of hair threatened to escape her coiffure. "How is *Zia* Armenia? Papa said she agreed to be his hostess this evening."

Nicoletta lifted a bare shoulder. "She invited us to stay with her, I think because she is lonely," she replied.

Vittoria sounded an unladylike snort. "Armenia has more lovers than any other woman in Roma," she claimed.

"Vittoria," Nicoletta gently scolded. Her eyes suddenly widened. "How would *you* know such a thing?"

Holding a gloved hand behind the whorl of an ear, the young woman said, "I listen to everything that is said in this house." A grin suddenly split her face. "You are planning to surprise your husband's family, no?"

Blinking at the sudden change in subject, Nicoletta turned to the clock on the fireplace mantel. "Indeed," she acknowledged. "I thought I was excited to see them again, but Donald will be over the moon happy. He is looking forward to showing off his new daughter."

"*Your* new daughter," Vittoria corrected her.

Nicoletta grinned. "We'll be moved out of Villa D'Avalos and back into the Villa Montblanc on the morrow."

"Why so soon?"

Grinning, Nicoletta said, "A certain grandmother will insist her grandchildren be close at hand. If *Donna* Bellingham could have another babe, she would do so." She allowed a long sigh. "Antony is spending his days with a tutor, and Amalia has been crawling for some time. I think she will be walking before the month is done. They grow up so fast."

Vittoria gave a start. "Papa said the same thing to me only yesterday," she whispered.

"Because it's true."

A commotion out in the corridor had them turning toward the door. A knock sounded, and Nicoletta hurried to answer it.

"I guessed right," Donald Slater said on a soft chuckle, referring to the identity of the bedchamber in which the two young ladies were ensconced. He lifted his wife's hand to his lips to kiss her knuckles. "I came bearing news. The butler announced that the Russos have arrived," he said, referring to an aristocratic couple they had befriended in Catania.

Their daughter, Nancy, was nearly as old as Antony, and the two youngsters frequently played together.

"Maria has been looking forward to touring Roma for years," Nicoletta remarked, referring to the Contessa Russo.

"As it happens, Russo only required an invitation to this come-out ball to finally arrange a holiday," Donald replied, his gaze darting to Vittoria. He let out a low whistle. "It's a good thing my brother isn't here, or you would find yourself a married woman before the week was out," he teased.

Nicoletta and Vittoria exchanged glances of amusement. "Remember, I haven't told him the surprise," Nicoletta whispered.

"What surprise?" Donald asked, bowing to his niece before he took her hand to his lips. The sound of chamber music could be heard from somewhere in the distance, the quick tempo suggesting the dancing selections had already begun.

She tittered as she curtsied. "If *Zia* Nikky hasn't told you, then I shan't either," she replied in her stilted English. Glancing at the clock on the mantel, her eyes once again widened. "I must go down now or Papa will accuse me of missing my own ball," she said, rushing from the bedchamber.

Nicoletta grinned as she watched her niece depart and then turned to regard her husband with an arched brow. "I am reminded of a certain night not so long ago," she murmured.

He took her into his arms and kissed her on the lips. "While I was parted from you, it felt like an eternity," he whispered. "But I shall never forget this gown," he added, pulling away to glance down the front of her bodice.

"It's too tight, isn't it?" she asked in her accented English.

He knew better than to agree, for if he did, she would spend the next half-hour undressing to don a different gown, and they would be the ones missing the ball. "It's perfection on you. Surely you know it's my favorite?" He dipped his head to drop a kiss on the top of first one mounded breast and then the other.

Nicoletta aimed a teasing grin in his direction. "If you're sure. Will you escort me down?"

"I will indeed," he answered, offering his arm.

The two took their time descending the two flights of stairs leading to the ballroom, neither one of them aware the special guests had already arrived.

CHAPTER 3
BACK TO THE START

Meanwhile, back in the Palazzo D'Avalos library

With the library door closed against the chaos happening at the other end of the corridor, David, Viscount Penton, could hear only the sound of his pulse pounding in his ears as he regarded the young woman who stood staring at him with fire in her eyes.

He blinked. Why was she staring at him as if *he* was the one who had attempted to take advantage of her behind the curtains of an alcove? "Are you well, my lady?" he asked, forgetting to put voice to his query in the limited Italian he had learned over the years. "Are you hurt?"

The raven-haired beauty straightened even more than she already was, as if she was willing her body to meet his six-foot height. Her chin, nicely rounded, meant she wouldn't look like a hag in her old age. She lifted it as if to make up for her lack of height, which meant he had a clear view of her entire heart-shaped face, a widow's peak emphasizing her regal appearance. Wide violet—or were those bluish brown?—eyes were lined with kohl, and pink tinged her cheeks. Her lush lips appeared bee-stung, which suggested the rake from whom he had rescued her had probably forced a kiss on them. "How *dare* you put your hands on me," she snarled.

The way she stood with her dove-gray gloved fists on her hips emphasized the width of the silver bell skirts of her ballgown. David was reminded of his mother. When she posed so, it usually meant she was angry or annoyed. A tongue lashing would soon ensue, leaving him suitably chagrined and apologizing profusely for his wrongdoing.

Why would this young woman have reason to be angry with him, though? "I only thought to help, *mia donna*. To rescue you from that... that *rake*."

He was about to ask why she was so annoyed when he noticed one of her perfectly combed black eyebrows lifting higher than the other, as if she was daring him to say more or to do something to verify her assessment of him.

Except he already had. He tried again, this time in Italian. "*State bene, mia donna?*" *Are you all right, my lady?*

She huffed and dropped her hands to her sides. "Your Italian is terrible," she said in heavily-accented English.

"Apologies," he said. "Did he... did he hurt you?"

Rolling her eyes, the young woman shook her head, which had a loose hairpin giving way so a lock of hair dropped to her shoulder. The diamond-encrusted comb holding the majority of her coiffure stayed in, though, sending sparkles of light dancing about the dim library.

David was fairly sure her murmured word was a curse, but he dared not antagonize her further by reacting as if he was shocked. He had heard his mother say something along the same lines when she didn't think anyone was within hearing range, and he had learned it was better to act as if he hadn't heard it. "It looks rather nice like that," he said, waving to her hair. "Makes you appear... alluring," he added, before he had a chance to consider how she would interpret his words.

He pointed to the Turkish carpeted-floor where the hairpin had landed so it was nearly vertical. He quickly knelt and retrieved it. Holding it between his thumb and forefinger, he offered it to her.

She rolled her eyes as she took it from him. "*Grazie,*" she murmured, although her gaze, still filled with the fire he realized was indicative of anger, seemed to reignite. "I am quite able to defend myself," she stated. "*Of* defending myself," she quickly corrected.

From the way she held the hairpin—as if she intended to stab him with it—David knew she spoke the truth. "That was quite obvious, *mia donna.*" When her eyes once again rounded, he added, "I could not help but hear that rake's howling from around the corner."

For a moment, he wondered if he would have heard it if he hadn't followed the couple out of the ballroom. The chamber orchestra, a quintet seated on a raised dais in one corner of the ballroom, had begun playing a waltz at the same time the young lady appeared descending the stairs, her entrance obviously a cue for the festivities to begin.

The butler had called out her full name in a litany that seemed to last longer than the usual announcement—how many names did Italians give their daughters?—while those already in attendance applauded. Once she was off the last step, she was met with murmurs of welcome and congratulations by a number of couples who then hurried off to begin the dancing, whirling about in a large circle beneath the gold gilt chandeliers. When he noticed she was no longer among them nor anywhere along the perimeter of the ballroom, he had gone in search of her.

She had been easy to spot given the ballgown she wore,

the furbelow-infested silver-on-silver silk the perfect comple-ment to her olive-tinged skin and raven black hair. On the arm of a conte's heir, Vittoria seemed glad for the aristocrat's atten-tions. Having learned about the *Don* Luciano's reputation from Lady Vittoria's great aunt Armenia upon his arrival—she had recognized and greeted David before insisting he escort her down the stairs into the ballroom earlier that evening—David decided he best see to the younger lady's welfare.

Since he now knew Vittoria could obviously take care of herself, he could at least offer her a way to avoid ruination in the aftermath.

"Might I inquire as to what you did to him? To have him screaming like a girl?" David asked, a grin lifting the corners of his lips. Although he didn't have any sisters, he did have a younger cousin, Grace, who used to make the same sounds as the rake had been making when she was antagonized by her older brothers, Randy and Tom, back when they had all been younger and playing along the banks of the River Isis. They wouldn't dare try nowadays, though—like the young woman who stood before him, Grace was quite able to defend herself.

The lady seemed torn for a moment. "I..." She waved a gloved hand in the direction of his crotch. "I squeezed his *testicoli*." She emphasized her point by forming her fingers into a fist.

Despite guessing correctly, David involuntarily jerked in response. "I shall be sure never to anger you, *mia donna*," he said in a quiet voice. His gaze darted to the library door when he realized the waltz music had ended. "Perhaps it would be best if you returned to the ballroom. Before you are missed," he suggested. "I will remain here for a minute longer so it will appear as if you have merely been in the lady's retiring room."

She angled her head to one side, as if she, too, were

listening for the music. "Very well. But don't expect me to pretend as if I don't know you when we see one another in the ballroom."

David gave a start. "Does that mean you'll afford me a dance?" he asked.

Pausing with her hand on the door handle, she stared at him as if he was a candidate for Bedlam. "You *have* to dance with me. *Twice*," she demanded, as if she expected him to withdraw his offer. She held up two fingers to emphasize her comment.

David bowed, and when he straightened, he wasn't surprised to see her already opening the door. He was fairly sure he knew her name, but just to be certain, he asked, "If that is to be the case, then might I learn your name, *mia donna*?"

She turned and dipped a curtsy. "*Donna* Vittoria D'Avalos. I will spare you all my other names."

Recognizing the family name as that of Nicoletta, his sister-by-marriage, David arched a dark brow. "D'Avalos?" he repeated. "A relation to the Marchesa Montblanc, perhaps?" he asked, knowing full well she was.

Vittoria once again lifted her chin. "She is my *zia*."

David pretended to be impressed. "This is your come-out ball," he murmured, remembering why it was their entire family had received invitations to the palazzo for this evening.

Vittoria dipped her head. "It is indeed. If you will pardon me, I shall return to my party."

She had the door half open when David called out, "Wait. Don't you wish to know *my* name, *mia donna*? Since we're pretending we've already met?"

She huffed. "You are *Don* David Slater, Viscount Penton, are you not?" she countered.

David blinked. "I... I am. How—?"

"You look *exactly* like my *zio*, Donald," she replied on a huff. Pushing her silver skirts against her legs so they would pass through the opening without snagging on the jamb, she angled her way out the door and closed the wooden panel behind her.

David remained standing where he was for several seconds, a look of befuddlement on his face. "Damnation," he muttered. "I think I'm in love."

CHAPTER 4
A GUEST ARRIVES

Meanwhile, at the top of the stairs to the ballroom

Handing over his greatcoat and topcoat to a footman, Patrick McAdams briefly studied the tapestry drapes framing the windows on either side of the double doors of Palazzo D'Avalos. From the outside, their detail had been obscured by the sheers that hung closest to the glass windows. Now that he could see them up close, he pretended to smooth his salt-and-pepper hair into place as he glanced into a carved plaster-framed mirror perfectly placed in the entry.

The jewel-toned tassels dangling from the edges of the drapes showed no signs of wear nor were they dusty, which meant they were fairly new. The drapes weren't bleached from the sun, either, which suggested they had been recently installed.

Conte D'Avalos obviously knew how to impress his guests—at least those who paid attention to such details. For one whose business was textiles, Patrick was impressed.

Daring one last look into the mirror, Patrick noticed how his face had tanned despite his wearing a hat whenever he was out of doors. He had a thought to acquire one with a broader brim before he crossed the wide marble corridor to stand at the top of the stairs.

He paused to regard the scene below and cursed softly. He hadn't thought his arrival was more than a half-hour past the time printed on the invitation, but from the number of people already dancing, he realized he was late.

"*Il tuo nome, signore?*"

He gave a start at the appearance of yet another servant and wondered how many were employed by Conte D'Avalos. Two footmen had seen to his coach and driver, two more flanked the entrance as if on guard to prevent uninvited guests from entering—although neither asked to see his invitation—and another had seen to his outer garments.

This one was different, though, his attire suggesting he was the head of the staff. "Uh, Patrick McAdams," he said, realizing the servant had asked for his name.

"*Titolo?*"

He was tempted to answer with "Proprietor". He was sure the only reason the conte had invited him was because Patrick had sent him a note requesting a moment of his time to discuss a business proposition. He hadn't thought a ball an appropriate occasion at which to conduct business, but he would take what he was offered.

Patrick dipped his head and said, "Mister... uh, *Signore* Patrick McAdams." He returned his attention to the ballroom, his gaze taking in the gold, glitter, and gilt on display. The colorful gowns and the even more garish costumes worn by the men had him reconsidering his choice of black formal attire. He chuckled softly. "It's worse than the Brits," he murmured.

"*Perdono, Signore?*"

Patrick lifted a hand and waved it dismissively. "*Niente.*"

The booming voice of the short butler sounded as he

called out Patrick's name. Blinking in surprise, Patrick scoffed before heading down the stairs. Although he was sure the announcement could have been heard in the next villa up the road, only a few of the people down below had paused in their conversations to glance up at him.

Which was fine with him.

The direction to which most turned showed him where their host was located, as if those in attendance sought to learn if the newcomer was known to their host. With his back to the wall, the conte was on the opposite side of the ballroom, a small half-circle of aristocrats paying homage.

"There you are," Patrick whispered, descending the steps as casually as he could manage given the black heeled shoes he wore.

Attending a ball with the intention of landing a potential client wasn't exactly how Patrick intended to do business in Rome, but from his research, he had discovered the Conte D'Avalos had influence and a sizable fortune mostly due to his marriage. The D'Avalos *contea* had also grown in size, some of the land featuring vineyards while the rest outside of the city was farmed.

There was also a sizable flock of sheep.

Patrick made his way in the direction of the conte, quickly learning he needed to stay on the carpeting that surrounded the checkered marble floor or he would cause a collision with one or more of the dancers.

As he nodded to those who took notice of him—he confirmed his choice of black satin pantaloons and black satin topcoat was at odds with most of the other men—he was glad he had worn his favorite silver embroidered silk waistcoat. The garment seemed to be attracting a good deal of attention.

Or perhaps it was merely him.

Before he had even reached the conte, he felt a prickle

on the back of his neck, a sure sign someone had taken an interest in his arrival.

When his gaze darted to a tall woman who was openly watching him, he was surprised when she didn't turn away. Instead, she merely lifted her glass of bubbly—Prosecco, he remembered learning the day before when he was buying wine—and took a drink, never taking her eyes off him.

He might have continued his stroll toward the Conte D'Avalos, but curiosity had him taking a detour in her direction.

As he grew closer, he was struck by her classical beauty and by how tall she was—nearly as tall as him. Rather than slouching in an attempt to hide her height, she stood proud, her bare shoulders held straight. She had every reason to, though, given her generous bosom and the way it was displayed by a bodice made of an exquisite silk trimmed in embroidery festooned with tiny beads.

"*Buonsera, mia donna,*" he said, bowing. He reached for the gloved hand that wasn't holding the glass and brushed his lips over the back of it.

"You're not British," she stated, only a hint of an accent tingeing her accusation.

Patrick blinked and straightened. "Uh, you won't hold it against me if I am not?" he countered in English. Now that he was even closer, he discovered he couldn't take his eyes off of her.

She was positively gorgeous.

One of her dark brows rose as a hint of a grin appeared on her red-rouged lips. "American?" she guessed.

He nodded. "I am Patrick McAdams, my lady. It's an honor to meet you."

"*Donna* Armenia D'Avalos," she said, dipping a perfect curtsy that only enhanced her rising moons.

A rock seemed to fall into the bottom of his stomach.

"The *Contessa* D'Avalos?" he asked, attempting to hide his disappointment.

Of course a woman of her beauty and grace would already be married. Probably had been for...

He considered how old she might be. Forty? Surely no more than fifty. But he quickly set aside thoughts of her age when he saw her expression of suspicion and realized he needed to explain his presence.

"I, uh, was invited by the Conte D'Avalos..." He paused and motioned in the direction of who he had thought might be the host of the ball.

She followed his line of sight. "Ah. My nephew, Edoardo," she said, a grin appearing to lighten her features.

"Your *nephew*?" he repeated. He dipped his head, a combination of embarrassment and surprise heating his face.

"You don't believe me?"

Patrick cleared his throat. "I thought he might be your husband," he admitted.

One of her eyebrows arched as her amusement became more apparent. "I don't have one of those," she stated, as if husbands were mere possessions.

For a moment, Patrick wondered if she was teasing him. Then he considered an alternative. "You're a widow?" he guessed.

She huffed softly. "I have *never* had a husband," she clarified.

He blinked as relief swept through him. "In that case, might I be allowed a dance with you this evening?"

It was her turn to blink. Several times. Patrick thought he saw an expression of disappointment darken her features. "You needn't ply me with the promise of a dance in order to gain an introduction to Edoardo," she said, the slightest hint of rebuke sounding in her voice. "I'll take you to him now."

Patrick reached out to capture her wrist before she could take a step, immediately regretting the move when she stared at his hand and then directed a glare at him. "Apologies, *mia donna*," he said, quickly releasing his hold. "I assure you, that was *not* my reason for asking."

She seemed to consider his words a moment before she relaxed. "Very well. Perhaps the next dance?" she offered, the music for the current dance nearing its end.

"That would be perfect," he said, glancing about for the refreshment table. He motioned to a footman carrying a tray of wide-rimmed glasses filled with Prosecco. "Would you like another glass of bubbly?" he asked, snagging two glasses from the tray.

For a moment, he thought she would decline, leaving him holding the two glasses. But she accepted the glass while a different footman saw to taking her nearly empty one.

"Might I ask what business you have with my nephew?"

Patrick drained nearly half his glass before he said, "I heard he has a flock of sheep." The sound of her titter had him grinning. "Pray tell, why do you find that amusing?"

"Forgive me, but I was sure you were after *Donna* Vittoria's hand in marriage," she said. "Rather than her sheep."

Patrick blinked. "Uh, no...." He drew out the word as if he might have made a mistake in attending the ball. "Is that why all these other gentlemen are here?" he asked, glancing around to see a number of young bucks in the ballroom. He was especially attentive when he heard names being called out at the top of the stairs.

English names.

"Most, yes," Armenia replied, her gaze going to the newcomers. "For *Donna* Vittoria. Not the sheep," she added, a grin lighting her face. "The music for our dance will be starting in a moment."

Quick to take her glass to deposit it on a nearby caryatid along with his, Patrick offered his arm, and she placed a gloved hand atop it. "I must warn you, it's been an age since I danced," he murmured, leading her to the edge of the marble dance floor.

"Whatever you do, please do not trod on my toes," she replied. "My feet are already in pain from these slippers."

"I shall endeavor to keep my feet off of yours," he replied. He glanced around and copied the way the other gentlemen held their partners, one hand at their waist while holding the lady's hand in the other.

With the first three notes, he knew the music was meant for a waltz, and he felt relief. This was a dance he knew.

So did she, for he knew immediately she had been born for it. Elegance oozed from her as she followed his lead, her steps sure on the marble despite her apparently sore feet. Beneath the hand at her satin-covered waist, he could feel the supple muscles of her torso, the fabric acting like liquid gold as they made the intricate turns about the floor. The skirt flared with every turn and folded when she was back before him.

"May I say you have the most beautiful shoulders?" he asked, his gaze sweeping across her collar bones as one of his gloved hands barely brushed over the smooth skin. Once again, she seemed to unconsciously react, briefly leaning forward as if inviting him to continue to touch her.

"I've not heard that particular compliment before," she replied. "*Grazie.*"

When he marveled at how effortless the dance seemed, he wasn't surprised when she said, "You needn't have worried, Mr. McAdams. You seemed to have remembered how to dance."

"Indeed," he replied. "Tell me, *mia donna*, is dancing your favorite pastime in Roma?"

She tittered again. "Hardly. I prefer walking, actually."

"From what little of Roma I have seen, I can certainly understand why. No matter which direction you go, there is something of interest to see." When they completed another turn, he asked, "Have you other interests?"

"Only to see to it my great *nipote* receives an excellent offer of marriage," she replied, her gaze suddenly darting about the ballroom as if she was in search of said niece. "And you? What are your interests, Mr. McAdams?"

Patrick considered how to respond. He had recently acquired property for his own company off one of the squares featuring three fountains—one topped with an ancient Egyptian obelisk.

The installation of a shingle soon followed.

Only a fortnight ago, he had moved into the apartment above the office space, hired a valet and a housekeeper, set up his office, hired a secretary fluent in both English and Italian, and now employed a network of caddies—young boys who acted as couriers—to see to the quick delivery of messages.

During the six months he had spent in England prior to his arrival in Rome, he had contracted with the British and North American Royal Mail Steam Packet Company for cargo space on their fortnightly runs from Liverpool to Boston. For shipments from Rome, he had an agreement with the Nattersley Shipping Company to accommodate his occasional shipments on one of their three sailing vessels that traveled between Rome and either Liverpool or London.

Now he had to fill the cargo space.

Although he had some suppliers in Devonshire and

Lancashire, he would require additional sources to make his enterprise profitable.

Italian sources for wool and silk.

Spinners and weavers he had in spades, the women either working in their own homes or gathering in a brick warehouse he owned in Boston to create beautiful fabrics.

There, his grown son, Patrick Junior, would see to the distribution of the textiles to their growing network of shops and drapers.

He was thinking of his son when he remembered Armenia had asked him a question. "I fear I've had little time for hobbies given my need to set up my office here in Roma. I am expanding my business to include more product from Europe."

Armenia nodded. "Hence the need for sheep?"

He chuckled. "*Sì.*"

"Have you found lodgings?"

"I bought an apartment near the Piazza Navona," he replied, deciding not to admit he had bought an entire building.

Her eyes widened as if she was impressed, but she said, "When we're close to the conte, simply dance us out of the circle, and I'll introduce you."

Furrowing his brows in confusion, Patrick asked, "I won't have the honor of finishing this dance with you?"

"Do not take offense, Mr. McAdams," she stated. "But I fear my slippers have become far too uncomfortable for me to enjoy this waltz."

"I could carry you," he offered, his grin giving away his tease. "You're probably light as a feather."

Beneath his hold, he felt her entire body shiver, and he secretly thrilled that he had discovered something that unnerved her. He did her bidding, though, and turned them out of the circle of dancers only a few feet from where

Edoardo D'Avalos stood holding court with a number of older aristocrats.

The satin-clad men parted their circle for Armenia, and Patrick felt a streak of jealousy at the thought that any of them might have shared her bed at some point in the past.

Odd that in the space of only one dance, he felt more affection for the lady than he had with anyone else since the death of his wife.

"Edoardo, there is someone here you simply must meet," Armenia said, holding out a hand to indicate Patrick. "*Signore* Patrick McAdams."

Patrick bowed deeply before shaking the hand that Edoardo held out. "*Mio don*, it's an honor," he said.

"Ah, you are the American who wished to make a deal with me," the conte said, grinning.

"About sheep, was it?" Armenia asked, arching an elegant brow as if she didn't believe the reason Patrick had provided.

"Come. I will speak with you in my study," Edoardo said, waving for Patrick to join him.

Patrick glanced around at the others and nodded before taking Armenia's hand to his lips. "Thank you for the dance, *mia donna*," he said.

Once again, he felt her shiver, but when he straightened, her attention had gone back to the ballroom.

"*Prego*, Mr. McAdams."

From her look of worry, Patrick realized she had lost track of her charge.

Since the conte didn't seem particularly concerned, Patrick followed the aristocrat out of the ballroom, down a short corridor, and into a study featuring a cluttered desk and a huge marble fireplace.

He would have to look for the conte's aunt later that evening.

CHAPTER 5
ARRIVALS MAKE FOR MERRY
AND THE BEGINNING

a few minutes earlier, in the ballroom

"Now *this* is a ballroom," Will Slater, Earl of Bellingham, murmured as he escorted his wife, Barbara, into the opulent, high-ceilinged testament to mirrors, marble, and gold. Down a short flight of stairs was the actual ballroom—their arrival had brought them into an open hall manned by several footmen collecting wraps and hats.

"It's positively gorgeous. Now I know from where Adeline took her inspiration for the ballroom in Morgan-field Manor," Barbara gushed, her gaze sweeping the ceiling to discover five huge crystal chandeliers, all their candles lit. Every tall mirrored panel on the walls was framed with gilt, and the black and white marble tiles formed a chess board on the dance floor. A generous band of Turkish carpet rimmed the room, which meant her tight slippers probably wouldn't pain her as much as they usually did at the end of such an evening.

"I wonder if there are any flowers left in all of Roma?" Helen Tennison Forster asked, her arm gripping her new husband's as if she needed him for support. The elegant urns sporting the giant displays of hot-house flowers were placed between the mirrored panels, their caryatid bases featuring carved marble cherubs.

Tom chuckled. "Those are probably from the D'Avalos gardens," he whispered.

Helen's eyes rounded. "We really must go out there when we've a chance," she said, waggling her eyebrows. If it hadn't been for the gardens behind Morganfield Manor, she and Tom wouldn't have shared the fateful kiss that eventually led to their marriage.

"I rather doubt there will be much to see in the way of flowers," he countered. "They're probably all in here." He leaned down and lowered his voice. "Dance with me? This will be our first as a married couple."

She tittered. "This will be our first *ever*. You never did dance with me the night we met," she reminded him.

"You must agree it was better that we spent our time together in the gardens," Tom replied, his brows waggling. "I find kissing you far more enjoyable than dancing."

That had been the night before Tom and his older brother, Randy, and the Slaters had departed on their Grand Tour. After spending nearly two years in several countries—Sicily, Greece, and Egypt along with stops on several Greek islands—they were at their final destination.

"Don't feel too offended. I've never danced with my husband, either," Diana Henley Forster said. She and Randy had stepped up to stand next to the younger couple since Randy, as the heir to the Gisborn earldom, would be announced directly following his aunt and uncle.

"I plan to make up for it tonight, my sweet," Randy said, his gaze darting about the ballroom. "Have you seen David? He should be announced before me," he murmured.

"He left in the first coach, quite some time before we did,

so he's probably already dancing," Tom said. He and Helen followed Randy and Diana when their uncle stepped forward to speak with the butler.

A moment later, and the booming baritone voice of the announcer sounded their names and titles.

"I don't know why I'm so nervous," Barbara murmured, displaying a tentative grin when those in the ballroom turned to regard them with expressions of curiosity as they descended the stairs.

"We have the advantage," Will whispered. "They don't know who we are." He nodded in the direction of an older man who was openly staring at them.

"How? We don't know *them*," Barbara countered, dipping her head when a young lady curtsied as they passed.

"Exactly. However, *we* were invited by a marchesa." His gaze fell on a middle-aged man holding court with the largest number of guests surrounding him. "Ah, I believe I have found our host." He led Barbara to the circle, and when the aristocrat acknowledged them with an expression of curiosity, Will said, "Conte D'Avalos?"

"*Sì*? Ah, you are *Don* Bellingham?"

"I am. *Posso avere l'onore di presentarvi mia moglie, Barbara, contessa di Bellingham?*" *May I have the honor of introducing my wife?*

The conte stepped forward and dropped a kiss on the back of Barbara's hand. "It is my pleasure. I am Nicoletta's brother, Edoardo, and the honor is mine—to finally meet the parents of my sister's husband," he said in heavily-accented English, waving a gloved hand to indicate the older couple as he made the comment for the benefit of the others who stood around them. He shook Will's hand and then greeted Randy, Diana, Tom, and Helen as they were introduced. "Is there not another with you? Donald's brother?"

Will glanced around the ballroom, his brows furrowing when he didn't see David. "My youngest son, David, Viscount Penton," he replied. "But I don't see him."

"Ah, yes, he is here. He was in search of my daughter so that he could secure a dance with her. I told him I would allow him two."

"That's very kind of you," Barbara replied. "I wished to tell you I am so sorry for your loss," she added. "Nicoletta wrote of the contessa's death in a letter we received whilst in Greece. Her grief was quite evident in her writing."

"*Grazie*," he replied, dipping his head. "Although this is my Vittoria's come-out ball, I admit to asking *Zia* Armenia if she might invite some *donne non sposate*," he said, referring to unmarried women. "I think it is time I see to marrying again."

"Then we shouldn't keep you from your other guests," Will said, giving the conte a bow. "Thank you for including us in the festivities."

"Of course. You are family. Do help yourself to refreshments, and enjoy the ball," Edoardo said, his attention going to another couple that was approaching from the dance floor.

The Slaters and Forsters all bowed and curtsied before they stepped away to line up near the edge of the dance floor.

"What do you suppose has become of David?" Barbara asked.

"He should be easy to see since he's wearing black," Will commented, his brow arching when an older couple passed them performing the waltz. The man was wearing a puce top coat and a lime green waistcoat. "Black doesn't seem to be the color of choice for gentlemen this evening."

"Except for that man who is speaking with the conte," Diana murmured, her attention returning to their group as her brows furrowed.

"What is it?" Randy asked, noting her look of confusion.

"The lady dressed in red. With the man in black. She looks..." She paused and shook her head. "Familiar, but... not," she stammered.

Barbara cast a sweeping glance behind her and around the ballroom. She inhaled softly when she realized the conte and the man in black were no longer in the ballroom. The woman, however, was still there, her gaze sweeping about as if she was in search of someone.

The music suddenly ended, which had those in the circle of dancers returning to the carpet at the edge of the marble floor.

Barbara glanced over at the woman again, and when their eyes met, she blinked. "She looks *exactly* like the Marchioness of Morganfield," Barbara whispered.

"Indeed," Will agreed. "And she's headed this way."

Barbara curtsied as did Diana and Helen while the gentlemen were quick to bow.

"My lords, my ladies, please do pardon me for not having greeted you upon your arrival. I am *Donna* Armenia, and I am supposed to be helping host this affair," the woman said. "I was detained by another guest, but I believe I caught all your names as you were introduced by the butler."

"*Grazie*, my lady. If I might say... you look so familiar," Barbara commented.

The statuesque woman seemed to consider the comment for a moment before her eyes widened with understanding. "You have met my sister, Adeline Carlington, no doubt. The Marchioness of Morganfield?" she clarified, displaying a hesitant grin.

"Yes, that's it, of course. Then you *are* Nicoletta's aunt?"

"Indeed I am."

Will reached for Armenia's hand and kissed the back of it before performing the formal introductions. "Her ladyship left an invitation for us and a note that we should attend this evening," he explained, motioning to Armenia.

She tittered softly and lowered her voice so only Barbara and Will could hear her next words. "Nikky and your son should be making their appearance at any moment," she said, her gaze darting to the top of the stairs. "He has no idea you have arrived in Roma—at least, Nikky hasn't told him—as she wished to surprise him with your presence."

Barbara inhaled softly. "We wondered when they might come up from Catania," she said. "But... they're not at the Villa Montblanc with us," she added.

"They're staying at my villa and will join you at their villa on the morrow," Armenia explained. "It was the only way she could keep you a secret from Donald."

"Well, *we* are certainly surprised," Barbara said. "I'm looking forward to spoiling their new babe. When we last saw Nikky and Donald, she hadn't yet given birth."

Armenia grinned in delight. "Amalia is a doll. A rather happy, almost toddling doll. Why, she'll have all of you wrapped around her tiny pinky before you quite know what's happened," she warned.

"We look forward to meeting her," Will said. "And I wished to thank you for the invitation and the means of transportation for us to attend this evening."

For a moment, Armenia appeared confused. "I cannot take credit for what my *nipote* has done," she replied, referring to the three coaches that had been sent to the Montblanc residence to transport them to Palazzo D'Avalos. She directed her gaze to the top of the stairs. "But you'll be able thank Nikky directly right now."

Everyone turned their attention to the top of the stairs when a trumpet sounded. The butler announced, *"Donna* Nicoletta, Marchesa Montblanc, and *Signore* Donald Slater."

A collective gasp sounded from their group. "They're *here*," Tom and Randy said in unison.

"Did you know about this?" Diana asked, turning a suspicious glance in Barbara's direction.

"I did not," she claimed. "But if they're here, that means the children are probably here, too," she added with excitement. "We'll be able to meet our granddaughter," she gushed.

"Oh, the marchesa is gorgeous," Helen murmured, which had Tom squeezing her hand.

"You're far prettier," he said in a whisper.

She grinned as Diana asked, "Is that David's brother?"

"In the flesh," Randy replied. "Seems you're to meet yet another one of your second cousins this evening."

Diana beamed in delight. "You say that as if you don't think I'll like him," she accused. "But I already do."

Randy furrowed a brow. "Oh?"

"Mother told me their story long before I met you," she said. "How they fell in love but couldn't marry. How he waited for her." She knew the rest of the couple's story from Barbara, and was sworn to secrecy when it came to the details of their son, Antony. "They look incandescently happy," she added, watching as the couple descended the stairs.

"Aren't we?" Randy asked, tearing his gaze from the approaching couple, their beaming faces a testament to their intention of surprising the family. His own displayed a look of concern.

Diana stood on tiptoe, held up a gloved hand to hide her mouth, and kissed his cheek. "We are."

He grinned, the tips of his ears turning bright red.

"Do you suppose they planned this?" Helen asked.

"*She* planned it," Will stated, his grin belying his accusation. "And kept it a secret from Donald."

As if his words caused their oldest son to glance in their direction, Donald did a double-take and beamed in delight.

"I do hope he won't be angry with her," Barbara said, her own grin widening into a smile. She had her arms held wide as Donald rushed up to embrace first her and then his father.

"Well, this is... this is—"

"A surprise?" Nicoletta finished for him, already enjoying the attentions of the others. "I have had to keep it a secret for an entire *fortnight*," she complained.

Donald scoffed as he shook hands with his cousins and kissed the backs of Diana's and Helen's hands. "I could not believe my mother's letters when she said I had new cousins," he gushed. "I wasn't sure if I should send best wishes or letters of sympathy," he added in a tease.

Diana and Helen giggled in response as their husbands pounded Donald's shoulders with their fists.

"Now there's a rather handsome couple," Randy remarked, his gaze suddenly directed on a regal man and woman who had stepped into the circle of dancers. The black-haired gentleman was garbed in a dark satin top coat and pantaloons while the bit of waistcoat that showed appeared made of spun gold. On his arm was an attractive woman about Nicoletta's age who wore a gown made of the same gold fabric. The fitted bodice emphasized her generous bosom and the sleeves, puffy at the shoulders, were tight around her forearms.

"The Conte and Contessa Russo," Donald stated. "They live near us in Catania. Nikky and Maria have been friends since their youth. Their daughter and Antony are nearly the same age and quite happy to play together."

Randy arched a brow. "I take it you are not friends with the conte?"

Donald allowed a look of surprise. "Russo and I play cards and go hunting on occasion. He's a crack shot with a pistol," he said. "But you're right. I cannot claim he is a close friend."

"Has it been hard? Living so far from England?" Tom asked, after catching the last of what Donald had said.

Donald shook his head. "Not really. As the Marchesa Montblanc, Nikky is well regarded in Catania, so life there is easy. Here in Roma, we're merely another aristocratic couple, I suppose."

"They accept you? Even though you're not Italian?" Randy asked, his gaze darting about in an effort to discover if anyone was watching them. He expected some to show curiosity at the presence of strangers, but most in attendance were either dancing or engaged in conversation.

Lifting a shoulder, Donald said, "Half of them don't know I'm British. The other half..." He shrugged again. "They either don't care, or if they do, it's because they're jealous I am married to Montblanc's widow because they wanted that fortune for themselves."

Tom leaned forward and lowered his voice. "So... you really are rich?"

Donald chuckled. "More than you'll ever be," he teased. His attention darted about the ballroom as if he was in search of someone. "Where's David?"

Their query was met with the opening strains of the next dance and the appearance of a young lady gowned in silver. Her head held high, as if she might be the lady of the house, she was perusing the crowd as if searching for someone. Her gaze settled on them, and she quickly made her way in their direction.

"*Zia* Nikky, you really must introduce me," she

demanded. Her high color suggested she had practically run from wherever she had been.

"Allow me," Donald said, capturing the girl's hand in his to pull her to his side. "*Donna* Vittoria D'Avalos, may I have the honor of introducing you to my mother and father, the Countess and Earl of Bellingham, and my cousins *Don* Randolph Forster and his wife Diana, and Thomas Forster and his wife, Helen. Tonight's ball is Vittoria's come-out," he finished before he once again glanced about the ballroom in search of his brother.

Murmurs of greetings and welcome were exchanged, the women quick to compliment the young lady on her gown.

"Did David not come?" Donald asked in confusion.

"Oh, *Don* Penton is around here somewhere," Vittoria said as she waved a gloved hand. "Acting like a rogue, of course, but I suppose you already knew that about him," she added, waggling her dark brows.

The others in the group stared at the young lady in shock.

"A rogue?" Barbara repeated in a whisper. She glanced up at Will, whose brows were furrowed in what appeared to be anger.

"Apparently I need to remind him of his manners," Will said under his breath.

They all turned when they heard David call from where he appeared as if from the same corridor as Vittoria had come.

"About time you all arrived," he said casually. "A nice surprise to see you again, sister," he added, lifting Nicoletta's hand to his lips. He was about to shake his brother's hand but realized something was amiss. "What is it?" he asked, his innocent manner quite at odds with Vittoria's claim.

While he displayed a look of confusion, she stared at

him with narrowed eyes. "Here he is now," she said, lifting her chin. "A rogue in Roma."

David's jaw dropped as he blinked several times. "I... I am *not*," he countered defensively.

Vittoria tossed her head before turning around at the exact moment a young man stepped up to claim her for the next dance. "*Mi scusi,*" she said before hurrying off.

Their party watched her go before they all turned and stared at David.

It was going to be a long night.

CHAPTER 6
DENYING AN
UNEARNED REPUTATION

a half-hour later

When it was finally time to claim one of his dances with the impertinent *Donna* Vittoria, David found it difficult to maintain a calm demeanor.

Especially when she greeted him by saying, "Well, if it isn't the rogue of Roma," as he approached her. She was in the company of his brother and Nicoletta.

David's eyes rounded in disbelief. "*Mia donna*, I do believe you have me confused with someone else," he said in answer to her claim he was a rogue. "*Don* Luciano, perhaps?"

He was glad to see her reaction of surprise. Having learned the name of the aristocrat from the footman who had seen to removing Luciano from the alcove, David was able to discover more information about him from the servant. Apparently two other footmen had been required to escort Luciano out of the residence by way of a side entrance, the servants forced to practically carry him to his equipage.

Just thinking of what Vittoria had done to the conte had

David holding his hands in front of his crotch.

When she had departed the library earlier that evening, David was sure she knew he was a gentleman. That he had no intention of taking advantage of her. But only a half-hour ago, upon finding his family surrounding the young miss, she had implied he was as bad as *Don* Diavala.

How *dare* she say he was "a rogue in Roma!"

He had attempted to defend himself, of course, although he had chosen to say something which only earned him additional censure from the young lady. "Why only moments ago, I found her in the clutches of a—"

"*Don* Luciano," she had interrupted. "*Don* Penton obviously misunderstood Luciano's intentions," she added, turning her gaze on her aunt.

Nicoletta's eyes rounded slightly. "*Don* Luciano only has one intention when it comes to young ladies," she had whispered. "And it shall not be mentioned in the company of our guests."

From the pouty expression *Donna* Vittoria had displayed, David thought she looked as if she was being admonished. Apparently she had known better than to engage with '*Don* Diavala', which had him wondering why she would allow the rake to escort her out of the ballroom and into an alcove in the first place.

Unless she had an ulterior motive.

Now that she stood before him, ready for their first dance, he was determined to defend himself. Perhaps his actions would speak louder than words, though.

"*Mia donna*," he said, bowing as she curtsied. He placed a gloved hand at her waist and lifted one of her gloved hands with the other. "Given the turmoil of earlier, I was unable to compliment you on your stunning gown," he said.

The music started, and he took an experimental step as he pushed her hand. She displayed a grimace. "*Grazie.*

When was the last time you danced?" she asked, obviously annoyed at his stutter-start. It had taken three or four steps before they were in sync with one another.

"Two years ago, at..." He allowed a grin. "At your *Prozia* Adeline's annual autumnal ball," he added, sure the mention of a relative could only help his case.

Vittoria's eyes rounded. "Did she give you permission to use her Christian name?" she asked in shock.

Nearly tripping—her large skirts seemed intent on inserting themselves between his legs—David gave a start. "Uh... apologies. I know her as Lady Morganfield, of course. However, I learned of your relationship to her from Nikky."

Her eyes once again rounded. "Has my *zia* given you permission to speak her name as such?"

David swallowed. "She is my sister by marriage," he countered defensively. "My brother introduced her with both her formal and informal names," he added.

Sniffing, she said, "Then I suppose you are allowed."

Annoyance made it difficult for David to maintain his civility. "Are you enjoying your party?"

She sighed dramatically. "As well as can be expected."

Careful to keep her from colliding with another couple, David was forced to stutter-step. "Congratulations on the crush."

From her look of confusion, he knew he had used a word she didn't recognize—at least as it pertained to the number of people attending the ball. Before he could amend his statement, she said, "I do not participate in the crush. That is for those who grow the grapes."

"Apologies. I was referring to the large turnout for your come-out," he explained. "We use the term 'crush' because, well, the ballroom feels crowded. As if we are crushed together inside it."

Her brows furrowed, and not in a nice way. "Are you implying my papa's ballroom is small?"

David couldn't help but roll his eyes in frustration. "Not at all, *mia donna*. My comment was meant as a compliment. You must be especially pleased there are so many here to celebrate you."

It was Vittoria's turn to stutter-step. She glanced both left and right after she recovered, as if to be sure no one had noticed. "*Grazie*."

Relieved he had finally said something with which she didn't find fault, David decided he best remain quiet for the rest of the dance. The thirty seconds seemed far longer before he was finally able to bring them to a halt, step back, and give her a deep bow. "*Mia donna*," he said.

Vittoria dipped a curtsy. "*Mio don*." She didn't wait for him to escort her to her aunt, but instead rushed off and disappeared into the crowd.

Scoffing softly, David shook his head and hurried off to find refreshment. He had downed nearly an entire glass of Prosecco when he realized he hadn't been able to learn just why it was she had allowed *Don* Luciano to escort her out of the ballroom only minutes after she had been announced.

"What secret are you hiding, you little shrew?" he whispered under his breath. He drank the rest of the bubbly before setting off to find another dance partner.

CHAPTER 7

RECONNAISSANCE
PROVES ENLIGHTENING

*M*eanwhile...

Patrick emerged from the conte's study and turned to bow. "I look forward to meeting your farm's foreman, *mio don*," he said.

"I will be sure he knows what's to be done. As I said earlier, my flock of sheep is hardly of a size to warrant your interest—"

"Ah, but the size is not what's important, *mio don*. The quality of the wool is," Patrick replied.

"I will not... what is the word? Quibble? Over the details. Your offer is fair, although your timing is not exactly perfect. I don't expect the flock to be sheared until late spring. However, I am quite sure my foreman will be happy to learn he doesn't have to see to transporting it all the way to Prato." He allowed a long sigh. "I would not even have sheep except my daughter insisted I buy them for her."

Patrick gave a start. "They are your daughter's sheep?"

The conte responded by rolling his eyes. "She was happy to have them on the occasion of her tenth birthday—she begged me for them, so I bought her ten—and then she promptly forgot all about them," Eduardo explained. "Now I have a huge flock. I spoiled her."

The two made their way back to the ballroom, where the crush of people had grown and the number of dancers had noticeably increased.

"Your daughter's come-out appears to be a success," Patrick said, noting the crowd of young bucks surrounding a young lady gowned in silver.

"Indeed. The sooner she is married, the more inclined I will be to find another contessa," Edoardo replied. "I find I miss my wife most at times like this."

"I, too, am a widower," Patrick said.

"Were you left with children to raise?" Edoardo asked, his dark brows furrowing.

"One son. He's... he's an adult now, though. Runs my company's office in Boston," he explained, his gaze sweeping the room in search of Armenia. "Might I ask as to your aunt's situation? I could not help but notice she was not in the company of an escort this evening."

Edoardo chuckled softly. "She rarely is. If you are asking if she is married, she is not. If you are asking if she is otherwise attached," he paused and shrugged. "This I cannot say."

Patrick scoffed. "Does she live here in the palazzo, *mio don*?"

The chuckle grew into a full-throated laugh. "*Zia* Armenia is in possession of the original Villa D'Avalos here in Roma," he said. "My father gave it to *Don* Montblanc as part of my sister's dowry, but upon Montblanc's death, he ensured it was given to Armenia."

The thought the marquess might have been enjoying the attentions of his marchesa's aunt had Patrick scowling on behalf of Lady Montblanc. From what he had ascertained during their meeting that evening, there had been a substantial age difference between Nicoletta and Mont-blanc. Had the marquess sought a dalliance with a woman closer to his own age?

"You needn't be consumed by the Green Monster," Edoardo said, a smirk appearing when he misinterpreted Patrick's reaction. "Montblanc wished for the property to be returned to a D'Avalos, but he didn't wish for my father to end up with it. He knew Armenia preferred living in Roma to Catania. Knew that she would see to keeping the property in good repair. So it has worked out for all," he explained.

"If I wished to escort her to an entertainment, is there someone with whom I should first speak?" Patrick asked. He didn't dare approach her until he knew he wouldn't be in someone's crosshairs.

Edoardo scoffed softly. "I'm not sure if you're aware, but *Zia* Armenia is probably old enough to be your mother," he whispered hoarsely. "She answers to no one but herself," he added.

Patrick inhaled softly. "I appreciate the information." He glanced around again and finally spotted the woman in question climbing the stairs. Despite the late hour, she still appeared statuesque, her shoulders and back straight as an arrow, not a hair on her head out of place.

His fingers ached to pull the pins from the raven hair. To spear the carefully constructed coiffure until the locks tumbled down around those gorgeous shoulders and back. To see it splayed across bright white bed linens. To feel it brushing over his bare chest.

Well aware his thoughts had his cock responding as if it would be experiencing a long-forgotten sensation, Patrick tamped down his erotic thoughts.

Knowing the lady's retiring room was on the same level as the ballroom, he surmised she was about to take her leave. "I wish to thank you again for seeing me this evening, *mio don.* I'll send the contracts by courier if I'm unable to bring them myself," he said, bowing to the conte.

"I look forward to doing business with you," Edoardo said, his own attention on his aunt as a footman helped place a mantle on her shoulders.

He wasn't surprised when Patrick McAdams made his way directly across the ballroom and straight up the stairs.

CHAPTER 8
A BALL ENDS WITH
AN EXPLANATION

*M*eanwhile, *in another part of the ballroom*

Struggling to keep a pleasant expression on her face as she danced with yet another young man, Vittoria couldn't when he stepped on her foot.

Her cry of pain and grimace couldn't be helped, nor did his murmured apology do anything to improve the situation. She was not only hungry and thirsty, she lacked the energy to pretend interest in the pimply-faced heir to a *marchese*. When the dance mercifully ended a few minutes later, she quickly curtsied and hurried off to find Armenia.

"She has taken her leave," Nicoletta said when Vittoria found her instead. "What is it?"

"I'm hungry, and my feet are killing me."

Overhearing her complaint, Donald joined them. "There is a table of food and refreshments," he said. "Come. Allow me to escort you."

Donald offered his arm and led her away as David stepped up next to Nicoletta. "Dance with me, sister?"

She smiled. "I was beginning to think you were avoiding me," she replied.

"Not intentionally," he said. "It seems I'm a bit of a novelty this evening."

"Ah, the young ladies find you intriguing?"

"I think it's more like their mothers," he replied. "I have yet to dance with someone close to my own age," he complained. "Other than *Donna* Vittoria."

The two moved into the circle of dancers and easily joined the flow. Despite the difference in their heights, David had no trouble with leading her in the dance. "Has my brother been good to you?" he asked.

Nicoletta gave a start. "He has," she replied. "I could not have asked for a better husband, nor a better father for our children," she claimed.

"I am glad to hear it, although you should know, he will probably spoil your children rotten."

Bursting into giggles, Nicoletta said, "I am aware." She quickly sobered. "What has you vexed this evening, brother?"

David winced. "Is it that obvious?"

"You are the amiable one. Handsome—"

"I look exactly like my brother," he interrupted.

"—always in good cheer, and an heir to a peerage," she finished. "Except this evening you seem... *vexed*."

"That's because I am," he admitted. "Would you promise not to take offense if I asked how it is your niece seems far more spoiled than you?"

Nicoletta giggled again. "Not at all. Vittoria has merely had a doting father that gave her whatever she wanted while mine used me for his own gains." Her face screwed into a grimace. "He used his sister—Armenia—even more poorly."

Shocked by her candor, David nearly lost his step in the dance. "Apologies. I... I did not mean to pry."

"No apology is necessary," she said. "Thankfully, Vittoria

has been spared from the machinations born of greed that drove my father to seek wealth any way he could whilst dispensing with it just as quickly," she continued. Her words were at odds with her pleasant expression, as if she had rehearsed them.

"But... your brother seems to be doing quite well," David commented, waving a hand to indicate their elegant surroundings.

"That's because he knows how to manage his estate, the *contea*, and his money," she replied. "As does Armenia, which is why Montblanc gave *her* the villa here in Roma."

Surprised by this last bit of information, David was suddenly curious about the spinster. "Am I to understand she has never wed?"

"Not once, and I assure you, she does not regret it."

David furrowed a brow. "Isn't she... lonely?"

"Probably," Nicoletta replied. "But she attracts men like moths to a flame." She paused and added more quietly. "Or rather, she used to."

"Might you be referring to that American she was dancing with earlier?" David asked. He glanced around, frowning when he couldn't locate the older gentleman in the crowd.

"They have both taken their leave," she said, a prim grin appearing.

David once again winced. "Are you implying—?"

"I'm not implying anything at all. But I admit, they made quite a lovely couple whilst they were dancing, don't you agree?"

"He was staring at her like he—"

"Like your brother did when he first danced with me," she interrupted, her grin broadening. "Armenia can take care of herself, David. Besides, Donald and I are staying at her villa, so I rather doubt she'll be hosting anyone else this evening."

David nodded his understanding. "Vittoria thinks I'm a rogue," he stated.

Nicoletta jerked in his hold. "I wouldn't take it personally. She... she has a tendency to think the worst of all men because that's what she's been raised to believe. Her mother was..." She sighed. "Really rather protective of her," she said.

"I saved her from that *Don* Diablo... Diavalo... whoever he is," he stated.

"*Don* Luciano is a libertine," she whispered. "*Grazie* for whatever you did to help her," she added. "I do hope she wasn't seen in his company."

"He was removed by some footmen after the incident," he said. "I rather doubt he'll go anywhere near her or Apollo ever again."

"Apollo?" she repeated in confusion.

"Let us just say the Roman god of medicine and healing may have caused an injury to a certain region Luciano was known to overuse."

Nicoletta's eyes narrowed, but a grin suffused her face. "Touché for him," she said.

His mood lighter than it had been all evening, David allowed a hearty guffaw. "Touché, indeed, *mia donna*."

CHAPTER 9
AN UNWELCOME PASSENGER

eanwhile, in the courtyard of Palazzo D'Avalos Armenia settled into the velvet squabs of her town coach and pulled her feet from the tight dance slippers, wiggling her toes as she allowed a sigh of relief.

Although she couldn't help but feel pleased at the thought of her niece's successful come-out—the appearance of Nicoletta's new family had brought a combination of joy and curiosity to the evening—she also hoped she might be spared from having to be at all the fêtes her nephew had planned for his daughter to attend. Watching handsome young men fawn over the girl was better left to a younger woman.

Other than the family dinner scheduled for the next night—Nicoletta planned to host Donald's entire family as well as her own—Armenia had nothing else on her calendar for the following day. With any luck, Edoardo would find a new wife, and Armenia would be relieved of her duty as a doting great aunt.

Or perhaps one of the young bucks at this evening's ball

would propose to Vittoria. The girl's dance card had been filled with a number of names of young aristocrats.

The town coach jerked into motion, the wheels clattering on the cobbles as it turned to make the exit from the courtyard of Palazzo D'Avalos onto the street. When it suddenly halted, nearly dislodging her from her seat, she glanced out the window nearest her. She expected to see another coach trying to make its exit at the same time.

Instead, the door suddenly opened.

"*Perdonatemi, mia donna.*"

Armenia gasped as a man quickly stepped up and into the coach, settling onto the bench opposite her. A familiar scent accompanied him, but it did nothing for the immediate fright she experienced.

"*Chi sei?*" she asked in surprise. *Who are you?* In the dark, she couldn't make out his features. The thought of trying to escape the coach was replaced with the need to remain where she was when it resumed its movement, the pair of horses neighing in complaint as the coachman urged them onto the street.

"Patrick McAdams, *mia donna*. We danced together earlier this evening," he said, as if he thought that would be reason enough to invade her town coach. "When I saw you didn't have an escort, I thought it best I see to your safe arrival at your villa." Despite the dark, she was aware he had removed his top hat and placed it on the seat next to him before rubbing his gloved hands on the top of his thighs.

Blinking several times, Armenia resisted the urge to scoff. "Although I appreciate your concern, *signore*, I assure you, I am in no danger." Her response sounded sharper than she intended.

Did she usually sound so annoyed when someone was attempting to help her?

Another thought had her rolling her eyes, if only for

how ridiculous it seemed. She was far too old for the gentleman to have invaded her coach for another purpose.

Seduction.

A decade ago, it wouldn't have been such a far-fetched thought. Many a penniless aristocrat thought she would be amenable to hearing platitudes and invitations to their beds. Now? She was sure she was old enough to be Patrick McAdams' mother. The thought of him attempting to bed her came and went in a flash. The effects of it lingered, though.

As did the scent of his cologne.

While most of the men who had attended that night's ball wore scents featuring cloying florals and tangy spices, his was far more subdued. Hints of citrus and amber combined with his natural musk to make for a masculine cologne.

"Perhaps, but if I learned on the morrow your coach had been set upon by thieves or... or involved in an accident, I would not be able to forgive myself," he claimed, interrupting her reverie.

Her heart rate returning to its normal rhythm, Armenia settled back into the squabs and regarded the American with narrowed eyes. "And after we have arrived at my villa, how do you expect to get to your lodgings this evening?" Once again, the query came out sounding harsher than she intended.

Despite the dim interior, she saw him wave a gloved hand in her direction. "My coach is following this one, *mia donna*," he replied.

Armenia gave a start. How had she not noticed the clatter of another coach—directly behind her—on the otherwise empty streets?

The words reinforced what she had already concluded only the moment before, though. He had no intention of attempting seduction, which meant his reason for being in her coach was probably as he claimed.

To see to her safety.

She tamped down the sudden disappointment she experienced, curious as to why it hurt more than it should.

"Did you enjoy the ball, *mia donna*?"

Glancing out the window in an attempt to learn how much farther they had to go, Armenia blinked back a tear. "I did. I rather expect Vittoria will find herself a married woman before the autumn entertainments have concluded."

"She certainly had the attention of many of the young men in attendance," Patrick agreed. "I wished to thank you again for dancing with me. You dance beautifully."

Armenia blinked again, fighting back the urge to sniffle. She extracted a handkerchief from her pocket and touched her nose. "The pleasure was mine," she replied.

"I rather doubt that. I nearly crushed your foot," he countered. "I suppose I didn't need to mention it has been years since I last danced." The comment held a hint of sadness—or perhaps it was regret.

"Did your meeting with my nephew gain the results you hoped for? I know that was your real reason for attending the ball, was it not?"

Despite the darkness, she could tell he was surprised by her query. "It was, although it wasn't my *only* reason for attending."

"Oh?"

"Uh, curiosity, I suppose. I wondered if the balls here were different from those I've attended in Boston."

"And?" she prompted.

"This one was far more... *more*," he said. "More glittery, if that is a word? More elegant? I certainly didn't expect to see men wearing colors I would deem more appropriate for ballgowns."

Amused, Armenia finally relaxed and grinned. "Roman men can be such popinjays on occasion," she agreed. *Always*, she almost added. "It's as if they aren't aware their time is coming to an end."

From the way he bent forward, his elbows moving to his knees, she knew he was surprised by her comment.

"What are you saying, *mia donna*?"

"I've been alive long enough to see what's coming, Mr. McAdams. The time for aristocrats in this country is nearing its end. At some point, the peasants will revolt, mayhap as they did in France, and we shall lose everything."

"Surely not in our lifetimes," he replied. "At least, I hope not. I just arranged to be the sole purchaser of wool from your brother's sheep for the next decade," he added.

Armenia gave a start. "*Wool*?" she said in disbelief. *Wool* had been the reason he was so anxious to gain time with her nephew?

He nodded. "I, uh, deal in silks and wools, *mia donna*. My textiles company might be based in Boston, but I'm required to import some of the materials or finished fabrics from here in Europe."

She couldn't suppress the scoff that escaped her throat. "Apologies. I suppose I imagined your business quite different."

"Oh?"

Tittering, she placed a gloved hand to her lips. "You seemed so serious—"

"I do have a tendency to look as if I'm on my way to a funeral," he admitted sheepishly. Despite the dark interior, she saw how he indicated the formal clothes he wore. "This evening's choice of attire being no exception."

"You wear it well, though," she replied. "I, however, prefer never to wear black. I am reminded too often of widow's weeds." She allowed a sound of disgust.

"Because you had to wear them?" he asked, his brows furrowing.

"Not as a widow, of course," she replied. "But both my father and my brother have died in the past decade." The coach turned, and she glanced out the window. "This is my villa," she said, noting how he had already leaned over to look through the opposite window.

"You are in town?" he remarked.

"I am," she acknowledged, struggling to force her feet back into her slippers.

He continued to stare out the window. "Is this the Via del Tor Millina?" The coach paused a moment to allow a gate to be opened before it passed through the entrance into a courtyard and slowed to a halt.

"One end of it," she replied.

"You're close to the Piazza Navona."

"I am," she acknowledged.

"My office—my lodgings—are not far from here," he said, attempting to gain his bearings from what little he could see given the tall buildings surrounding them.

The coach door opened, and he hurried to step down. He turned to offer his hand as Armenia clutched at her skirts, one of her slippered feet tentatively testing for the location of the step.

"With your permission, *mia donna*?" Patrick asked. He raised his hands to her waist and easily lifted her out of the coach, lowering her until he was sure her feet were on the marble that made up the floor of the courtyard.

Armenia had to suppress the urge to yelp at the unexpected move. "*Grazie*," she murmured.

The two horses pulling his town coach stopped directly behind her coach, the neighs of complaint rending the otherwise quiet night.

"I'll see you to your door, *mia donna*," he said, offering his arm.

Hesitating a moment, Armenia finally placed her arm on his and was reminded of how it had felt during their dance earlier that evening. Remembered how she had caught him staring at her.

Probably wondering my age, she thought.

"Have you a butler? Or someone to see to the door?" he asked when it didn't open at their approach.

"I told DeLuca I wouldn't require his services this evening," she replied, reaching out to push down on the door handle. The carved wooden panel opened inward. The vestibule beyond, lit by a single candle lamp, included a wide marble staircase that wound up in a large spiral. The upper steps beyond the entry disappeared in the gloom. "*Buona notte, Signore* McAdams," she said, climbing the single step before turning to face him. Given her height— she was nearly as tall as him—she had the advantage of being able to look down at him. She dipped a slight curtsy.

Patrick took her hand to his lips and kissed the back of it. "Might I be allowed to pay a call on you? Perhaps escort you... on one of your walks?" Given she stood on the threshold with the candlelight behind her, she appeared as if in silhouette.

Armenia blinked, surprised he remembered her mentioning she liked to walk. "Tell me, *Signore* McAdams, do you *truly* like to walk?"

"I do," he replied. "I have been on a quest to find as many fountains as there might be here in Rome," he added.

Turning her head slightly, she glanced to where DeLuca usually left her correspondence and saw only one missive on the silver salver. "If you're not intending to find *all* of them..." she hedged.

"I hear tell there are three-thousand," he said.

She tittered. "In the middle of the city, you might find four-hundred," she said. "I could take you to four on the morrow, if you're not too early," she replied. "Otherwise you'll have to attend my morning *toilette*," she warned, arching a dark brow as if she was challenging him.

Patrick swallowed. "You say that as if it would be a hardship," he said in a hoarse whisper.

She lifted a shoulder. "For some, it is." She watched as his brows once again furrowed, but before she knew quite what was happening, he leaned forward and kissed her on the cheek.

The move may not have been made with any other intention than a farewell between friends, but a shiver shot through her at the simple courtesy.

"I will come for you around eleven o'clock," he said. "Perhaps we can find a place to enjoy a luncheon afterwards?"

She nodded. "I'll try to be ready by then," she teased.

He displayed a grin. "*Buonanotte, mia donna.*" He turned and made his way to his coach, easily stepping up into the equipage before the horses were set into motion.

Watching from where she still stood in the doorway of Villa D'Avalos, Armenia felt a pang of dismay.

For the first time in a very long time, a man hadn't insisted he be allowed to spend the night with her. She would have had to deny him given she was hosting Nicoletta, David, and their children for one more night. In the morning, they would return to Villa Montblanc to play host to David's family.

Finally closing the door, she removed her mantle, hung it up on a hook by the door, and made her way up the stairs to her bedchamber.

I suppose I am too old for him, she thought.

CHAPTER 10
THE MORNING
AFTER A BALL

he following morning
From her seat in the breakfast parlor of Villa Montblanc, Barbara watched as a phalanx of footmen passed by the arched doorway, their direction suggesting they were on their way to the front door. "They're here," she said with excitement.

Will glanced up from the Italian news-sheet he had been attempting to read. "They must have awakened rather early," he remarked, knowing immediately she referred to Donald's family.

David was already on his feet. "I'm off to meet my niece," he announced. "With any luck, I'll have her playing cards before the week is out." He disappeared from the breakfast parlor.

Everyone else in the room scoffed in surprise, but soon they, too, rose and hurried to follow David. The coaches had already come to a halt in the courtyard when they emerged into the bright sunshine.

The carriages weren't carrying Nicoletta, Donald, Antony, and Amalia, though—merely their trunks. "*Donna*

Montblanc sends her regards," a servant explained in halting English. He held out a folded paper. "We are to wait for you and take you to the Palazzo D'Avalos."

David opened the note and quickly read it before announcing, "It seems our hosts don't plan to come here until later in the day. They have requested we join them for a late breakfast at Palazzo D'Avalos before we go on a walking tour of Rome."

"Why, that sounds delightful," Barbara remarked. "I'll only be a moment. I shouldn't need more than a hat and a pelisse on such a fine day."

"Me as well," Diana and Helen said in unison, following the matron back into the house.

"Mayhap a parasol, too. The sun is rather bright," Helen added as she blinked several times.

"Gentlemen, we need hats," Will said, following the ladies back into the villa.

Fifteen minutes later, they filed into the carriages and set off for Palazzo D'Avalos.

eanwhile, in Vittoria's bedchamber at Palazzo D'Avalos

"After such a successful ball last night, it's important you be seen in the company of visitors to our city," Nicoletta said, watching Vittoria's lady's maid iron another curl into her hair. She held Amalia in the crook of her arm, the babe happily jabbering.

Vittoria glanced at her aunt's reflection in the mirror over her dressing table. "Are you referring to your husband's family?" she asked, her suspicion evident in how she narrowed her eyes.

"*Sì.* Donald and I are going to take them on a walking

tour, but we'll have the coaches follow us in the event the sun is too much. Will you join us?"

Sighing in resignation, her niece lifted a shoulder. "I will if I can wear my newest walking gown."

"It is why we had the modiste make it for you," Nicoletta countered. "I expect our guests to arrive within the hour—"

"The *hour*?" Vittoria repeated in shock. "I still have to dress, and I haven't had a bite to eat since before the ball last night."

"There is coffee and cornetti on its way," Nicoletta assured her. "But we'll have a real breakfast before we depart. Oh, and you might wish to leave that lock of hair down in front of your shoulder," she suggested, waving a finger to indicate her own coiffure. "Much like you did last night."

The lady's maid paused with said lock held aloft, a hairpin held in anticipation of it being added to the ornate coiffure she had started a half-hour earlier.

"Why?" Vittoria asked, turning her head to regard her aunt directly.

Nicoletta simply winked and took her leave of Vittoria's bedchamber.

*A*malia fell asleep in her arms as Nicoletta made her way downstairs. The familiar clatter of horse hooves in the courtyard had her hurrying to the entry at the same time the butler opened the doors to admit Donald's family.

"Oh, me first," Barbara murmured as she reached out to take Amalia from Nicoletta's arms.

"You are welcome to her," Nicoletta said, grinning at the sight of her guests. She giggled softly at hearing her mother-in-law's cooing as Barbara held the babe. "I do hope you're all comfortable in your rooms at the villa?" she asked, turning a cheek so David could kiss it.

"The accommodations are far finer than what we could ever imagine," Diana assured her. She glanced over at Randy. "We certainly didn't require an entire apartment for only the two of us."

"That's the only way they come," Nicoletta replied, letting out a squeak when Will pulled her into an embrace.

"I wasn't able to greet you properly last night at the ball," he said, as he released her from his hold. "Is my son treating you right? Is he being a good husband?"

She nodded. "The very best, Papa," she replied.

Donald appeared from the stairs, Antony holding onto his hand. His shout of welcome set off another round of greetings. "Are you settling in over at the Montblanc house?" he asked, shaking hands with his cousins after he let go of Antony's hand so the boy could bow to their guests.

Antony was quick to run to Will, who lifted him into the air before settling him onto a hip with a complaint about how tall the boy had grown in the year since he had last seen him.

"We are, and if you don't kick us out, Helen and I would like to stay for the rest of our lives," Tom teased.

"I already told Nikky we didn't require an entire apartment," Diana said. "After our accommodations on those river boats in Egypt, our bedchambers seem almost too large."

"They're all like that, I'm afraid," Donald said, offering his arm to Nicoletta before leading the group further into the residence. "I believe the Malgeri were once a very large family, and several generations all lived under the same roof."

Although there were individual guest rooms in the Villa Montblanc, there were a number of multi-room suites suitable for married couples. Even David had been led to one, which had him claiming he was tempted to host a guest or two of his own in the massive suite.

His comment was met with chiding glances from both his mother and from Randy. "Careful, cousin," Randy warned. "After last night, you already have a reputation as a rogue," he added.

David scoffed in response. "It wasn't me. It was *Don Diavala*," he claimed. "Conte Tucci's heir," he amended when Randy raised an eyebrow at hearing the nickname. "Other than dance with her, I didn't try anything untoward with Lady Vittoria. I swear it." He lowered his voice, intending for only Randy to hear his next comment. "I wouldn't have anyway," he said with a sneer.

"Oh?" Barbara asked, moving so she stood closer to her youngest son. "I thought she was a rather lovely young woman."

"If you only knew," David said under his breath.

As everyone paired up and made their way into the parlor, Donald cleared his throat. "We haven't yet had our breakfast—"

"We were in the middle of ours when the coaches arrived," Tom interrupted.

"—so we thought to host you for one here before taking you on a walking tour," Donald finished. They took seats around the large parlor, the women opting for one of the long settees. "However, we are waiting for one last person to join us before we go in."

"My brother sends his regrets. He had business at his *latifundia* today," Nicoletta said.

"His farm," Donald clarified. "We're waiting for the young lady of the hour."

"She'll be down in a moment," Nicoletta said, grinning as Barbara finally gave up her hold on Amalia so that Diana could have a turn holding her youngest cousin. "When she gets to be too much, please tell me, and I'll ring for her nurse," Nicoletta said.

"I want a turn," Helen said.

"And you shall have it, but only after my arm grows too weary," Diana said, her gaze on the baby who had awakened during all the commotion. Apparently Amalia was unbothered by it, though, her gray eyes wide as she stared at Diana. A tentative grin appeared, which had Diana gasping in surprise.

"How is it you are so good at holding a babe?" Randy asked from where he sat in an adjacent settee, his brother flipping up his topcoat's skirt to settle in next to him.

Diana glanced up in surprise. "I am a woman," she stated. "We come by it naturally. My work in archaeology proves it." She rearranged Amalia so the girl was perched on her lap, eliciting a squeal of delight from the year-old babe.

Randy ignored Tom's attempt to jab an elbow into his ribs, but it was Tom who was awestruck when Diana placed Amalia into Helen's arms. He watched as his wife held the babe, one of her fingers stroking the girl's cheek as she spoke quietly and grinned in delight.

One of Amalia's arms escaped the blanket in which she was wrapped, and it waved about before settling onto Helen's breast, the tiny fingers gripping the bodice of her gown.

"Oh, I want one," Helen said, lifting her head to discover her husband was watching her.

Tom blinked, well aware everyone around the room was suddenly staring at him. "And you shall have one, my sweet, but do remember, we have to be married in an Anglican church before it's born," he reminded her.

Although he and Helen had been married by the former chaplain of a British ship whilst they were in Egypt, he knew the marriage wouldn't be considered legal in England. Any offspring would be illegitimate. As soon as they were back on British shores, he intended to secure a marriage license and see to it they were properly wed.

Helen displayed a pout. "Oh, I know," she replied, her attention back on the babe.

*M*eanwhile... Having consumed a cup of coffee and part of a cornetto, completed her toilette, and finished dressing, Vittoria headed to the parlor. She nearly froze on the threshold upon seeing Nicoletta's family-by-marriage— seemingly all of them—seated in the velvet settees and upholstered chairs scattered about the room.

She recognized Donald's parents from having met them the night before and wasn't surprised to see that Antony was seated next to his grandfather while his sister was enjoying the attentions of one of the young women.

The odd man out in the parlor was leaning against the fireplace mantel.

"*Mia donna*," David said, immediately straightening to give her a bow.

Recognition had Vittoria blinking, but before she could remember exactly why, all the other men in the room stood and bowed in her direction. She dipped a curtsy and managed a smile. "*Buongiorno*. Pardon my tardiness."

A chorus of greetings followed before Donald said, "Now that we're all here, let's eat our breakfast. I can hardly wait to show you our favorite sights here in Rome."

"We don't have to see them *all* in one day," Will said. "We're going to be here for at least a month."

"It's a large city, Father," Donald commented, lifting his daughter from Helen's arms before he kissed her forehead and handed her to a nurse who had appeared after Vittoria's arrival. He turned to his son. "Your tutor is waiting, *mio don*."

From Antony's look of shock, it was obvious he was disappointed. "*Sì*, Papa." He made the rounds, bowing to the women before stopping to allow his mother to give him a kiss on the cheek.

"I'll see you before your dinner, *mio don*," she said.

He glanced around the room. "May I join you for dinner? I promise I will be on my very best behavior," he said.

She grinned. "Of course, *mio don*."

Anthony beamed in delight as he headed out the door.

"He's practically a young man already," Barbara lamented.

"He's not even eight years old," Nicoletta said, her gaze following the Marquess Montblanc as he took his leave. "And he's growing up far too fast for me." She allowed Donald to help her to stand and placed an arm on his. "Lead the way, my darling."

The other couples paired off and followed Donald and the Marchesa Montblanc, leaving Vittoria with the only single gentleman in the room.

"*You*," she said in a hoarse whisper.

"Me," David acknowledged, arching a brow before he smirked. He offered his arm. "It is best we don't dawdle. My brother tends to walk fast."

She huffed her disdain. "So you really are David Slater," she stated, as if she hadn't made mention of his name only the night before. As if she hadn't included a comment about his resemblance to his brother.

"Of course," he said, making a show of taking her hand and placing it on his arm. "Viscount Penton." He had them exiting the parlor before she could put voice to a complaint. "But you can call me—"

"Whatever I wish," she finished, lifting her chin defiantly.

David gave a start. "*Mia donna*?"

She rolled her eyes. "What is the word in English? Rake?"

Given how close they were behind Tom and Helen, David was forced to keep his voice low when he responded. "I am many things, *mia donna*, but a *rake* is not one of them."

"Perhaps the better word is *libertino*," she offered.

He visibly stiffened, and from the way the muscles of his jaw moved, it was apparent he was biting back an angry retort. "I think you have me confused with that libertino I found you with in that alcove last night. *Don* Diavala, was he?"

She gasped. "How *dare* you. You obviously have me confused with a... a..." She struggled to sort the English word.

"Tart?" he supplied.

"*Sì*." She immediately regretted agreeing with him, sure he had laid a trap for her given her limited English.

He smirked as he pulled out a chair for her at the dining table. "Touché."

"*Grazie*," she murmured, rearranging the skirts of her sapphire blue walking gown once she was seated. She was relieved he didn't take the chair next to her, but she struggled to keep from rolling her eyes when he ended up in the seat directly across from her.

Although the conversation grew livelier as footmen delivered platters of food and poured coffee and wine, Vittoria elected to remain quiet unless someone directed a question to her.

With only one older brother and no other siblings, she wasn't used to eating breakfast among so many people. The ease at which they enjoyed one another's company was unnerving. Her aunt Nikky acted as if she was familiar and comfortable with everyone, despite having met Diana and Helen for the first time only the night before.

Nicoletta was a marchesa, though, her time as a wife to the late Ricardo Malgeri, Marchese Montblanc, long enough for her to learn the art of hosting guests and the diplomacy necessary to navigate the shifting whims of the Italian aristocracy.

Once Vittoria was married, she would be expected to do the same. The thought had her dark brows furrowing, her appetite suddenly gone. She drank her wine, well aware she was being watched from across the table. Lifting her gaze, she pinned David with a withering stare.

"Did you enjoy your come-out ball?" he asked.

Sure he intended to lay some sort of trap for her, Vittoria lifted a shoulder. "Most of it," she replied. "The dancing, of course. The rest... not so much."

Vittoria expected David to put forth a word of protest, but it was Donald who said, "What, pray tell, happened, dearest niece?"

Vittoria stiffened. About to say that his brother had accosted her in an alcove, she was prevented from doing so when David said, "*Don* Luciano thought to trap *Donna* Vittoria in a dark alcove, but she was most effective in rendering his advances moot."

Vittoria blinked and did her best not to put voice to a word of protest.

The rest at the table turned to stare at her.

"I told your brother he shouldn't include *Don* Luciano in the invitation list," Donald said, his quiet words meant only for Nicoletta.

From her place at the opposite end of the table, she rolled her eyes. "Unfortunately, *Don* Luciano's father is a *conte*," she replied. "And no longer of a mind to attend the entertainments."

"*Don* Luciano is a libertino of the worst kind," Donald countered.

"Yet it sounds as if our niece defended herself?" Nicoletta countered, a dark brow arched in query as she turned her gaze on her niece.

"She was actually quite fierce," David stated, his gaze directed on Vittoria. "I should not wish to find myself on her list of those upon which she desires to come to harm," he added.

Vittoria managed a pleasant expression despite what she wished to be doing to David.

Kicking him in the groin, for starters. Seeing to it a certain statue impaled him, leaving him unable to father children. "Really, *Don* Penton, must you be so... so graphic?"

"I am merely stating your skills, *mia donna*," he answered. "Should I possess your ability to render a man unable to procreate, I should be most proud," he said.

The other men at the table visibly winced at the comment, and the women hid their smirks behind their napkins.

Not sure how to respond, Vittoria aimed a pleading glance in her aunt's direction.

Nicoletta responded with widened eyes and a lift of her shoulders. "*Don* Luciano is not one we would wish to join the D'Avalos family by way of marriage," she said. "Better he be injured and gone from the premises than for you to be forced to marry him because someone discovered you with him," she added.

"I could not agree more," Donald stated.

Anxious to change the subject, Nicoletta raised her voice. "So, our plan for the day is to take you all on a walking tour of Roma. We won't see everything, of course, but enough for you to let us know what you wish to revisit on future excursions," she explained.

"When can we start?" Helen asked, her gaze darting to her husband, Tom.

"In a few minutes," Nicoletta responded. "Do be prepared to climb a few hills—there are seven all told—and of course we won't climb all of them today, but if they should be too much for you, we shall have a couple of coaches following us so you needn't feel as if you must walk the entire time."

"Well, that sounds quite acceptable," Barbara stated.

The others at the table nodded their agreements, and when Nicoletta indicated she was done, everyone rose from the table and made their way to the vestibule of the Montblanc house.

The fact that Vittoria still directed a look of derision at him had David realizing it was going to be a long day.

*D*onald was about to don a pair of gloves but paused when a footman motioned to him. "I'll only be a moment," he said to the others, before making his way to where the servant and butler were engaged in a quiet conversation.

"What has happened?" he asked in Italian.

"There has been an accident. The Russo carriage overturned last night on its way home from the ball, and the Conte Russo and his contessa have died," the butler explained.

Inhaling sharply, Donald glanced back at Nicoletta. Although slightly older than Nicoletta, Maria, Contessa Russo, had been a good friend to his wife back when the marchese was still alive. Their children frequently played together. "What of their daughter? *Donna* Nancy?" he asked in a quiet voice.

The footman lifted a shoulder. "She was not with them, but one of the servants said they are worried as to what's to become of her and of the household staff that came with them from Catania."

Relief had Donald sighing softly. "Send word to their villa that she and her nurse are to be delivered to the Mont-blanc villa. We will host them until arrangements can be made," he instructed. "Until relatives have learned of their fate. Have one of the rooms off the nursery prepared, and be sure there are quarters for the nurse. Have our things moved back there as well."

"Right away, *signore*."

When Donald rejoined Nicoletta and the others, she directed a pleading glance in his direction, but he merely shook his head. "Later," he whispered.

CHAPTER 11
A HOUSEKEEPER
PROVIDES OPINIONS

M eanwhile...

Despite having stayed out far later than he planned the night before, Patrick awoke at his usual time. The servant he employed to see to his clothes and his apartment, Giovanni Ricci, shaved him before holding out his typical uniform for a day—navy topcoat, white shirt, white cravat, embroidered waistcoat, cream colored pantaloons, and stockings. The only difference from day to day was the color of the waistcoat.

"Let us do the..." He sucked air through his teeth, trying to imagine what color frock Lady Armenia would choose for their outing. "The yellow waistcoat," he finally decided.

Breakfast was already on the table when he made his way through the corridor towards the center of the apartment. Giovanni's mother, Signora Ricci, an older woman who was as round as she was tall, greeted him with her usual string of Italian words—half of which he still hadn't been able to interpret—and used a pudgy finger to point at the pile of correspondence next to his plate. "For you," she added.

He watched as she filled his plate with poached eggs, buttered toast, and a slice of ham leftover from the dinner she had made several nights ago.

Although most inhabitants of Rome didn't consume such a big breakfast until later in the morning—they ate very little with their coffee—Patrick was used to eating a hearty breakfast first thing. Despite the amount of cajoling he had to employ to convince her, Signora Ricci seemed pleased with the arrangement—once she learned she didn't have to make him another meal until dinnertime.

"The ball was good, no?" she asked, pouring him another cup of coffee.

He glanced up from the note he had written for himself the day before, a reminder of what he needed to accomplish in the office below his apartment before he set off to collect Lady Armenia.

"Very good," he replied. He lifted one of the missives from the pile of correspondence she had placed next to his plate.

"You meet *Don* D'Avalos?"

Chuckling softly, he popped the wax seal from the back of the envelope. "I did. He has agreed to sell me all his wool." He wasn't sure she understood anything he said in English, but she was always attentive.

"You meet his daughter? Maybe you marry her?" she asked in her stilted English.

He had to resist the urge to laugh as he shook his head. "I did not have the honor. She was... otherwise engaged with much younger gentlemen, including several from England," he said, watching for her reaction. He was fairly sure Sophia Ricci had agreed to be his housekeeper and cook as a means of gathering gossip she could share with her friends when she went to market every day or so. That he gained a valet in the process by way of her son was simply a bonus of her hiring.

"Young men from *England*?" she repeated, her eyes wide.

He nodded. "Indeed. From what I could gather, they are on their Grand Tours," he explained. "And they are somehow related to the man who is married to the Marchesa Montblanc."

Her eyes rounded. "*Signore* Slater?" she said in awe.

Patrick blinked, surprised she would be familiar with him. From what he had heard the night before, the husband of Armenia's niece usually lived in Catania with the marchesa and their children. "Do you know him?" he asked.

Sophia slapped one of her hands against her ample bosom several times. "I see him. When he is walking with the marchesa. Very nice man. Always tips his hat when he sees me," she claimed, miming the move lest he not understand her heavily-accented English. "So polite. His mama raised him good."

Patrick gave a start. "Well, as it turns out, his mother was there last night, as was his father," he said, suppressing the urge to grin when he saw how her eyes once again rounded. "The uh...." Here he paused in an attempt to remember what he had overheard. "The Earl and Countess of Bellingham," he stated. "They were with their nephews and their wives," he went on, happy to have her undivided attention. "The oldest is an heir to an earldom. There was another young man, too. Uh..."

"*Don* Penton?" she guessed, her eyes even rounder.

Scoffing in surprise, Patrick asked, "How did you know?"

Signora Ricci shrugged a shoulder. "A good guess," she replied. "He is *Signore* Slater's little brother," she stated.

Patrick had to resist the urge to call her out for saying David Slater was "little." From what he remembered, the two appeared to be about the same hieght. "I think you mean *younger*," he murmured.

"Donna Vittoria will need to be careful with that one," she added, wagging a finger before she turned to resume her work at the sink.

"Oh?" he responded, curious as to what she might have heard in the market square. Feeling spiteful on behalf of David Slater, he said, "It seems to me any young man would need to be careful when it comes to *Donna* Vittoria."

The housekeeper turned from the sink and gave him what he could only interpret as an evil eye. "*Donna* Vittoria D'Avalos is a sweet, perfect young lady," she claimed.

"She is?" He didn't mean for his query to sound with disbelief, but from the behavior he had paid witness to the night before, he would have thought Vittoria a spoiled rotten brat.

"She is a perfect young *donna, signore*," Signora Ricci insisted. "Penton is a *briccone*."

Patrick glanced at Giovanni, hoping the servant could supply the English translation.

"*Libertino*," the young man whispered.

Stunned the viscount had such a reputation—he hadn't paid witness to any actions that would put David Slater into the category of a rake—Patrick turned his attention to his missive. "Thank you for telling me. I shall be sure to pass along the information should anyone ask me," he said.

The few lines of masculine scrawl were merely an acknowledgement that a delivery of wool had been made to the dock and loaded on *The Fairweather*. The sailing vessel was due to depart for England on the morrow.

Since he had shared what he knew from the ball, perhaps Signora Ricci would be able to provide him with information on a certain woman who lived only a short distance away. "Might you know anything about *Donna*

Vittoria's aunt? Great aunt... *prozia*, I think. Uh... *Donna* Armenia D'Avalos?"

A scoff sounded from the servant as she executed the sign of the cross over her left breast. "She is a... an *una puttana*. You would be wise to avoid her."

"*Una puttana*?" he repeated in confusion.

"A whore," Giovanni whispered, but he rolled his eyes as if he thought his mother's assessment wasn't to be believed.

Patrick settled back in his chair and allowed a sigh of disappointment. He had a hope that his housekeeper might be in his corner when it came to the aristocrat's aunt. Instead it seemed he would need to keep his regard for Armenia a secret from her.

Turning his attention back to his breakfast, Patrick downed the meal quickly and descended the stairs to his office.

He decided it best he see to the rest of his correspondence in private until it was time to leave for Villa D'Avalos.

CHAPTER 12
A WALK IS A BIT BUMPY

*M*eanwhile...

Arm-in-arm, Nicoletta and Donald and their guests departed the courtyard of Palazzo D'Avalos and headed in the direction of the river. Once again, David was forced to offer his arm to Vittoria when his uncle and cousins paired up with their wives.

Vittoria allowed an audible sigh but threaded her arm through his elbow. "Are you sure you wish to be seen in the company of a tart?" she asked in a hoarse whisper.

David gave a start, surprised she would even speak to him. "I'm not sure if you are aware, but tarts come both sweet and sour," he said.

She furrowed her dark brows. "What are you saying?"

Chuckling softly, he said, "I have a confession to make."

"There is a church very close," she countered, waving a gloved hand in the direction of a gothic building featuring a pair of ornate spires.

For a moment, David was confused until he realized she was speaking of a confessional in a Catholic church. "No, not that sort of confession. One meant only for you," he replied.

She inhaled softly. "Tell me," she urged.

David cleared his throat, his gaze going from her to the building they were passing. "Had I arrived to the ball only a few minutes earlier than I did last night, I might have employed tactics similar to those that had *Signore* Luciano leading you to that alcove." He paused them a moment so he could study the architecture of the buildings on both sides of the narrow lane in which they walked.

Vittoria narrowed her eyes. "So... you admit you are a rogue?"

He waggled his brows as if to reinforce words that could only confirm her suspicions about him being a rake.

"Only to suffer the same fate as him?" she went on, a look of triumph suffusing her face.

"Had *I* been the one joining you in that alcove, you would have been enjoying the encounter, I assure you," he claimed. "You would not have given a thought to injuring my person, but then, I would have made sure your indiscretion went unnoticed by everyone in attendance."

Vittoria huffed. "You... you insufferable—"

"I prefer my tarts sweet, by the way," David added, a grin bringing a dimple to his lower left cheek.

"Then I suppose I must be sure to be forever sour in your—"

"Oh, Vittoria, shall we show our guests our favorite staircase?" The query came from Nicoletta, who, with her husband, was walking alongside Donald's parents. Behind them were Randy, Diana, Tom, and Helen. Several in their party looked back at Vittoria.

She blinked. "*Sì.* Perhaps someone will enjoy a dip in the fountain there," she replied, directing a glare at David.

He gasped. "I have not found the heat especially oppressive, but if you're feeling faint, my lady, I could certainly assist you in a thorough dousing if you'd like."

Vittoria's mouth dropped open as her eyes turned to slits. "You wouldn't *dare*," she countered in a hoarse whisper.

"Continue to test me, and I'll…" Although he seemed about to continue, David suddenly sobered when he noticed Randy had turned to glare at him. "You are correct. I would not." He didn't add that he could certainly allow his imagination to come up with a suitable image that would keep him entertained should he ever be bored—Vittoria D'Avalos, sitting in the middle of a marble fountain, not only drenched, but suffering the indignity of a nearby statue peeing on her.

Not on her head, though. He found her coiffure especially fetching, the single lock of hair on her shoulder making him wish he could slide his hand beneath it so he could feel the silken strands against his bare skin.

Perhaps he really did need to seek out a priest in a confessional.

The two ceased their conversation as they followed the others to the Piazza Trinità dei Monti and the Spanish Steps.

"*D*avid and Vittoria seem to be conversing rather well," Nicoletta said, her comment directed to her husband.

"That is no surprise to me," Donald replied. "Everyone finds David rather amiable. I'm not sure what you have in mind for them, though."

Nicoletta grinned as she squeezed his arm. "I think they would make a *perfect* match," she claimed. "Don't you?"

Donald made an odd sound in his throat. "Your niece and my brother?" he asked in disbelief. Although he hadn't been a witness to whatever Vittoria claimed had occurred the night before, her assessment of David had convinced Donald the girl wanted absolutely nothing to do with him. The fact that David was even sporting enough to escort her on this day had him realizing his younger brother was more mature than he had been when they departed on their trip from England only two years prior.

He remembered a time when he had been on his own Grand Tour—it hadn't even been ten years ago!—and he had wanted nothing more than to seek out female companionship. A chance to sow his wild oats. Then he had met Nicoletta in Catania, and all thoughts of other possible liaisons had dissipated.

Given David's age and the fact that he had already been betrothed had Donald believing his brother would prefer to explore Rome on his own with an entirely different agenda than the one they were pursuing on this day.

One that included young ladies, and not of the aristocratic sort.

Nicoletta glanced over at Barbara, who was pretending not to overhear their exchange. "What, pray tell, do you think of Vittoria?" she asked.

Barbara arched a brow, her attention briefly darting to her husband to discover his attention was directed at the building they were passing. "She is a lovely young lady who will no doubt cause my David a good deal of trouble," she replied, her lip quirked. "I saw how he watched her last night."

"I fear I might have overheard words suggesting they were... *annoyed* with one another," Donald murmured, glancing back to see the two in question had fallen behind their group. From the way their heads were bent, it was apparent they were speaking to one another, and not in a pleasant manner.

"Annoyed?" Nicoletta repeated. "Do you suppose he missed his dance with her?"

"No. I saw them dancing," he said.

The marchesa inhaled softly. "Are you quite sure?"

He nodded. "A surprise, I know, since our niece's dance card was quite full. I believe their words were exchanged well before she took her first dance partner. Mayhap before we even made our appearance at the ball."

Nicoletta paused at a stone bench and lifted a dainty foot to rest it on the edge. Donald was quick to check the fastenings of her half-boot to see they were fine. He couldn't help but notice her attention was on her niece, though.

"Are we pretending something?" he asked in a hoarse whisper, his gaze following hers to see that David and Vittoria had fallen even further behind their party. From the way the young woman's hands waved about—she wasn't even hanging onto David's arm—he knew they were engaged in an argument of some sort.

Nicoletta lowered her foot to the bricks making up the street and lifted her other foot to the edge of the bench. "*Sì*, and you're performing your part perfectly," she murmured.

"*Grazie*," Donald replied, grinning when Diana and Helen mimicked what his wife was doing, their husbands quick to check their footwear for embedded stones. He angled his head in the youngest couple's direction. "We'd best let them have their disagreement," he murmured.

"I'm not sure whom I should be more worried about," Diana whispered. "Although I know David can hold his own in an argument, I don't believe that's quite what's happening."

"Lady Vittoria truly believes David is a rogue," Helen remarked.

"And she's being a shrew about it," Donald said on a huff. He turned to see a look of shock on his wife's face.

"Apologies, my sweet. but I've never seen her behave like this."

Nicoletta sighed her disappointment. "No need to apologize, darling. I am well aware something must have happened last night to have them behaving so." She allowed another sigh. "I was so hoping they might make a match."

Donald blinked in alarm but didn't reply.

CHAPTER 13
INTERRUPTING A BATH

Meanwhile, a mile to the southwest

Patrick regarded the entrance to the courtyard of Villa D'Avalos and wondered how long the testament to marble architecture had been standing. The Corinthian columns framing the wrought iron gates were stained with rust but otherwise intact. The marble blocks making up the courtyard walls, which he realized were also the outside walls of at least one of the interior rooms of the villa and of the carriage house, were mostly white, their veining a combination of pale yellow and gold.

A doorway separate from the gate was set off to one side, a reminder that most people probably didn't arrive by coach but rather on foot. He tested the black wrought iron handle and was surprised when it easily moved and the wooden door swung inward. When he closed it, he was careful to ensure the latch caught.

Glancing around the courtyard, he discovered flowering oleanders in between the evenly spaced columnar cypress trees. From their perfect shape and size, it was evident a gardener tended the property.

Armenia's coach wasn't in the courtyard, but there were tracks on the marble floor leading to the carriage house, and their arched wooden doors were closed. The faint odor of horse manure suggested the stables were probably behind the carriage house.

Patrick made his way across the courtyard and paused before the front doors. Another set of Corinthian columns flanked it—a detail he hadn't noticed the night before given the dark. Glancing up, he was surprised to see the building stood at least three stories tall. Remembering the stairs beyond the doors, he realized the servants quarters were probably on the ground floor to the right.

He pulled his pocket watch from his waistcoat and checked the time—a minute past eleven. Well, her ladyship couldn't claim he arrived too early if he knocked now.

Grabbing the large ring beneath the iron lion's head knocker in a gloved hand, he pounded it three times and stepped back. He didn't have to wait long for one of the panels to open.

"*Signore* DeLuca?" he said, remembering the name Armenia had used the night before.

"*Sì?*"

"*Signore* Patrick McAdams for *Donna* Armenia," he said, holding out a calling card.

The butler didn't take the card but stepped back and bowed as Patrick entered the vestibule. "*Donna* Armenia *è al piano di sopra. Seguimi.*"

She is upstairs. Follow me.

They climbed the curved staircase, the servant continuing to climb even when a landing indicated they had reached the first floor. From Patrick's brief glance, it was apparent the villa was kept in good repair. Paintings framed in gilt lined the walls, their placement below ornately carved moldings. A wide marble landing at the top of the stairs branched off into two corridors, a Turkish rug running the length of both.

They passed four closed doors before reaching the end of the west corridor. DeLuca knocked on the door and said, "*Signore* McAdams *è qui.*"

There was a moment of silence before a feminine voice called out, "*venire.*"

Reaching for the door handle, DeLuca paused and gave Patrick a beseeching look.

"What is it?" Patrick asked. "Uh... *sbagliato?*"

"*Potrebbe essere arrabbiata.*" He lifted both shoulders and hurried back down the hall as if he feared his mistress.

"Angry?" Patrick repeated, not sure if he correctly understood the man's comment. He slipped into the room—a sort of parlor featuring a marble fireplace and feminine furnishings from the century prior—but no one was seated at either of the chairs or on the settee. A chandelier hung in the center, but none of the candles were lit. "*Donna* Armenia?"

"In here," he heard from somewhere to his left.

He made his way through the only open door on that side of the room and stopped short at seeing Armenia lounging in a footed bathtub set in the middle of a bathing chamber. If she hadn't been there, he would have taken a moment to appreciate the marble fountain that dominated one wall or the chandelier that matched the one in the parlor. Perhaps he would have glanced out the windows hung with lacy curtains that faced both west and south.

Instead, his gaze was caught by her. At first, he thought she was naked, her raven hair caught up in an ornate chignon at the back of her head, her bare arms resting on the curled edge of the tub, the level of the water barely covering her breasts. After staring for only a moment, he realized she wore a sleeveless shift. Beneath the water, though, the fabric was practically translucent, and he could make out the rosy areolae of her breasts and the dark triangle at the top of her thighs.

Apparently his cock thought the display was an invitation, for it reacted before he even realized what was happening. "Uh... apologies," he said, turning away. "I didn't mean to—"

"One would think you had never seen a woman in a bath before," Armenia chided.

He swallowed, willing his manhood to settle down. "That's because... well, I... I haven't," he struggled to reply.

"Liar," she accused, although there was humor in her voice.

Finally facing her, his brows furrowing at hearing her accusation, he scoffed. "I have not," he insisted. When she didn't attempt to cover her breasts with one of her arms, he glanced around until he spotted a pile of bath linens on a chair at the end of the tub. "Where is your lady's maid?" He headed to the chair and took the opportunity to glance out the window to see the tops of the buildings across the street. Beyond was the river. At one time, the villa probably had a clear view of the Tiber.

Armenia straightened in the tub, pulled her knees to her chest, and wrapped her arms around her legs. "I dismissed Marcella after she finished my hair," she replied, turning her head in an attempt to discover what he was doing.

Patrick plucked a linen from atop the stack and shook it out. "She's done a beautiful coiffure," he remarked. "But don't you usually bathe first and then have your hair done?"

Blinking several times when he moved to stand next to the edge of the tub, the linen held up so it hid his face from her, she scoffed. "*Sì*, usually," she replied. "But I decided I wished to bathe after she had already finished it. I was not thinking straight this morning."

He dropped the linen a fraction, his gaze studying the fabric. "This isn't linen," he murmured thoughtfully. Realizing what she had said had him dropping the bath linen more, and he furrowed his brows. "Why weren't you thinking straight?"

Armenia stared at him a moment. "Because I didn't remember I was to expect you until she had already finished." She lifted an arm. "Help an old lady to stand, will you?"

"Old lady?" he repeated, glancing around the bathing chamber. "I don't see anyone matching that description."

She glanced up at him, her expression unreadable. "Perhaps you require spectacles."

"Ha ha," he replied. Doing her bidding required he drop one corner of the towel so he could offer a hand. He tried not to look as she stood, her other hand gripping the edge of the tub until she was on her feet.

Noting the tub was elevated due to the clawfeet located at the four corners, he feared she might be injured should she slip during her attempt to get out of it. "From wherever did you get this tub?" he asked.

"I had it shipped from Holland," she replied.

"Cast iron?" he guessed. What other material could it be made from that would allow it to have feet? Unless she'd had a sculptor carve it from marble, and it didn't appear to be made of stone.

"Yes, and the towels are made of cotton," she said on a huff, obviously not impressed he would notice. She watched as he recaptured the other corner of the towel and held it up to wrap it around her. He took another from the stack, shook it out, and tossed it over one of his shoulders. "What are you...?" She couldn't finish the sentence when he simply scooped her into his arms and lifted her from the tub.

"Apologies, but I think this is safer for you," he said. "Where…. where do you dress?"

"You're going to be soaked through," she said in dismay.

"It's merely water… isn't it?"

"Well, I didn't add any oils to the bath water, if that's what you're asking."

"Good. That will make it less likely I'll drop you."

She scoffed, her attention on the open doorway. "Through there and into my bedchamber," she said, pointing with a forefinger. "Although I *can* walk. I shouldn't want you to hurt your back."

"You're light as a feather. Tall, but…" He hefted her, which had her crying out in surprise. "Light."

"I cannot help my height," she said as he angled her through the door and into the sitting room.

"Nor should you. It suits you," he said. "Makes you appear statuesque."

"What's *that* supposed to mean?" she asked, sounding defensive.

"You look like a Roman goddess. You're an aristocrat, are you not? When you stand, you don't slouch like some of the other tall women tend to do, as if they think it's fashionable to…" He paused on the threshold of the arched opening into the bedchamber. A maid had already seen to making the canopied bed, its red velvet counterpane topped with a number of satin-covered pillows.

"Fashionable to?" she prompted.

He glanced down at her, and for the first time since they had left the bathing chamber, he realized she had lifted her arm to grip his shoulder, as if she thought he might lose his hold on her. "Slouch," he murmured. He lowered his arm and bent down until her feet touched the carpet. "Your shoulders are rather regal. You are wise to show them off as you did last evening." In direct opposition to his words, he took the towel he had draped over one of his shoulders, unfolded it, and wrapped it around her shoulders. "I would offer to help dry you, but I..." He swallowed.

"Your top coat is soaked," she said in dismay.

"It's wool. Superfine. It will dry," he assured her. He glanced back in the direction of the sitting room. "Should I wait for you in there?"

"I'll need help with my corset and buttons," she said.

His cock once again reacting as if it thought she was inviting him to her bed, Patrick took a deep, steadying breath. "So, you don't intend to ring for your lady's maid?"

All at once, her shoulders dropped and a sigh of frustration sounded. "I can, of course."

"Uh, oh, dear," he said, understanding suddenly dawning. "You wanted me to... to bed you?" he whispered. It wasn't hard for him to sound disappointed he had missed his cue.

She visibly swallowed. "Not at first, no," she replied. "I almost told DeLuca to send you away," she added. "As I said, I wasn't thinking straight."

His brows furrowed in confusion. "Wh... what changed?"

Huffing as she turned and made her way to a massive maple wardrobe, Armenia opened the doors and plucked a deep green walking gown from a peg and tossed it onto the bed. "I thought you a... I thought you were a rogue," she accused.

"*Me*?" he asked in disbelief. "What have I done to give you that impression?"

"Well, *nothing*, as it turns out. Well, except when we were dancing, and you made that remark about my shoulders." She shivered at the reminder of how his gloved hand had caressed the top of her shoulder during their dance. How he had leaned forward. She was sure he was going to brush his lips over them. He hadn't moved that close, though. The brief disappointment she had experienced had surprised her.

She opened a bureau drawer and pulled out several undergarments, tossing them onto the bed with more force than was necessary.

"You have gorgeous shoulders," he countered. "Among other rather beautiful attributes."

She inhaled sharply. "Most men would have started with *those*," she said, adding several petticoats to the pile of undergarments.

"I would not think it appropriate to comment on a woman's... *bosom*... during a ball," he replied. "Even if yours is rather... impressive."

Clutching the wet bath linen he had wrapped around her, Armenia glanced down to discover one of her breasts was no longer covered, the damp shift plastered to her skin so her nipple showed through the translucent fabric.

"*Exactly* like a Roman goddess," he murmured, struggling to keep from taking a step closer. If he had, he wouldn't be able to stop himself, and the clothes that were piled atop the bed would have ended up on the floor to make room for her once he had her stripped of the linens and the wet shift.

In only a moment, he imagined the different ways he could bring her pleasure, to have her writhing beneath him, begging him, calling out in his name, or murmuring a string of naughty Italian words before he buried himself in her. Although it had been some time since he had been with a woman, he was fairly certain he hadn't forgotten the basics.

The basics wouldn't be enough for her, though, would they? She had probably been with a number of lovers. Skilled lovers.

A whore, his housekeeper had said. The reminder was like being doused with a bucket of cold water.

Armenia must have sensed the change in him, for she quickly readjusted the linen. "I thought perhaps you were attempting to seduce me," she murmured. "I was sure of it when you climbed into my coach last night."

He winced as he scratched the side of his face with a forefinger. "That was rather brash of me," he admitted. "I happen to come from a city where women require protection from footpads and thieves and worse," he explained. "So when I learned from the conte that you didn't have an escort, I thought to act as one on your behalf."

She relaxed at hearing his explanation. "You certainly know how to make an impression," she said in a whisper.

"Well, first impressions are important," he replied. He dipped his head. "If you'd still like, I'll help you dress, and we'll go for a walk. You can show me... four... mayhap five fountains. Enjoy a luncheon."

"And then?" she prompted, sounding breathless.

"And then... if you wish, I'll escort you back here, and..." He swallowed. "If you'd like, I'll, uh, make love to you," he whispered.

Her eyes widened in suspicion. "But not because *you'll* want to," she challenged.

It was his turn to scoff. "Oh, my lady, you could not be more wrong."

She blinked several times, especially when he quickly moved to the bed and pulled the shift from the pile of cotton underthings. "If I don't get you dressed this minute..." He shook his head.

"You'll what?" she challenged.

"Well, I'll be no better than the rogue you believed me to be when I climbed into your coach last night. But I am a gentleman, *mia donna.*"

Gathering up the edges of the shift, he held it out as she dropped the damp towels, and he pulled the damp garment off her body, careful not to disturb her hair. He was just as careful with the dry shift, placing the opening over her head as she pushed her arms through the sleeves.

Try as he might not to stare, he couldn't help but steal quick glances of her bare body. Although she did possess heavy breasts, their nipples tight and puckered in the cool air, she was otherwise lean. Not skinny, though, for her hipbones didn't show in relief, nor did her collarbones. Her thighs were long, and her calves gently curved in an S-shape that ended in narrow, long feet. For a brief moment, he imagined what they would feel like gripped around his thighs as he rode her in a spirited round of sexual congress.

He gulped back a curse. If he wasn't such a damned gentleman, he would take her right now. Pick her up and dump her onto the red velvet counterpane. Suckle her breasts and stroke her belly and thighs. Insert a finger inside her most private place and use his thumb to rub her clit until she begged him to stop.

Would she, though? How many times could she be pleasured in a single bout of lovemaking?

She didn't strike him as one who would be satisfied unless she was pleasured at least three times.

Three times.

Well, he could manage that. His manhood obviously thought so, too, for it had begun to throb. He was glad for the long skirt of his top coat, for his erection would have been quite evident given the tight fit of his pantaloons.

Whore.

Once again, the word had him gaining control of himself. At some point, he would have to discover why his housekeeper would say such a thing about Armenia.

He returned his attention to her face, struck by his inability to guess her age. He saw no wrinkles but for a few lines that radiated from the sides of her eyes. "You would have made an excellent model for Botticelli," he remarked.

She made an odd sound in her throat. "No one has ever said anything like that to me before."

He turned and fished the corset from beneath a petticoat. "I'm sure they thought it," he offered, secretly pleased he seemed to have scored a point in his favor with the compliment. Once she had the corset in place, he saw to tightening the strings before tying the ends into a bow.

"You have seen Italian art?" she asked.

"Not as much as I'd like. Perhaps you can be my guide here in Rome," he said, arching a brow. "Stockings next?" he guessed, holding out the pair of black knit garments.

"I can finish the rest on my own," she said, motioning to the sitting room.

"You're sending me away?" he asked, pretending offense.

"You passed the test," she said, arching a brow.

"Oh." Chuckling softly, he dipped his head and made his way to the sitting room to wait for her.

He exhaled a breath of relief as he took a seat even as he knew what he had to look forward to later that afternoon.

Some Italian artistry at its finest.

CHAPTER 14
THE SPANISH STEPS
LEAD TO A SINKING SHIP

*M*eanwhile, in Piazza Trinità dei Monti

For all of five minutes, neither David nor Vittoria said a word. The air between them crackled with a sort of energy that could only be described as invigorating in the worst possible way.

Vittoria glanced up at the *Obelisco Sallustiano*, a Roman obelisk made to imitate those in Egypt and erected directly in front of the doors to the Chiesa della Santissima Trinità dei Monti. Even its hieroglyphic inscription was copied from another obelisk.

"I can only imagine what you'd like to do with that should you be able to lift it," David commented dryly.

Blinking in confusion, Vittoria allowed her gaze to go from the bottom to the peak of the structure, her attention lingering on the cross that crowned a fleur-de-lis at the very top. "I do not know of what you speak," she claimed.

"Impale me with it?" he hinted, remembering what the statue of Apollo had done to *Don* Luciano the night before.

She gave him a quelling glance. "I would not do so with a cross," she countered. Her eyes narrowed. "Are you quite sure you don't require a confessional?" she added. She and David followed the others in their party into the Catholic church for which the plaza was named.

David countered her quelling glance with one of his own. "I am happy to wait outside should you wish to unburden yourself," he countered, his gaze taking in the interior of the late Renaissance church. Knowing the structure had been home to Minim Friars for most of its existence, he expected to see more of a French influence in its interior. He also knew Napoleon had it looted of its original decorations, though. The Bourbons had restored it nearly a quarter of a century ago, and although it was quite beautiful, it struck him odd that the ceiling was entirely white.

When Vittoria didn't provide a reply to his last comment about waiting while she went to a confessional, he glanced in her direction. He suddenly regretted his words, for she appeared to be on the verge of tears. "Apologies. That was unkind of me," he said.

"I thought it rather knightly," she countered.

Blinking, David struggled to sort her meaning. "Knightly?" he repeated.

She nodded. "Chivalrous," she stated, pronouncing the word slowly in her Italian-accented English.

"Oh," he replied. "Then... I will wait for you. There is certainly much to see in here, if we're allowed to linger," he added.

She shrugged and lifted a handkerchief to the edge of one eye. "I am not sure why, but I always have the urge to cry when I come here."

"Well, it is beautiful," he said. As far as churches were concerned, he had been in a number of them during their Grand Tour. None stood out as particularly jaw-dropping, although he was looking forward to the Church of St. John on Malta. They planned to stop in Valletta on the way back to England to see the co-cathedral's art and its exquisite Baroque interior.

"But it is not the most beautiful of all the churches in Rome," she said in a whisper. "Wait until you see St. Peter's Basilica."

The two gave a start when they realized someone was directly behind them.

"Are we ready to descend the steps?" Donald asked in a hoarse whisper.

David glanced over his shoulder at his brother, surprised to discover the rest of their party were already making their way out of the church and down its double staircase. "The Spanish Steps?" he asked.

"Indeed," Nicoletta said happily. "But first allow me to show you where your English poet John Keats lived," she added, pointing to a house to her left. "He died there, too, when I was a young girl."

"I admit I am not terribly familiar with his works," Barbara said.

"That's because you and I were recently married and busy with two boys and the farm," Will reminded her.

"How many steps are there?" Barbara asked as they made their way across the piazza. She stopped short upon seeing the terraced stairs leading down to a fountain. "Oh!" The steep decline from the double staircase in front of the church to the terraced steps below resulted in momentary vertigo.

"One-hundred-and-thirty-five," Donald stated.

"My knees are already causing me pain," Will quipped, but he led Barbara down the first set of stairs, pausing at the landing to allow the others to join them.

"The view from here is quite spectacular," Diana breathed.

"Because you want to dig it up?" Randy asked, grinning.

She directed a grimace at him and shook her head. "It feels as if it's already been dug up and is on display," she said happily, bouncing down the stairs as she held onto her husband's arm.

Tom and Helen joined them, the younger couple serpentining their way down to the Piazza di Spagna in an effort to avoid the stairs that had been damaged or were crumbling from the effects of time.

"Shall we?" David asked, glad Vittoria once again threaded her arm through his. He couldn't imagine how she would be able to descend so many stairs given the bell-skirted gown she wore. "I promise to catch you should you stumble. These stairs are not in very good condition."

"I will be fine," she replied, "but I do prefer climbing them instead of going down them."

"Won't we be doing that later?" he asked, glancing back to see how far down they had come from the church.

She gave him a quelling glance. "Nicoletta has carriages following us for a reason. We'll walk all the way to the Pantheon, but we'll be riding home."

He chuckled softly as he led them down a path of stairs that were mostly intact. "Such a shame they are so damaged."

"That's because they're French," she replied with derision.

"What?" David scoffed softly.

"The Bourbons had them built. They've been here since seventeen-twenty-five," she explained.

"Well, I think their age has something to do with their condition," he countered. "Tell me about what we're heading towards," he added, lifting his chin to indicate the fountain below them.

"That is the Fontana della Barcaccia," Vittoria replied.

"It's shaped like a boat," David remarked.

"Indeed. Papa told me it was designed by Pietro Bernini—"

"The pope's architect for the Acqua Vergine?" David interrupted.

"The very same," she replied, her arched brow indicating she was impressed he knew of the aqueduct that fed several fountains in Rome. "He designed it in honor of a boat that was left shipwrecked here in the piazza when the Tiber flooded in fifteen ninety-eight."

David glanced in the direction he thought the river might be and frowned. "That must have been some flood," he murmured.

When they finally reached the Piazza di Spagna, David rushed them to the edge of the fountain. For the briefest of moments, he once again imagined Vittoria in the structure, wet but for her head. For some reason, the idea of her in a sinking boat had him realizing he would go in after her. Save her from drowning, for surely her gown and petticoats would drag her under the surface. "If I remember my readings about the aqueduct, the fountains along it are all gravity-fed," he mused.

Vittoria appeared confused. "Gravity-fed?" she repeated, shaking her head slightly.

"Oh, the, uh, the water in the aqueduct is essentially running downhill, which means these fountains are able to spout their water simply due to gravity." He glanced around. "The next fountain on the line is probably in that direction," he said, pointing toward the south.

"We're headed there next," Donald said, joining his brother. Nicoletta stepped up alongside him, a small flask held in one gloved hand. "The water here is drinkable if you're thirsty," she said.

"Really?" David asked in awe.

"Most of the fountains feature fresh water," Donald said.

He held out his own flask and David took a sip while Vittoria saw to filling her own. The silver *mensa* had obviously been in her pocket, for she didn't carry a reticule.

"Very refreshing," David remarked.

"Even more so if you douse yourself in it," Vittoria teased.

David blinked. "Careful, my lady, or you shall be taking your second bath of the day," he warned, although his grin was wide.

Vittoria's eyes rounded. "How is it you know I took one already?"

Seeing her shock had David smirking. "I could say it was a lucky guess, but you smell of lemons and something lightly floral," he murmured, only loud enough for her to hear.

Inhaling softly, Vittoria turned away from him before her blush was evident.

"We had best be on our way," Nicoletta said. "The next fountain we'll see is my favorite of all."

"Mine, too," Donald said, offering her his arm as he surreptitiously bussed her on the cheek.

Shrieks of delight had them turning to see their cousins splashing water on each other and on Will and Barbara.

"The sooner the better," David said.

Chuckling, the four of them led the others out of the piazza and in a southerly direction.

"Downhill all the way," Vittoria murmured.

When David glanced in her direction, he saw she displayed a pleasant expression. Something about seeing her happy seemed to put him in a much better mood.

He had come to realize he really didn't like a shrew.

CHAPTER 15
A FOUNTAIN AND
SOME GOSSIP

half-hour later

Although it had only taken Armenia another twenty minutes to finish dressing, she rang for coffee and insisted they enjoy the tiny servings prior to setting out in the direction of Piazza Navona.

Her walking gown was a bell-skirted affair featuring a rather high neckline, long sleeves that ballooned in the middle but were tight at the deep cuffs, and a matching mantle. A small hat, a dark green felt with a single peacock feather, didn't hide the best of the coiffure Marcella, her lady's maid, had spent nearly an hour creating that morning.

Patrick had offered an arm upon their exit from Villa D'Avalos and saw to the door at the courtyard entrance, which gave her an opportunity to study his clothes. She thought his choice of a yellow waistcoat interesting—had he expected her to wear yellow?—but it was perfect with his navy coat. She thought his buff pantaloons might have been Nankeen, but the way they hugged his muscular calves had her realizing they were made from some kind of knit fabric.

Upon closer inspection of his top coat, she expected to see water stains but found no evidence the coat had suffered from its earlier soaking. What little of his waistcoat that showed hinted at silk embroidered with tiny birds.

Once they were on the street, she asked, "How is it you knew your top coat would not be damaged from its bath this morning?"

He chuckled softly. "You might say it is my business to know. I deal in silks and woolens," he reminded her.

Giving him a look of disbelief, she said, "When you told me you wanted to speak with my nephew about his sheep, I did not realize you were asking for his wool."

He chuckled. "I'll take as much as I can find here in the Kingdom of the Two Sicilies," he said. "I have cargo hold space secured on ships that sail to England and on steamers that cross the Atlantic," he explained. "I have customers all over America demanding the very best wool and silks."

"Has it completely dried? Your coat, I mean?" she asked. They emerged from the tight confines of Via di Tor Millina and into the plaza, the bright sun and few clouds already promising a warm day.

"Indeed. I believe it was before we had even left the house," he replied. "I tend to choose superfine for my top coats as it can survive a good soaking in the rain."

She inhaled softly. "How is it I didn't know this?"

He reached over with his free hand and pinched a section of her mantle. "Your wrap is made of it," he said. "The die matches perfectly with your gown. Cotton twill, is it not?"

Blinking, she shook her head. "I have absolutely no idea."

He sounded a scoff. "You don't choose the fabrics for your clothes?" he asked in surprise.

"Well, the colors, yes, but I leave the fabric choice to my modiste."

"Then you are very trusting," he commented.

"Madame Clos du Bois has made my gowns for..." Here she paused, not sure she wanted to admit how long she had employed the old woman who, despite her name, was no more French than she was. "A very long time," she finished.

He chuckled. "She has done well with your gown. The small bows along the striping are perfectly spaced and not overdone at all."

"Oh?" she glanced down at the tiny decorations as if seeing them for the first time.

"Some modistes tend to over-decorate a gown, which means they can charge more for it," he commented. "Lots of frills and furbelows are fine for a young lady fresh from the schoolroom, but for true ladies, restraint should be practiced." He paused before adding. "The gown you wore last night was absolute perfection. You wore it very well, and the color was..."

Red.

Whore. His housekeeper's comment once again had him sobering.

"Flattering?" she guessed.

"Yes," he agreed. "Yes. I was trying to think of the name for the red. Some French word for poppy, I believe."

Armenia arched a brow but decided not to challenge him. "Coquelicot," she murmured.

"That's it," he said, raising a gloved finger.

"I'll be sure to let Madame Clos du Bois know," she said. Apparently the man knew fashion as well as fabrics.

As for the reason for their walk, she was reminded of it when they approached the fountain located in the middle of the piazza. "When you said you wished to see four fountains, it's rather unfair we came here first," she remarked. Piazza Navona featured three fountains, evenly spaced out along the long, narrow plaza.

"I've only visited the Fountain of the Four Rivers," he replied, using the English name for the Fontana del Quattro Fiumi. "So the other two will be new to me." He pointed in the direction of his office and lodgings. "I live in a building just there," he added.

She followed his line of sight and frowned. "You rent space?" she asked, wondering if she might know his landlord.

"I actually bought part of the building," he replied, stopping before the section of the fountain dedicated to the Nile River. The man depicted in the statuary bore a remarkable resemblance to paintings of Moses. "The ground floor has my office as well as one for my secretary, and I live in the upper floors."

Armenia gave a cursory glance in the direction of the ornate fountain, the carvings by Bernini so familiar to her, she could recite all four rivers—the Ganges, the Danube, Rio de la Plata, and the Nile—even though she hadn't actually seen any of them in person. In the center was a Roman obelisk topped with a bronze bird.

"Do you employ servants?" she asked, moving to stand before the side of the fountain dedicated to the Danube. The statue of the muscular man portraying the river was turned toward the obelisk, apparently because Faith was said to be descending on the world from the obelisk.

"I must," he affirmed. "I have a young man who sees to my clothing, and his mother, who is my cook and housekeeper."

"Convenient," she commented, moving to the side of the fountain depicting the Rio de la Plata, its statue appearing awestruck by Faith since it was unknown in its part of the world.

"Indeed. Although I do wonder as to how many people know everything there is to know about me around here." He waved to indicate the surrounding area.

She paused before completing the circle around the fountain. "What do you mean?"

"I rather imagine Signora Ricci enjoys exchanging gossip with the other housekeepers in this area. Perhaps even with yours."

Inhaling softly at hearing the familiar name, Armenia removed a glove and reached out to dip her hand in the water. "No doubt," she said, pretending nonchalance. Perhaps the Signora Ricci he employed wasn't the same Sophia Ricci who had at one time been a housemaid in Villa D'Avalos back when her brother, Enrico, was still alive and master of the house. Been employed and then dismissed when it was discovered she was with child.

How long ago had that been? Twenty years, at least. Mayhap twenty-five years. As for who had fathered the child, Armenia didn't know, nor had she ever asked. She had learned long ago that when dealing with her older brother, she couldn't believe half of what he told her.

Despite her efforts to keep her private life unknown to the servants of Villa D'Avalos, Armenia knew they shared gossip when she entertained a member of the opposite sex, even if it was only for a coffee or a meal. As to how far that gossip extended, she had no idea. Gossip was a commodity in Rome, though, as important as news of business or politics.

"Do you know her?" Patrick asked.

The query pulled Armenia from her brief reverie. She shook the the water from her hand, as if she found it offensive. "If she is the same woman, Signora Ricci has worked as a servant for a number of households in this area," she remarked.

"'A number of households' implies she's either not a very good employee or she's—"

"A gossip," Armenia stated. "Be mindful of what you say in her presence, and you should be fine." She knew from his reaction she had said too much.

"Did she spread rumors about you?" he asked, his concern evident in how his brows furrowed.

Armenia lifted a shoulder. "Probably, but I learned long ago not to pay any mind to gossip."

"Liar," he murmured quietly.

About to deny his claim, she instead said, "Given Signora Ricci's age..." She paused and did a quick addition in her head. "You will likely find her a loyal employee. She cannot afford to be relieved of yet another position." Armenia placed her arm back on his, expecting they would resume their walk.

"How long have you known her?" he asked.

She lifted a shoulder and considered the query a moment. "Since long before I gained possession of Villa D'Avalos."

"Gained possession?" he repeated.

She saw his look of humor and relaxed. "My brother gave it to the Marquess Montblanc as a dowry when he married off my niece, Nicoletta, to the marquess. Not even ten years ago," she explained, her body quaking at the reminder of Enrico's betrayal.

Villa D'Avalos had been her childhood home. Her refuge in Rome. For Enrico D'Avalos to have given it away as a dowry was unforgivable. He had gone to his grave knowing how angry it made Armenia. It also left the immediate family with property only in Catania.

"How did you get it back?"

She lifted a shoulder. "Montblanc gave it to me. In his last will and testament," she replied.

Noting how Patrick stiffened at hearing the news, Armenia wondered about two things at once. Did Patrick assume she and Montblanc had been lovers? And was he jealous?

The oddest flutter in her chest had her inhaling softly.

CHAPTER 16
A MAGICAL FOUNTAIN

eanwhile, at the intersection of Via De' Crocicchi, Via Poli and Via Delle Muratte

Although he had seen drawings and paintings of the largest Baroque fountain in all of Rome, David Slater, Viscount Penton, wasn't prepared for seeing the Trevi Fountain in all its glory.

The eighty-year-old travertine structure was huge—over one-hundred and sixty feet wide and nearly ninety feet tall —and it marked the end of the Acqua Vergine aqueduct in spectacular fashion.

"Is that Neptune?" Randy asked, pointing to the central figure standing atop a chariot made of a shell and pulled by two hippocamps and two tritons.

"The Titan Oceanus," Diana replied. "At the very top of the façade is the papal coat of arms."

"Is that a real building behind it?" Helen asked, her feet at the very edge of the pool of water in front of the fountain.

"Indeed. The Palazzo Poli. It's a private residence," Donald replied. "The columns you see framing Oceanus are free-standing. They are not connected to the triumphal arch, which was also added to the palazzo's façade."

"A rather robust triumphal arch," Will commented in awe. He crossed his arms as he studied the various statues making up the fountain.

"It is quite impressive," Barbara breathed. "I don't suppose one of those could be added to the front of Ellsworth Park?"

Alarmed, Will turned to discover her aiming a teasing grin in his direction. "We'd have to update the entire façade," he murmured. "Although it would enhance the Georgian architecture," he mused.

"Who are the statues on either side of Oceanus supposed to be?" Helen asked, directing her query to Diana.

"In the niche on the left is Abundance, and Salubrity is on the right," she replied.

"The entire set of statues and bas reliefs are meant to depict the Roman legend of the Acqua Vergine aqueduct," David chimed in. "Over there is Agrippa approving the project..." He pointed to one of the reliefs before redirecting his arm. "And that woman there is a virgin guiding thirsty soldiers to the water," he added.

"And the basin in front represents the sea," Donald finished for him.

"It feels lovely standing here," Helen remarked. "Oh, this is the best wedding trip I could ever hope to have," she added, directing her comment to Tom.

"I am in agreement, my sweeting," he said, bussing her on the cheek.

"Where are we off to next?" David asked, earning him a quelling glance from Vittoria.

"Another fountain on the same aqueduct," Donald replied.

Furrowing his brows, David offered his arm to Vittoria

and tried to sort where they might be going. "Do you know?" he asked her.

She lifted her chin. "Of course. But I'm not telling *you*."

David rolled his eyes. For the space of a half-hour, he had thought he might have improved in her estimation.

Apparently not.

CHAPTER 17
ANOTHER FOUNTAIN
AND TALK OF LOVERS

*M*eanwhile, in Piazza Navona

The look on Patrick's face continued to betray his sudden jealousy, and Armenia realized she needed to clear up the misunderstanding about her and the Marchese Montblanc or risk losing her escort.

"I assure you, Montblanc and I were never lovers," she firmly stated.

The tenseness seemed to flow out of Patrick as quickly as the water from the nearby fountain. "Yet, he gave you a *house*," he countered in disbelief.

"He knew how much it meant to me, probably because Nicoletta told him," she explained. "The bequest was written so that no male relative could claim it without my approval," she continued. "Still, it was a pleasant surprise."

"And a source of gossip, no doubt," Patrick said, offering his arm again. He seemed troubled as they made their way toward the south end of the piazza.

"If you're implying he wanted me to be his lover, I assure you that was never the situation. He was old enough to be..." She paused, dipping her head. "Well, almost my father, but he was beholden to Nicoletta. He loved her. Deeply," she said, allowing a long sigh. "And her son," she added, grinning as she remembered how Montblanc spoiled the boy in his early years as a toddler.

Patrick seemed lost in thought, as if he was conjuring an image of the marchesa he had briefly met as she and her second husband, Donald Slater, made the rounds of the ball the night before.

"If you're thinking *Signore* Slater was after Nikky's fortune when he married her, you needn't be concerned," Armenia stated. "She is as in love with him as much as Montblanc was with her."

"And Mr. Slater?"

She gave a start before she tittered. "Donald fell in love with her first, I think," she said, her gaze on her mind's eye. "My brother knew it and used him. Poorly."

Patrick furrowed his brows as they stopped before the Fontana del Moro—the Fountain of the Moor. The statuary in the middle of the water featured an African man holding a dolphin, and there were other carved figures surrounding him. "How so?"

Armenia began her stroll around the fountain, her arms crossing as she studied the marble statuary. "He had already promised Nikky to Montblanc, but she didn't know it. Enrico encouraged Donald to court her. I thought it because he hoped to marry her off to the highest bidder, but he never had any intention of allowing Donald to marry her. Even if he was the son of an heir to a marquessate in England."

Patrick joined her on the other side of the fountain. "Sounds as if your brother had an ulterior motive," he murmured.

"Oh, he did. I often wondered if he did it to make Montblanc jealous so he would ask for her hand, but in reality,

Enrico wanted Montblanc's vineyards on the side of Mount Aetna," she explained. "And he wanted his daughter to have a title."

"Did he get them? The vineyards?"

Armenia chuckled softly. "He did. Had them less than a year before he died, though, so he never had an opportunity to drink any of the wine from his own vines," she said, obviously pleased. "My nephew—Edoardo—has them now."

"Huh," Patrick responded, offering his arm. "Is the wine any good?"

"The Nerello is excellent, of course," she replied, referring to one of the varietals most commonly grown on the slopes of the volcano.

Instead of heading toward the northern end of the piazza, he led them east along the Piazza di Pasquino. "So Mr. Slater was forced to wait until Montblanc's death before he could marry Lady Montblanc?" he guessed.

"Indeed," she said, a grin lighting her face.

"For... how long?"

She lifted a shoulder. "Six... seven years, I think. When Donald met Nikky, he had been on his Grand Tour, but when he learned what my brother had done during a ball, he left for England the very next day," she explained.

"Am I to understand *Signore* Slater is the oldest son of the Earl of Bellingham?" Patrick asked, remembering the details from overhearing some of the conversations from the night before.

"Oldest, but illegitimate. His parents are married now, but Bellingham got a child on Barbara before he left for his tour as a commander in the British Navy," she explained. "She is an earl's daughter, and they were betrothed at the time."

"So... that's why his younger brother... uh, Lord Penton, is the heir?" Patrick concluded.

"Exactly."

"Just looking at the two of them—you can tell they share the same parents. Does *Signore* Slater resent Penton, do you think?"

Armenia considered how to respond before she said, "I think it has worked out for the best he is not in line to become the Marquess of Devonville."

Patrick furrowed his brows. "Because?"

"Donald won't be forced to return to England to claim a title. His son is now the Marchese Montblanc."

"Stepson, you mean," Patrick murmured, leading her toward the Pantheon. If they had timed their arrival for when he originally wanted to be there, they would be inside the circular building when the sun was at its zenith and lined up with the hole in the center of the concrete roof. Given Armenia's bath and the time it took to dress her, they would be arriving a bit too late to see the full effect of the sun's rays on the temple's floor.

When Armenia didn't offer a reply, he glanced over to see her staring at him with a look of expectation on her face.

Appearing confused, Patrick narrowed his eyes. "Uh... is that not the right word for it? Stepson?" he asked. "I admit to not knowing the Italian word." When she continued to stare at him, one brow arched, he quickly reviewed the story in his head before realization dawned.

Nicoletta's son was also Donald's son.

Apparently Nicoletta's father believed the Marchese Montblanc was too old to get a child on her, so he had encouraged *Signore* Slater's attentions as a means of ensuring an heir.

Poorly used indeed.

He scoffed, his gaze darting about as he remembered everything he had heard the night before. "*Damnation*," he whispered.

"I cannot confirm whatever it is you think you have sorted," she warned. "But relationships are not always what they seem in that family."

Wondering if she was implying there was even more to the story, Patrick made an odd sound in his throat. He wasn't sure he wanted to know any more.

CHAPTER 18
THE HEART OF ROME

eanwhile, a half-mile away

Since Vittoria wouldn't tell him where they were going next, David called up to his brother. "What are we about to see?"

"A column in honor of your favorite Roman emperor, and another fountain, of course," Donald replied.

"Hadrian?" David replied, excitement in his voice.

Donald stopped in his tracks and turned to regard his brother with confusion. "I thought Marcus Aurelius was your favorite."

Shrugging, David said, "Well, he was, before we started this Grand Tour. Now that I've seen so many of Hadrian's accomplishments, I fear Marcus Aurelius has fallen to the second spot in my estimation," he explained. His eyes suddenly rounded as they entered the Piazza Colonna. "Is that the Column of Marcus Aurelius?" he asked in awe.

"Indeed. It's been here since one-ninety-three," Donald replied. "Carved marble topped with a bronze statue of St. Paul."

"What are all those columns back there?" Barbara asked, her gaze directed to the west.

"That is Palazzo Wedekind," Donald replied. "The temple of Marcus Aurelius used to be located there, and that colonnade in front of it originated in Veii but was brought here," he explained.

In addition to the intricately carved marble column at the center of the piazza, there was a recently restored fountain. "Is this one of Giacomo Della Porta's fountains?" Diana asked, her gaze on the two sets of twin dolphins that had been added at either end of a long, rounded octagonal basin made of pink marble.

"You are correct," Donald said. "Fontana di Piazza Colonna. This is one of the sixteen fountains he built following the reconstruction of the Acqua Vergine. It was built as a means to supply clean drinking water to Roman residents."

"From where did they get their water before the fountains were built?" Barbara asked. She sat on the edge of the basin and removed a glove before dipping her hand into the cool water.

"The Tiber," Nicoletta replied, her shiver an indication she found the idea of drinking water from the river revolting.

"This one is gravity-fed as well, I take it?" David remarked.

"Indeed. That central white marble vasque was placed there only a decade ago," Donald explained as he refilled his flask. "The same time the dolphins were added," he said, pointing to the statues. The dolphin tails were wrapped around seashells, and water spouted from their mouths. Around the outer perimeter were sixteen carved lion heads tucked into an indentation that formed a unique shape to the fountain's basin.

"Compared to what we saw earlier, this one is rather simple," Helen remarked.

"So as not to detract from the monument," Donald replied, his gaze following the spiral carvings as they ascended the column.

"Quite an impressive feat of carving," Randy said. He had been staring at the column for nearly their entire time in the piazza. "The story of his campaigns during the Marcomannic Wars," he added as he studied the scenes depicting battles, sieges, and sacrifices involving the Sarmatians and Germanic tribes.

"Is the Rain Miracle included?" Diana asked, joining her husband to stare at the spiral relief carvings.

"What?"

"The episode when the Roman soldiers were saved from thirst by a rainstorm," she clarified. She raised a finger. "There it is. About two-thirds of the way up. They say it was Divine Intervention."

"I cannot believe you can see that clearly enough from all the way down here," he said. "And that you remember such details from your reading."

She shrugged. "I cannot help it."

"Nor do I want you to," he replied. "Having you on my arm means I don't have to carry a bunch of books."

She grinned as they joined the other couples and made their way out of the piazza, heading west.

"We must be nearly done for the day," David said, his words meant for Vittoria.

"Almost," she replied.

"Another fountain?"

She lifted a shoulder. "Maybe," she teased. "But you'll have to be on your very best behavior."

He turned his head so quickly to stare at her, his neck

made a sound of protest. "I am *always* on my best behavior, my lady," he countered.

She directed a quelling glance at him before remaining quiet for the rest of walk.

CHAPTER 19
ANOTHER FOUNTAIN, ANOTHER REVELATION

eanwhile, in the Piazza della Rotunda
Patrick and Armenia paused in front of the Fontana del Pantheon—the Fountain of the Pantheon—and studied the statuary. Sculpted out of marble by Leonardo Sormani, it featured four dolphins at the base of an Egyptian monolith, *Obelisco Macuteo*.

"It's ingenious, really," he commented, his mind still on what Armenia had implied but not admitted only the moment before. "*Signore* Slater didn't have a title, but he could ensure his son had one?" he added, his gaze directed on the obelisk.

Armenia shook her head. "It wasn't like *that*, Mr. McAdams. Donald..." She sighed. "He would probably prefer his son was merely a commoner. He is not a social climber in the least, despite growing up with an earl for a father and another earl for an uncle. His grandfather is a marquess and good friends with my sister's husband, who is also a marquess," she explained, watching to see how he would react.

"Which means he probably hasn't had to work a day in his life," he argued. "Although…"

Turning to regard Patrick with an expectant expression, Armenia knew he was recalling scenes from the ball the night before. He had probably met Will Slater and the younger men with him. They were all strapping lads with broad shoulders, possessed of physiques that were at odds with the typical English aristocrat.

"They have all labored in the Gisborn farm fields," she stated. "Quite scandalous, if my sister is to be believed," she added, waggling her brows as she grinned.

"Your sister?"

"Adeline Carlington. The Marchioness of Morganfield," she stated. "Her husband was on his Grand Tour when they met, and he took her home to England with him," Armenia explained. "As for Donald, these days he's a… a writer. His first book was published in London two years ago, and he's nearly finished with another."

His opinion of the young man obviously improved, Patrick nodded in the direction of the Pantheon. "We should get you out of the sun," he said. "And into a temple suitable for a Roman goddess such as yourself."

She arched a dark brow. "You know it's really a church," she said, moving past the colonnade of Corinthian columns to stand before the huge bronze doors.

"A church?" he repeated.

"The Basilica of Sancta Maria ad Martyres," she said. "Raphael the painter is buried here."

"And here I was only interested in seeing the hole in the roof," Patrick remarked. He opened the door for her, obviously amazed at how easily it swung on its hinges despite its size. "A marvel of Roman ingenuity," he added his gaze going up.

Armenia made the Sign of the Cross after stepping over

the threshold and then placed her hand on Patrick's arm as she watched his gaze take in the huge, circular interior and its coffered concrete dome. Sets of columns were separated by alcoves containing statuary. Directly across from the entrance, an altar was placed in the apse from where a Roman emperor had at one time ruled.

"How is this not a wonder of the ancient world?" he asked in a whisper, his gaze sweeping the interior before rising to the oculus, the only source of light in the building.

"All the Roman statuary was removed in favor of the Christian versions, and the original red porphyry columns were replaced with granite copies," Armenia explained. "All twenty-eight of them."

"Twenty-eight," Patrick murmured. "Which is exactly the number of coffers in each circular row in the ceiling," he added thoughtfully. "Twenty-eight is a perfect number."

"A perfect number?" she repeated. "Because there are twenty-eight days in a lunar cycle?" She turned to find him displaying an expression of awe, his features cast in the light that beamed down through the oculus. For a moment, she was nearly as awestruck, for the oddest sensation deep in her belly had her inhaling softly.

Patrick tore his gaze from the ceiling. "Uh, it's a number that equals the sum of its proper divisors," he replied, grimacing. "Six is the first, for example. Its divisors are—"

"One, two, and three," she interrupted. "One plus two plus three equals six."

"Exactly," he said, grinning in delight, which had her allowing one in return. "Twenty-eight is the next one," he said, turning to face her. "And then, uh... four-hundred and ninety-six, if I remember correctly. The ancient Greek mathematicians were fascinated by them," he added.

"Would they always be even numbers, do you suppose?" she asked.

He furrowed his brows. "I honestly don't know if an odd number has been discovered yet." He seemed to stare at her a moment before he shook his head. "An exercise for another time, I should think," he said. "Shall we make our way to the next fountain?"

"What were you thinking just then?" she asked.

Patrick blinked a few times, a flush of red coloring his face. "Uh... I was thinking how lovely you look with this beam of light shining on you," he said before he swallowed.

Armenia inhaled softly, and not only at hearing his words. For a moment, she wished her villa wasn't a ten-minute walk away. "*Grazie*," she murmured.

She wasn't sure if she was the one to lean toward him or if he made the first move, but a second later, her lips were touching his. Before she quite realized it, he had an arm around her waist and had deepened the kiss. She was forced to open her mouth and allow him to plunder it with his tongue.

Forced? No. She knew she willingly participated in the intimate act, even if it was entirely unexpected.

Unexpected and yet wanted.

How had he known what her body was begging for whilst they stood in the beam of light? Was her desire for him so obvious? Had he spent the night before imagining them kissing like this? Clutching one another in a beam of celestial light as if they were being blessed by the Roman gods?

Even when Patrick angled his head in the other direction, requiring her to do the same to keep her lips on his, she knew she wouldn't be the first to break such a kiss. She wouldn't be the first to come up for air. She wouldn't be the first to give up her hold on his arms.

The sound of a clearing throat was all it took for the kiss to suddenly end. For the two of them to break apart, their blinks of surprise giving away the fact that they had both been lost in the kiss.

The beam of light no longer enveloped them, the sun having moved beyond the edge of the oculus. Gasping, Armenia turned to discover a red-faced priest regarding them with a quirked lip.

"*Scuse*," Patrick said, lowering his head.

"*Per favore perdonaci, Padre,*" Armenia chimed in, dipping a curtsy.

"*Sei venuto a fare la confessione?*" the priest asked.

Did you come to make the confession?

"No," Patrick replied. "I came to..." He paused, glancing at Armenia before he said, "*Proporre il matrimonio.*"

The comment earned him two wide-eyed stares.

CHAPTER 20
LAMENTING
LOST TREASURES

*M*eanwhile, outside in the Piazza della Rotunda

A pleasant breeze reinvigorated the group following Nicoletta and Donald as they entered the Piazza della Rotunda.

Donald was quick to look back in an effort to make eye contact with his brother. "Now *this* is one of Hadrian's accomplishments," he said, grinning when he saw how David was already awestruck by the sight at the south end of the piazza. "A temple for all the gods."

Another obelisk blocked part of the view of the main attraction—the Pantheon. The building featured a façade reminiscent of a Greek temple with eight Corinthian columns across the front of its portico. From the groups's vantage, the only way to know the temple was round was by noting the domed roof, an expanse of concrete larger than any other known atop a structure.

"You dog. You saved the best for last," David accused, quickening his steps. Vittoria was forced to hurry as well or let go her hold on his arm.

"The best?" Randy repeated, grinning when Diana

hurried on ahead to study the obelisk. "We haven't even seen the Colosseum or the Roman Forum," he reminded them.

"How well do you remember your Latin?" Donald asked as he and Nicoletta joined David and Vittoria. He pointed up to the large inscription above the columns.

M·AGRIPPA·L·F·COS·TERTIVM·FECIT

David guffawed. "Quite well, since I've had to use it nearly every day of this Grand Tour," he claimed. He turned his attention back to the inscription, his brows furrowing. "This makes no sense," he said.

"Why do you say that?" Donald asked.

"The M is for Marcus, so Marcus Agrippa, son of Lucius, made this when consul for the third time," David recited. "But... Hadrian built it."

"Ah," Donald replied. "I think perhaps Hadrian was merely giving Agrippa the credit for an earlier version of the temple that burned down," he explained.

"Or, more likely, the temple burned but the façade did not," Vittoria said.

David turned and regarded her with wonder. "Yes," he said softly. "That's probably it exactly."

Vittoria blinked, her gaze darting to Nicoletta before she lifted a shoulder. "Although it might have been built as a temple to all the gods, it is only for one now."

David glanced over at his brother, who said, "It's a Catholic church now—Santa Maria Rotunda—and has been a church for over a thousand years."

"Huh," David replied. "That's probably why it's in such good stead. And it doesn't hurt that the columns were made of granite shipped from Egypt," he added. "Each one solid rather than made up of drums," Diana noted with appreciation.

"All thirty-nine feet of them," Donald said, arching a brow.

"The portico seems rather odd," Tom remarked, his brows furrowed. "Almost as if there was one built in front of another."

"That's because it is," Donald agreed. "The columns arrived already carved and ready to erect, but they were too short for the original portico design by about ten feet, so an accommodation had to be made," he explained. "A short cella of sorts was built behind the portico. And then, the original bronze ceiling of the portico was removed when Pope Urban the Eighth demanded it be melted down to make cannons to fortify the Castel Sant'Angelo—"

"Hadrian's Mausoleum," Diana interjected, her attention turning to the obelisk.

Donald waved a hand in her direction. "Also known as Hadrian's Mausoleum," he added. "There used to be bronze tiles atop the roof, too, but Emperor Constans the Second ordered they be stripped and sent to his residence in Syracuse along with all the other bronze and copper treasures he looted whilst he was here," he said in disgust. "This was after the temple had already been converted to a church," he added.

"What did *he* use them for?" Tom asked, obviously bothered by the story.

"He intended they be shipped to Constantinople, the capital of the Byzantine Empire at the time."

"But?" Tom prompted.

"They didn't make it. I... I don't recall what happened," Donald said, his face screwing into an expression of concern as his gaze darted to Diana.

"Constans was assassinated in Syracuse, as were many of the people who lived there," she said. "His ill-gotten gains ended up in the hands of the conquering Saracens," she added.

"What did *they* do with them?" Tom asked.

"Took them to Alexandria in Egypt," she replied. "Where they were no doubt melted down for the valuable metal."

"Oh," Tom's expression of disappointment was shared by Donald.

"So many lost treasures," he murmured.

"Which is why I make sure to keep mine close," Randy murmured, leaning over to bus Diana on the cheek.

She tittered, her gaze briefly locking with Vittoria before the young lady's attention was captured by Tom doing the same to Helen. From the expression on Vittoria's face, Diana knew the young woman had never paid witness to such public displays of affection.

She closed the distance between them in three steps and whispered, "If you have a choice when it comes to a husband, make sure he values you as he would a treasure and you will have a happy marriage."

Vittoria's eyes widened, but she nodded her understanding. "*Grazie*," she whispered.

CHAPTER 21
A COURTSHIP OF A
DIFFERENT KIND

*M*eanwhile, inside the Pantheon

Armenia stared at Patrick, her eyes wide at hearing what he admitted to the priest. "I think perhaps you don't realize what you said." She turned to the priest. "*È americano e non parla molto bene la nostra lingua.*" *He is an American and does not speak our language very well.*

"Ah," the priest replied, a grin lighting his face. "*Quindi non hai bisogno di confessare i tuoi peccati?*" *So you don't need to confess your sins?*

"*No, non oggi,*" she replied, dipping another curtsy. She wound her arm through Patrick's and practically dragged him out of the rotunda and through the short cella.

He was chuckling by the time they made it to the portico. Instead of heading straight out into the crowded piazza, he led them to the left and then north on Via della Rotunda. "I wonder if that's ever happened before?" he asked.

"Certainly not to me," she replied, displaying a look of dismay. "I don't think I've ever been so... so embarrassed." She paused and turned, her gaze sweeping the Piazza della

Rotunda to discover a number of people milling about. Upon spotting her niece, Nicoletta, and her husband, Donald, along with all their guests, she quickly turned so her back was to them. "Could we go to the next fountain now?"

Quickly sobering, Patrick glanced back in an effort to see what had her vexed, but there were far too many people for him to discern which one of them might have bothered her. "Of course." He slowed his steps once the road took a sharp turn to the left.

They walked in silence until the street thinned in between two tall buildings to become Salita dè Crescenzi. Stopping, he turned to stand in front of her. Lifting the hand she was using to grip his forearm, he kissed the back of it and then kissed her forehead.

"What was that for?" she asked.

"On the one hand, I should probably apologize for having chosen that particular spot to do what I wished I had done last night," he murmured.

Armenia inhaled softly at hearing his confession. A fluttering in her stomach had her realizing she had desired him as much as he did her. "And on the other?" she prompted.

"I am not sorry, my lady," he admitted. "Uh, well, I am sorry a priest paid witness to our kiss, but I certainly don't regret it. I was... uh, well, I admit I was..." He stopped and swallowed. "Overcome." He saw how her elegant dark brows arched in surprise, and he lifted a shoulder in a helpless shrug.

"Overcome?" she repeated, determined to keep a passive expression on her face.

"Do you understand what is meant by the word 'bewitched'?" he asked.

Armenia blinked. "I... I think I do."

"*That* is what you've done to me," he murmured,

glancing around them to ensure no one was watching. "From the moment I saw you last night, I... I had to meet you. I wanted to know you. Everything about you," he claimed, once again offering his arm so they could resume their walk. "It's a most unsettling but exciting situation in which I find myself."

Settling into a comfortable stroll, Armenia was quiet for a moment before she said, "I appreciate your candor, Mr. McAdams."

"Please, call me Patrick," he said, turning them north onto Via della Dogana Vecchia.

"All right..., Patrick," she replied, as if she was trying to say the word for the first time. "Tell me, are you aware of what you said to the priest?"

Patrick considered the query a moment before he said, "Are you referring to when I told him I was proposing marriage?"

She scoffed. "*Sì*. So... you *knew* what you were saying?"

He nodded. "Of course. It's a perfect place to propose marriage, don't you think? Surrounded by a perfect number of columns under a perfect number of coffers and bathed in that beam of light as we were..." He paused to watch her before adding, "Pray tell, is there a better place here in Roma? One you would prefer to receive a proposal of marriage? One where you might actually agree?"

Sighing softly at hearing him reiterate his intent to propose, Armenia pretended to consider suitable locations for a marriage proposal. She finally listed a few. "In front of the Trevi Fountain, of course. Or on the Spanish Steps, probably at night. Or in the afternoon, on the grounds of the Villa Borghese," she mused. "I had never thought of the rotunda of the Pantheon until you reminded me of its attributes," she added.

"*Grazie,*" he said, turning them onto the Via del Salvatore. If his building wasn't directly ahead of them, they would have been able to see the Piazza Navona.

"For what?"

"For giving me some other options," he replied. He was quiet a moment before he blurted, "I don't regret kissing you, *mia donna*. I hope you don't regret it either." He waited a moment before he dared a glance in her direction.

When she didn't respond right away, he considered why, and he suddenly widened his eyes in alarm. "Oh, my God. That priest... is he... is he *your* priest?"

She returned his glance and shook her head, a grin finally appearing when she saw his expression. "No, nor have I ever seen him before," she assured him.

"So... no regrets?" he prompted.

She angled her head to one side, her expression inscrutable. "Well, we weren't struck by lightning, so I suppose not," she whispered.

He turned and placed the hand he was still holding so it rested on his forearm. "I am glad to hear it," he said.

They made the slight turn at the Palazzo Madama and another onto Corsia Agonale before emerging onto Piazza Navona. He led them to the north, reminding her they still had one more fountain to visit.

"There's not much to see with this one," she warned.

"No statuary?" he asked in surprise as they approached the simple fountain.

"None. Just a water spout," she said as they stopped before the pool of water contained by an ornate marble surround.

"It definitely needs statuary," Patrick remarked. "Something bold. Jupiter or Neptune," he said, his free hand fisting as if he was holding a trident. He briefly posed, his arm upraised as his expression turned fierce.

"You could offer to model for it," she teased.

"Mayhap you could be the model for one of Neptune's nymphs," he countered, before shaking his head. "No, that wouldn't do."

She stared at him, obviously offended. "Because I'm too tall? Or because my bosom is too large?"

"Because it would mean the sculptor would see you naked, and I can't abide the thought of another man seeing you like that," he answered.

Blinking, she was about to put voice to a complaint but thought to tease him instead. "Are you saying you would be jealous?"

He nodded. "*Sì*. Absolutely. Remember, I have every intention of proposing marriage. Again," he claimed.

She chuckled, obviously not believing him as they completed their walk around the simple fountain and headed for Via di Tor Millina and her villa.

"I promised you a luncheon," he said. "Do you have a favorite place for a midday meal?"

She didn't answer right away, which had him slowing his steps lest they go too far in the wrong direction.

"Villa D'Avalos," she stated.

He blinked. "You wish to eat at your home?"

"*Sì*. My bedchamber."

"Uh... by yourself, or...?"

"With you, of course. On my bed."

Patrick had to resist the urge to grin like a schoolboy at hearing her words, but he couldn't help how his steps quickened.

He was starving in more ways than one.

CHAPTER 22
THE PANTHEON PROVIDES
A PLACE TO PROVE ONESELF

eanwhile, in the Piazza della Rotunda
"Oh, how I wish I had brought my sketchbook," Diana lamented, her gloved hands gripping the edge of the dark marble fountain in front of the Pantheon. In the middle was a carved marble base upon which the granite tower was mounted. She leaned forward in an effort to make out the hieroglyphs that decorated the *Obelisco Macuteo*.

"Careful, my sweet, or you're going to find yourself soaking wet," Randy said from where he stood next to her, sure she was about to fall into the basin of water.

She glanced up at him, her eyes suddenly darkening. "What do you have in mind?" she asked, arching a teasing brow.

Randy inhaled slowly, realizing how his words had been interpreted. "Oh." He glanced around. "Well, if there was a niche... or a reasonably private place, I would gladly see to your immediate pleasure," he whispered.

Tittering, Diana reddened at hearing his claim. "Later. When we're in that wonderful bed," she whispered in reply.

"I'll be ready," he promised. His gaze went up the obelisk. "Is this one from Egypt?" he asked.

"Indeed. This once stood in the temple of Amun-Re in Heliopolis," she replied. "And there are two cartouches up there," she added, pointing with excitement to the very top. "It's probably Rameses the Second." She allowed a huff. "There is just so much to see here, and," she waved to the others who wandered about the piazza. "They have no idea of the history through which they walk."

"We'll come back, of course," he assured her. "We have at least a month," he reminded her.

"Can we go inside?" Barbara asked, pausing in front of the fountain to enjoy the cooler air.

"We should be able to, even if it is a Catholic church now," Will commented. "The artist Raphael is buried here. Wait until you see the oculus in the ceiling."

Barbara inhaled softly. "You've already been here, haven't you?"

He nodded. "*HMS Greenwich* put into port near here on more than one occasion," he replied. "Never for very long, though, so I appreciate we now have the time to see it all at leisure." He offered his arm and the two made their way past the columns of the portico and to the entry.

Despite their size and weight, the twenty-five-foot high bronze doors opened easily, and the group filed into the cella and through to the rotunda.

Almost immediately, everyone craned their necks in an effort to study the dome above them.

"How high is it up to that hole in the ceiling?" Randy asked.

"One-hundred-and-forty-two feet," Donald replied. "The same distance as this room's diameter."

"What happens when it rains?" Barbara asked.

"There are drains in the floor to capture the water,"

Nicoletta replied, using a gloved hand to point out one of them.

"It feels so much larger inside than it looked from the outside," Helen remarked.

"Indeed," Tom agreed. He pointed to the niches located around the perimeter. "I take it those didn't always hold Christian statues."

"Those used to display statues of the Roman deities," Donald confirmed. "Including an ivory statue of Minerva sculpted by the Greek artist Phidias, and we know there were statues of Venus, Jupiter, and Mars."

"Pliny the Elder wrote about the decorations in his *Natural History*," David remarked, his gaze darting about the interior of the rotunda. "The original capitals of these columns were made of Syracusan bronze, but they were obviously looted," he added sadly.

"Two of the original marble capitals are in the British Museum," Will commented. "As for the rest—"

"'Decorated by Diogenes of Athens, and the caryatides, by him, which form the columns of that temple, are looked upon as masterpieces of excellence'," Diana quoted from *The Natural History*.

Donald glanced over at Randy, who merely shrugged. "She remembers everything she reads," he whispered.

"Diogenes also did the statues up on the roof," Vittoria stated. "And one of Cleopatra's pearls was cut in half so that each half—"

"'Might serve as pendants for the ears of Venus, in the Pantheon at Rome'," Diana finished for her, her delight evident in finding someone who was familiar with the passage.

"Pearls?" Barbara repeated. "What's this about?" she asked, joining them to learn more.

Vittoria looked to Diana, but the young matron made a

motion that she should answer. Obviously uncomfortable at being the center of attention, Vittoria dropped her gaze to the floor. "Well, it all started when Cleopatra inherited a pair of enormous pearls from the Kings of the East," she began. "She was hosting Marcus Antonius at her palazzo in Alexandria and was quite put off by how he was indulged with all the lavish arrangements. When he asked what could possibly be better, she, well, she made a wager." Here Vittoria stopped and directed a pleading glance in Diana's direction.

Diana took up the story, quoting from Pliny the Elder's account in volume two of *The Natural History*. "'To this she made answer, that on a single entertainment she would expend ten millions of sesterces'—a Roman coin," she interjected. "'Antony looked upon it as a thing quite impossible; and a wager was the result. On the following day, she had an entertainment set before Antony. Upon this, Antony joked her, and enquired what was the amount expended upon it; to which she made answer that the banquet was only a trifling appendage and that she alone would consume at the meal to the value of that amount. The servants placed before her a single vessel, which was filled with vinegar, the sharpness of which is able to dissolve pearls'."

"Oh, dear," Barbara breathed, already concluding what had happened to one of the large pearls.

"'Antony was waiting to see what she was going to do'," Diana went on. "'Taking one of them from out of her ear, she threw it into the vinegar, and directly it was melted, swallowed it. Lucius Plancus, who had been named umpire in the wager, placed his hand upon the other at the very instant that she was making preparations to dissolve it and declared that Antony had lost—an omen which was fully confirmed'." Diana allowed a long sigh. "Such an important historical loss merely to prove a point," she lamented.

Randy offered his arm, and she joined him to take a turn about the round room, following Barbara and Will as they did the same.

"But that was just one of the pearls," Vittoria said, her words directed to David, Helen, and Tom. "After Cleopatra's suicide, Octavian brought the other pearl to Rome, where it was divided and reshaped for the statue of Venus made for this very temple."

"Oh, where might she be?" Helen asked with excitement, her gaze darting about in search of a statue of Venus. The few steps she took landed her nearly in the middle of the room, the light from the oculus bathing her in the midday sun.

"Gone," Vittoria replied sadly. "All the Roman statues were removed when it was made into a church, and although some might have ended up in other temples, the fate of Venus and her pearl earrings is unknown."

Visibly bothered, Helen sighed as Tom wrapped his arm behind her waist and pulled her to his side. "Another lost treasure," she murmured sadly.

"We may not know what happened to Venus," he agreed, "but I do have an idea of what to buy for you when we are next at a jewelry shop."

Helen gave him a watery grin. "Pearls?"

"Pearls for my pearl," he whispered. "Which is exactly what you look like standing here in this gorgeous light."

"Oh, thank you, darling," she whispered. She lifted herself onto her tiptoes and kissed him on the cheek.

Although she thought to turn away before she could pay witness to Helen's kiss, Vittoria found she could not. She watched the couple's intimate exchange, unaware she made a faint whimpering sound at seeing the chaste kiss.

From where he stood next to her, David was watching with curiosity. Suppressing a grin, he leaned closer to Vittoria. "Was it the promise of pearls or Helen's reaction to his words that has you staring so?" he whispered.

Inhaling sharply, she turned and regarded him with a look of shock. "Neither," she finally said, giving her head a quick shake.

David furrowed his brows. "Then what, pray tell, has you vexed?"

Vittoria looked as if she might cry. "After what *Donna* Forster has told me, I fear my expectations are too high," she whispered.

Glancing around to discover the others were well away from where they stood, David ushered her to the edge of the room near the entrance and faced her. "What expectations?" he asked gently. For once, she wasn't displaying her usual sneer in his company.

"To have a husband who would regard me as *Signore* Forster does *Donna* Helen," she replied. "He loves her," she added, almost in disbelief.

David allowed a slight chuckle. "He does indeed. He has for a couple of years. Even so, it still took him some time to realize they were perfect for one another."

When Vittoria didn't appear convinced, he added, "Now Randy—*Don* Forster—claims he didn't fall in love with Diana at first sight, but *I* think he did."

"Why?" Vittoria asked, her curiosity evident.

"Because Diana didn't want to have anything to do with him. She would have been happy spending her life as a spinster," he explained.

Scoffing, Vittoria shook her head. "But she... she obviously *adores* him," she argued, her gaze darting to where the couple in question was studying one of the statues in a niche. Even as she watched, Randy lifted a hand to place it at the back of his wife's waist.

"Oh, she does now," David agreed. "Because Randy

proved himself able to accept a woman who is far more clever than he is."

Furrowing a dark brow, Vittoria appeared as if she didn't believe him. "Would you, *mio don*?" she asked. "Accept a woman who is more clever than you?"

David blinked. "I... I suppose it depends," he stammered.

Vittoria angled her head, lifting her chin as if she was daring him to continue.

Swallowing, he made an odd sound in his throat. "You know you really shouldn't do that," he murmured.

It was her turn to blink. "Do what?"

"Act like you want me to... to kiss you," he whispered.

Her eyes widening with shock, Vittoria was about to put voice to a protest but was saved from doing so when a man's voice sounded from behind David.

"*Ho già interrotto un bacio qui oggi, e non vorrei farlo di nuovo.*" *I've already interrupted one kiss in here today, and I shouldn't wish to do it again.*

David jerked sideways at the same moment Vittoria took a step back, her skirts flattening against the wall. She was quick to recover, though, dipping a deep curtsy at the same moment David determined their interloper was a priest. He bowed.

"*Non l'avrei permesso, padre,*" she said. *I would not have allowed it, Father.*

The priest glanced between David and Vittoria. "*Desideri confessare i tuoi peccati?*" *Do you wish to confess your sins?*

"No, *Padre. Grazie,*" David replied. He offered his arm to Vittoria. "*Stavamo semplicemente ammirando la vostra chiesa.*" *We were merely admiring your church.*

Nodding, the priest stepped away and made his way further into the rotunda.

David leaned closer to Vittoria, his lips entirely too close to her ear. "I wonder who he caught kissing in here earlier," he murmured. "Terribly cheeky of whomever it was," he added with an arched brow.

Vittoria shivered when his breath washed over her cheek. She gave him a quelling glance, though. "No one we know, I am quite certain," she replied, although her attention was on her mind's eye.

She was fairly sure it was *Zia* Armenia she had seen on the arm of a man she recognized from her come-out ball the night before. The two had departed the Pantheon whilst their party was still in the piazza, their attentions on the obelisk, the fountain, and the temple's façade. Would they have kissed inside the Pantheon, though?

Perhaps she would have to ask during that night's dinner.

CHAPTER 23
LOVERS IN THE AFTERNOON

eanwhile, at Villa D'Avalos

Excitement, anticipation, and disbelief combined to make Patrick experience a moment of light-headedness. Perhaps he was hungrier than he thought—in more ways than one. "Tell me, my lady, when you say you wish to have your luncheon in your bed, are you...?" He paused and swallowed.

She glanced up at him as he opened the door to her courtyard. "Speaking of food or proposing lovemaking?" she finished for him. She stepped under the arched opening. "Perhaps a bit of both," she said on a sigh. "I am hungry. I'll have DeLuca send up a cold collation."

"That sounds... uh, very good," he stammered, closing the iron door until he heard the *clunk* of the latch when it engaged.

She watched him a moment before they made their way across the marble tiles. "Why, Patrick, for a man who claims he was about to propose marriage, you seem terribly nervous all of a sudden," she accused.

"That's because I am," he admitted, opening the door to

the villa when DeLuca didn't immediately appear. When the butler stepped into the entry from somewhere off to the right, Patrick realized his guess that the servants quarters were on the ground floor was confirmed.

"Why?" She seemed genuinely curious as she shook the mantle from her shoulders and handed it to DeLuca. She rattled off a series of orders in Italian to the servant before lifting her skirts to make the climb up the stairs.

"I fear I am about to humiliate myself," Patrick murmured, following her up the stairs he had climbed earlier that morning.

Had it just been that morning?

A quick glance at his pocket watch confirmed they had only been gone for a couple of hours.

Armenia glanced back at him, a brow furrowing in confusion. "Why?"

He dipped his head. "Uh, I haven't been with a woman —in bed—in a very long time."

For the first time that afternoon, she seemed uncertain of what to say. "Because...?"

He lifted a shoulder and sighed. "Travel, business, lack of opportunity." He followed her down the corridor to her apartment. "I'm not very social when I'm concentrating on business," he explained, relieved when they were in the sitting room outside her bedchamber and he could close the door behind him. "My son is constantly nagging me to..." He stopped speaking and stiffened when he saw her take a step back, her eyes wide with censure. "What is it?" he asked.

"Your *son*?" she repeated. "You are... *married*?" A hint of anger sounded in her words.

For the first time that afternoon, Patrick realized they hadn't discussed his personal life. "No. Uh, I mean, I... I was," he stammered.

"Divorced?" she guessed, her accusatory expression changing to one of curiosity.

"A widower," he stated. "For several years now. It's just been my son, Patrick Junior, and myself."

Armenia visibly relaxed, although she still seemed unnerved. "No mistress?" she asked. "No... prostitutes?"

An odd sound came from his throat. "If you knew anything about the ladies of the evening in Boston, you would not be asking," he said. When he noted her eyebrow once again arched, he added, "Uh, they will rob you blind and leave you with venereal diseases or... syphilis," he said, shuddering with disgust. "There is something to be said for celibacy."

Apparently satisfied with his response, Armenia moved into her bedchamber. "When you said you thought you were about to... what was the word you said?" she asked, turning her back to him so he could undo her buttons.

"Humiliate myself," he replied, quickly setting the jets free of their holes. It was far easier to undo them than it had been to button them earlier that day. "Uh, embarrass?" he clarified, thinking she didn't understand his English. "It's not that I don't know how to... to pleasure a woman," he said in a quiet voice. He pulled the ties of her corset and petticoats. "It's only that—"

"You think it's been too long?" She turned around, pulling her arms from her bodice as one of her petticoats fell to the floor.

"Maybe," he replied. He swallowed and kept her gaze as he felt her gloved hand sweep down the front of his top coat. His erection, one he'd been fighting since they had been climbing the stairs, was evident behind his pantaloons, and he inhaled sharply when she pressed her palm around the bulge.

"Maybe not," she whispered, her eyes never leaving his.

"And you?" he challenged. Given her beauty and his housekeeper's opinion, he feared she bedded a different man every week.

She stiffened. "My favorite lover and I parted when Nikky and Donald were courting," she murmured, her gaze darting to the side. "He had already taken up with someone... *younger*," she whispered.

"Then he was a fool," Patrick stated, groaning when she acknowledged his comment by tightening her hold on his arousal. "May I kiss you?"

She blinked and seemed to think on her answer for a time before she finally said, "This is where *I* may... humiliate myself."

His brows rose in surprise. "You're not about to say you haven't kissed a man," he warned, reaching for his pocket watch. "At least, not in the past half-hour, I suppose," he teased.

She captured her bottom lip with a tooth as her gaze swept down to his cravat. "Before you took me by surprise in the Pantheon, it had been a very long time since I had engaged in such intimacy," she finally replied.

"It had been a long time for me as well," he murmured, thinking of when he had last kissed his late wife. He wondered if he would have done so if he hadn't have learned she was near-death. Not everyone had the benefit of knowing when it might be their last chance at convincing someone they were loved. "Yet we seemed to do it very well," he whispered, his throat thick as he was reminded of the sorrow he had experienced only the year before. Reminded of the guilt he felt at having spent too much of his time on his business and too little of it in Grace's company.

Had someone asked him why he had chosen Rome from which to run his European base, he might have claimed it was merely logical given the shipping routes available. But deep down, he knew its reputation as the City of Love might mean he could find another woman with whom to share his life. His modest fortune.

He was determined to give it a try. That he had crossed paths with such an interesting and gorgeous woman so early in his tenure in the city only proved he had chosen well.

He leaned forward and kissed her forehead as he reached around her waist to pull her closer. "Do you need to be anywhere this afternoon? Do you... have any appointments? Or are you expecting any callers?"

She shook her head. "Only DeLuca with our luncheon," she said. "I told him to leave it in the sitting room."

A grin appeared to lighten Patrick's face before his lips brushed hers in a tentative kiss. When she didn't back away, he touched his lips to hers again with a bit more force, finally capturing them in a kiss that had her relaxing into his hold.

When she slid the hand that had been pressing his manhood up the front of his coat to grip his shoulder, he moved a hand to the back of her waist and pulled her hard against the front of his body. Given her height and the half boots she wore, she didn't need to stand on tiptoe to continue the kiss, a situation he found he rather liked. They could battle for one another's lips without bending or struggling for balance. He reveled in their mutual hunger for one another as their tongues tangled and her soft mewls sounded.

When he ended the kiss, he left his forehead pressed to hers. "*Grazie*," he whispered.

Armenia blinked several times, as if she was awakening. "*Grazie*?" she repeated in confusion.

"*Sì*," he replied, chuckling softly. Given his one hand was already at the back of her waist, he moved the other to join it and began loosening the laces of her corset as he continued to nip her lips with his.

Meanwhile, she had already started on his buttons, and by the time she had his coats pushed from his torso, he was pulling the gown from hers.

Layers of twill passed between them as he lifted the gown over her head. He didn't send it to the floor, though, but held it out, shook it, and carefully draped it over the back of a nearby chair.

She watched in fascination, apparently expecting he would discard the gown on the floor. She followed his lead and did the same with his top coat and waistcoat. When her back was to him, he reached out and undid the ties of her second petticoat until it dropped in a heap at her feet. Then he lifted the corset over her head.

He grinned at seeing her in only her shift and stockings, the thin cotton hinting at what he had seen earlier that day.

A body made for bedding.

A pair of breasts meant for suckling.

A pair of legs so long and lean, he could hardly wait to feel them wrapped around his hips.

"How do you like it?" he asked in a whisper.

She inhaled softly. "Like... what?"

He swallowed. "What brings you the most pleasure, *mia donna*?" He reached out and slid his hand along the side of her torso, his thumb barely skimming over the protrusion of her nipple evident in the fabric. Both of her nipples were hard, he hoped evidence of her arousal and not because she was cold.

From the sound of her inhalation of breath, he knew his touch had caused something. Bending down, he placed his lips around the silhouette of one nipple and gently suckled it through the fabric.

Armenia immediately captured the sides of his face in

her hands, her fingers spearing his dark hair. "For whatever you do, I wish to be on the bed," she whispered. "You will use no restraints, nor anything that can elicit pain," she added.

Patrick had to swallow a curse. What poor excuse of a man would dare restrain this woman or cause her pain in pursuit of pleasure? "Noted," he whispered.

He had to suppress a grin when she let out a yelp as he lifted her into his arms and carried her to the edge of the bed, finally lowering her until her feet were firmly on the floor. Keeping one arm wrapped around the back of her waist so he could smooth his large hand over her flared hip, he reined in the excitement he felt over what they were about to do. If he lost control, he was sure she would dismiss him from her bedchamber.

Armenia watched as he tossed the pillows onto nearby furniture and stripped the bed of its counterpane. When she stepped out of his hold and moved to the window, he asked, "Where are you going?"

"To draw the drapes. I rather doubt anyone is watching, but..." She lifted a shoulder before closing the velvet panels on both windows, casting the room in near darkness.

Patrick took the opportunity to shed his shirt and shoes, and he was about to push down his pantaloons when she returned to the bed. He watched how she lifted her shift from her body, tossed it aside, and then bent to climb onto the mattress, her olive skin a dark contrast to the white bed linens. When she was in the center, she leaned on one hip and one hand and arched an eyebrow.

"Oh, do please continue," she murmured, a smirk lighting her face. She used her other hand to point to his pantaloons.

"You minx," he accused, grinning. He pushed the garment from his body, the front catching on his arousal before he could free it. He stripped his stockings, leaving him completely nude. "May I remove your stockings, my lady?"

Armenia seemed uncertain at first. "Promise you won't snag them? They are new, and today is the first time I have worn them."

"I will be very careful." He waited until she had settled onto the bed and bent her knees before he climbed onto it. Braced on his own knees, his arousal jutting out from the dark hair at the base of his torso, he reached down with both hands and captured the top edge of one of the stockings between his thumbs and forefingers. He pulled the ribbon garter free before he carefully rolled the edge to get it started, and then used his palms to coax the rolled stocking over her knee and down her calves, making sure to skim her skin with the tips of his fingers as he did so.

He reveled in hearing her soft sighs and short pants for breath, in seeing how her heavy breasts had settled onto the tops of her arms, secretly pleased there would be room to rest his head after he finally allowed his release. Despite her age, her belly was nearly flat, but then he realized she had probably never born a babe.

"You never did tell me how you like it," he said, rolling down the second stocking. It popped off the end of her narrow foot, and he dropped it to the floor next to the first. He placed a kiss on one of her knees and grinned when her leg shivered in response.

"When in Rome, do as the Romans do," she murmured.

Patrick blinked before he understood what she was referencing, and then he chuckled softly. "I am at your command, *mia donna*," he whispered. He used his hands to push apart her knees and lowered his mouth to one leg to leave kisses from the inside of her knee all the way to the top of her thigh.

He matched his moves on the other side, pleased when she finally seemed to relax her legs and allow her knees to fall to the sides. Not sure if his hunger for food or his hunger for her drove him, he settled himself between her legs, gripped her hips, and dropped his head until his nose was buried in her soft curls.

From the scent of her musky dampness, he knew she was already wet, but he was determined she experience as much pleasure as possible before he buried himself in her.

Reaching out with his tongue, he swiped it along her folds, glad he'd had her hips held down when she attempted to buck beneath him. A slower swirl of his tongue allowed him to find the swollen bud of her womanhood.

Her soft cries drove him, the tip of his tongue circling the sweet red pearl before he suckled it and licked it. Her thighs clamped around his head, rendering him deaf to her mewls and words of, "*Sì, sì, sì*." When he finally drove his tongue deep into her wet channel, her chest rose from the bed. He thought he heard a muffled, "*Fermare*," but reason no longer prevailed. He was determined she experience as long an orgasm as he could manage to manifest in a body obviously meant for lovemaking.

He would have thrust his tongue into her again, but she drew her knees to her chest and rolled to one side, removing her quim from his view.

Momentarily confused, Patrick lifted his head to find her staring down at him. "Did I do something wrong?" he asked.

She seemed to struggle for air. "*No, sei uno scemo.*" *No, you foolish man.*

"Are you all right?"

She nodded, although she seemed to have to think about it before she did so. "Come inside me," she whispered, once again opening her legs to him.

He crawled forward, positioning his erection at her

opening. "*Grazie*," he whispered, pushing into her in small increments until he was buried to the hilt. He struggled for breath, dipping his head so he could kiss first her lips and then both of her nipples. "My Venus," he whispered.

He pulled nearly all the way out of her before he thrust into her. Her chest rose from the mattress, and her legs wrapped around his back as he emitted a groan of satisfaction. "I am not going to last long," he whispered, thrusting into her again and again. At some point he knew her hands were gripping his sides, her ankles hooked around his hips, and he remembered what he had imagined earlier. All at once, his body responded before he could regain control, and he knew he would be lost to the throes of his release.

Apparently, Armenia knew as well, for she displayed a look of unadulterated joy as her insides gripped his manhood and milked him for all he was worth.

The sensation of intense pleasure was so sudden, so startling, he was forced to cease his movements before a growl escaped his throat.

He straightened his arms, determined he wouldn't fall atop her, but it was no use. Every bit of his strength seemed to leave him all at once, and he lowered himself to rest atop her, his head landing between her breasts before he passed out.

CHAPTER 24
A CARRIAGE RIDE
PROVES PROBLEMATIC

*M*eanwhile, back at *Piazza della Rotunda*

"I think it's time we head back home," Donald murmured, his attention on the priest who had been speaking with David and Vittoria.

Or scolding them.

He couldn't tell for certain, but he would discover more when he had a chance to be alone with his brother later that evening.

"There will be a luncheon waiting for us," Nicoletta replied, which had Donald hurrying off to gather the others in their party.

"Our carriages await," he said as they filed out of the Pantheon. Indeed, two town coaches and a barouche, all emblazoned with the Montblanc coat of arms, were lined up along one side of the piazza.

"I would prefer to be out of the sun," Barbara said, hinting she wanted to ride in one of the town coaches.

"And you shall, my sweet," Will said, helping her into the first coach. They were joined by Nicoletta and Donald while

Randy, Diana, Tom, and Helen hurried into the second coach.

David furrowed a brow, as if he suspected his brother might have planned the seating arrangements. He glanced over at Vittoria. "It appears we're to share the barouche," he commented.

"If we must," she replied, lifting a shoulder as she opened her parasol. She allowed the tiger to help her into the open equipage, taking a seat so she faced the direction of travel.

Tempted to join her on the same bench, David realized her gown wouldn't allow it—she had positioned herself in the center of the seat and spread her skirts so they nearly covered the entire bench. Her parasol was already opened, and she held the ivory handle in one gloved hand while the other rested on her lap. With her chin thrust out and tipped up a fraction, she appeared as spoiled as she behaved.

David settled onto the opposite bench and leaned his head back until sunlight bathed the lower half of his face. "You're quite fortunate to live where the sun shines so frequently," he remarked.

Vittoria sniffed. "Hardly. It can be terribly hot," she countered.

"But tolerable in the winter," he said.

She lifted a shoulder dismissively. "I suppose."

"You don't have to trudge through snow?" he asked.

Blinking, she appeared confused for a moment. "Trudge?" she repeated. "There is rarely snow here."

"Ah," David replied, nodding.

"What is 'trudge'?" she asked.

"How one must walk when the snow—or the mud, I suppose—is deep," he replied. "It's... unpleasant. And very damaging to half-boots and slippers." He gestured down to where the toes of her half-boots poked out from beneath the hem of her gown. They suddenly disappeared, and he lifted his questioning gaze to discover her face had taken on a blush of color. "What is it?" he asked.

She shook her head. "Nothing."

"Why did you hide your feet?"

"My feet are none of your concern," she replied.

David sounded a scoff. "If you have a rock in your shoe—"

"I do not."

"Or lodged in the sole of your—"

"My boots are none of your concern." She seemed to tuck them even farther back from the edge of her hem.

Furrowing his brows, David regarded her a moment before he said, "Are they giving you pain, my lady?"

She gave him a suspicious look. "Always."

David blinked. "Well, then why did you wear them?"

It was Vittoria's turn to blink. "They are what is worn," she replied.

"Well, surely there must be a shoemaker who can craft you a pair that don't cause you pain," he argued.

"I rather doubt it," she said on a huff, her attention on one of the buildings they passed.

"Must be why Donald insisted he rub Nikky's feet every night," he murmured absently.

Vittoria's eyes rounded, her gaze turning to him. "What is this?"

David lifted a shoulder in response. "I think he learned to do it from Father," he said, as if he was talking to himself. "Something about the return on effort far greater than the cost."

Visibly swallowing, Vittoria seemed to display even more color than she had only the moment before. "I cannot imagine of what it is you speak," she said, once again turning her attention to something outside of the barouche.

Determined he find something of interest to the both of them, he asked, "Have you ever been to England? To see your aunt in London?"

Once again, Vittoria blinked and seemed to struggle with how to answer his query. "I have not."

"But you have traveled? Outside of Rome?"

She seemed uncertain of how to answer before she finally lifted a shoulder. "I have been to Naples, Messina, Taormina, Catania..." She shrugged again. "And Roma."

"That's all?" he asked in surprise.

Her chin rising defiantly, Vittoria was obviously offended. "It is enough," she stated.

"How old are you?"

Her eyes once again rounded as a scoff sounded. Before she could put voice to a scold, David held up a gloved hand. "Apologies. I did not mean it... like it sounded," he stammered. "I merely expected the daughter of a conte to be more *worldly* is all." He knew if looks could kill, he would have been dead earlier that morning. Now he was wishing the floor of the barouche would open up to allow him to escape the equipage.

"How worldly were *you* at eighteen years of age?" she asked.

David blinked, his mouth opening and closing as if he were a fish. "Oh," he finally responded. "I had only traveled in England at that age," he admitted. "Oxford, London, the Cotswolds. Derbyshire." He stopped and struggled to remember any other places he might have been. "Oh, and Bath, of course."

One of Vittoria's brows arched. "Of course," she mocked.

Sighing, David was about to give up on attempting further conversation when his attention was drawn to a structure on the horizon. "Is that... is that the Colosseum?" he asked in awe.

Vittoria followed his line of sight and said, "It is."

"Will we go see it on the morrow?" he asked, wincing when they passed by a building that prevented him from seeing the ancient site of gladiatorial battles.

"I believe that is the plan," she replied. "You will need to climb a number of stairs if you intend to go to the top."

"We can go inside?" he asked, turning his attention back to her.

"Of course."

"Have you been?"

She lifted a shoulder. "I have."

David scoffed softly. "You were not impressed?" he guessed.

For a moment, she seemed unsure of how to answer. "If I did not know its main purpose for existing, I think I would have enjoyed it far more than I did," she replied. "It's quite large, with excellent sight lines from nearly every seat, and views of the city and the Forum from the arched openings."

"I'll have to be sure Diana brings her paints," he murmured.

"Paints?" Vittoria repeated.

He nodded. "In addition to her avocation of archaeology, Lady Forster is quite a talented painter."

Vittoria furrowed a brow. "You do not seem... *bothered* that she has an avocation."

"Because I am not. She's rather clever. Remembers everything she has ever read, seen, or heard, which makes her an excellent resource should I have a question about something from the past," he said, grinning.

Vittoria narrowed her eyes, her suspicion evident. "Why is it *you* did not marry her?"

David was stunned by the query. "Uh... I suppose because I am not attracted to her in a manner befitting marriage," he replied. "Whereas Randy was quite smitten with her from the moment he first saw her."

"Smitten," Vittoria repeated quietly. "I do not know this word."

His eyes widening, David considered how to provide a definition. "Uh... almost love at first sight. Interested in a romantic sense. Attraction to another, I suppose." Angling his head to one side, he asked, "Have you ever been smitten?"

Vittoria shook her head.

"Liar," he accused, but he was grinning as he said it.

"Have you?" she countered defensively.

"Of course. Probably... a half-dozen times," he admitted, his grin widening when he saw her reaction of shock. "The last time was with a young lady with whom I was betrothed."

Her dark brows furrowing in confusion, Vittoria asked, "Did you... did *you* break it off?"

David inhaled softly and let the breath out in a *whoosh*. "It was a mutual decision which allowed her to accept an offer of marriage from another. From Diana's brother, in fact. They are married now, and quite well suited for one another." He struggled to swallow the lump that threatened to close off his throat. Not having thought about Lady Jane Fitzsimmons for some time, he was surprised by his reaction.

"You loved her," Vittoria stated in a hoarse whisper, leaning forward to study his face.

Blinking several times, David nodded. "I suppose I did," he said.

"Were you a rogue with her?"

"No!" he replied, perhaps a bit too forcibly.

"Is that why you were betrothed?"

"No. Not at all. In fact, I offered a betrothal as a means of protection. So she would have an excuse to put off unwanted suitors," he explained. "I even gave her a ring, which..." He attempted to clear his throat. "She still wears to this day. As her wedding ring." He took an unsteady breath before looking up to discover Vittoria staring at him. "I gave it to Marcus since he didn't have one, and she adored the one I had given her."

"A family jewel?" she asked in awe.

He shook his head and waved a hand dismissively. "No. I had bought it in a jewelry shop in London. Which reminds me, I probably should be on the hunt for a replacement. Might you know of a jeweler where I could obtain another?"

It was Vittoria's turn to blink. "There are many here in Roma," she replied.

"Good. Perhaps you can help me choose one," he suggested, anxious to see how she would respond. For the first time that afternoon, she seemed to have forgiven him for the events of the night before. "It would be good to have the opinion of someone of your sex," he said. "Of your age."

"Perhaps," she replied haughtily. "Or, far better, you can simply take the next woman with whom you are *smitten* and ask her opinion," she said before rolling her eyes and directing her gaze beyond his shoulder.

David allowed a long sigh and decided he best keep quiet for the rest of the ride back to Villa Montblanc.

CHAPTER 25
AN ORPHAN ARRIVES

Upon the group's return to Villa Montblanc, a small carriage was pulling out of the courtyard, and their equipage was forced to stop until the drive was clear.

"That is the Russo carriage," Nicoletta said, her brows furrowed. "But it's empty. Surely Maria would not have—"

"*Donna* Russo has not paid a call," Donald said, clutching Nicoletta's gloved hand. "*Donna* Nancy and her nurse will be joining us for a time," he added. Nicoletta's confusion was evident until he added, "There's been a terrible accident, my sweet. The Russos have both died."

Everyone in the coach inhaled sharply and stared at Donald.

"No," Nicoletta said under her breath.

"When...?" his father started to ask before Donald added, "Last night. On their way home from the ball. I only learned of it before we departed this afternoon."

"On that awful curve, no doubt," Nicoletta whispered, referring to a location where a road's sharp turn was hidden in the dark.

"I didn't wish to speak of it earlier. To cast a pall over our outing," Donald explained.

"But Nancy is all right?" Nicoletta asked, her eyes wide with fright. The coach jerked into motion again, and she gasped at the sudden movement.

"She was with her nurse at their villa when it happened."

Nicoletta lifted a hand and crossed her heart. "She will be devastated," she whispered.

"Does the girl have any other family?" Barbara asked. "Aunts or uncles?"

"We will host her until we can discover the answers," Donald stated. "It is the least we can do for her given how helpful *Donna* Russo was during Nicoletta's first few years as a marchesa." He glanced out the window as the coach came to a halt in the courtyard and a footman hurried out from the villa.

"She was with me when I delivered Antony, and I was happy to be with her when she gave birth to Nancy," Nicoletta said. "She had a difficult labor. I worried Nancy would not survive the night, but she proved us all wrong."

"How old is she?" Will asked.

"Nearly as old as Antony," Nicoletta replied. "Maria..." She paused to swallow the lump in her throat. "She has raised her to be a proper young lady even as she allows her to be a child. Antony is quite taken with her. They play together sometimes."

"She sounds adorable," Barbara remarked.

"Does Nancy have a brother?" Will asked. "Older siblings?"

Donald shook his head. "There are no sons. No other daughters. From what I know of Conte Russo, there may be no close heirs. Mayhap a cousin in Naples," he said, lifting a shoulder in resignation.

"We will not allow Nancy to go to Naples," Nicoletta stated. When the others stared at her, shocked at hearing the insistence in her voice, she added, "The family there is rotten. Maria has said so."

Will and Donald exchanged knowing glances. "It sounds as if Antony might be gaining another sister?" Will asked gently, at the same moment the tiger opened the coach door.

Before anyone made a move to depart the coach, Barbara suddenly gripped Will's arm, and he turned to stare at her. "What is it?"

She directed a glance at Donald and then at Nicoletta before she turned her attention back to her husband. "What if David and Donald were to gain a sister?" she asked in a quiet voice. "I've always wanted a daughter," she reminded him. She gave Nicoletta an apologetic shrug. "*Another* daughter," she quickly amended.

Will took her hand from his arm and kissed the back of it. "Let's not get ahead of ourselves," he whispered.

Donald dipped his head. "I hardly think it appropriate *we* take her in."

"Why ever not," Will asked, his voice kept low.

Donald dipped his head. "Antony informed me he planned to make her his marchesa when he was of an age to marry," he replied with a soft chuckle. "They have played together since they were babes."

Nicoletta allowed a watery grin. "Perhaps it would be best for her to live with you," she said, her gaze on Barbara. "Seeing as how I will be giving birth to another babe before the spring entertainments."

Will and Barbara stared at her while Donald merely appeared embarrassed. "You're going to have another baby?" Barbara asked, her face lighting in delight. "Why, why that's *wonderful.*"

"Congratulations," Will said, punching his son on the arm.

Donald beamed. "I've been wanting to tell you since I first saw you at the ball," he claimed. "Nikky wouldn't let me."

Nicoletta dipped her head. "I have not yet told my brother nor *Zia* Armenia."

Donald rolled his eyes. "I am fairly sure *she* already knows," he murmured, finally rising to make his way out of the coach. He turned and helped his wife down before offering a hand to his mother.

"What makes you say that?" Barbara asked, watching Nicoletta as she hurried off towards the front door.

Glancing around to be sure no one else was within earshot, Donald said, "Because *Donna* Armenia is the one who first told me," he said, arching a brow.

*B*y the time their party were all inside, the fate of Nancy's parents was known to everyone. Barbara had already gone up to the nursery with Nicoletta, their steps quickening until they were nearly running.

"Do you think anyone has told her?" Barbara asked with worry.

"I don't believe so," Nicoletta replied. "I don't think her nurse would be brave enough." She allowed a sigh of frustration. "*Donna* Nancy was here only the day before yesterday, playing with Antony as if she didn't have a care in the world."

They slowed their approach to the nursery and glanced in to see Nancy and Antony embracing one another.

"Look who has come to see me again, Mama," Antony said, beaming in delight. "Hello, *Nonna*." He quickly bowed as Nancy held out her skirt to one side and dipped an awkward curtsy as Nicoletta and Barbara entered the room.

"*Sì*," Nicoletta replied. She knelt before the girl and then noticed the nurse hovering in the doorway to the girl's new bedroom."Does she know?" she asked in Italian.

The nurse quickly curtsied and then shook her head. "Only that they were badly hurt, *mia donna*. We have been waiting for someone to come with news of what is to become of us."

Before she had a chance to greet the child, Barbara inhaled softly when Nancy rushed forward, her arms wide until she collided with her skirts and embraced Barbara's legs. "*Nonna*," she said happily.

Awestruck, Nicoletta stared at the girl. "Why do you think she's your grandmother?" she asked in Italian.

Nancy was about to answer, but Barbara had already knelt to pull the young girl into a hug. "Oh, you precious girl," she said on a sigh.

"Nancy doesn't have a *nonna*," Antony said. "I told her I would share mine," he explained. "You," he added. "I hope it was all right."

"It's perfect," Barbara said, before kissing the girl on the side of her head. "Could you tell her I would also like to be her new mother?"

Antony furrowed a dark brow, the expression making him appear much older than his years. "Did her *madre* and *padre* die in their carriage?"

Surprised he knew of the accident, Barbara dared a glance at Nancy before she nodded. "They did."

His shoulders dropping as if he had been expecting the news, Antony nodded. "I will tell her, but..." He dipped his head.

"But?" Barbara prompted.

"She already knows, *Nonna*. Nancy hears the servants when

they don't know she's listening," he whispered. He turned to discover Nancy staring at him. Tears already threatened to roll down her cheeks, as if she understood their conversation. He spoke to her in a quiet voice before pulling her into an embrace.

Barbara had to swallow the lump in her throat before she could ask, "Will you tell her you will share your grandfather as well? That is, if you're willing?"

Antony inhaled sharply before he shared the news with Nancy. When she responded with a query that made her sound excited, Antony chuckled.

"What did she ask?" Barbara questioned, her attention on her grandson.

"She wants to know if *Nonno* will spin her around in circles like he does with me," he replied.

Barbara grinned despite the tears that streamed down her cheeks, but it was Will who answered from somewhere behind her. "Just try and stop me, young lady," he said. With his hands at her waist, he lifted her into the air and spun her around over his head.

Nancy squealed with excitement, her laughter infectious. When both Will and she were dizzy, he lowered her until her slippered feet touched the floor.

"I shall never tire of hearing a child's laughter," he commented, his gaze on Barbara.

"Does that mean we can keep her?" she asked in a whisper.

He shrugged. "If no one else claims her, we'll take her back to England with us," he replied in a quiet voice. He turned his attention on Nicoletta. "But you do realize it means you'll have to travel to England on occasion so these two can renew their acquaintance?" he asked, waving to Antony and Nancy. The young girl's brown eyes were wide as she stood and stared up at him, apparently well aware she was the topic of a serious discussion even if she couldn't understand their words.

Nicoletta allowed a watery grin. "I told Donald we could go whenever he thought he could spare the time," she replied.

"How about every year?" Donald asked. He had joined them in the nursery, hanging back in the doorway to watch. "We stay for a month—"

"When it is the hottest month of summer here," Nicoletta suggested.

"So... with travel, we'll only be away for ten weeks or so?" Donald finished, stepping forward to reach out to Nancy. He whispered something in Italian, and she was suddenly shy.

"You have yourself a deal, young man," Will replied. He paused and asked, "What did you say to her?"

"I told her I was going to be her new brother, but she seems a bit dubious," he said, feigning offense.

"That's because you did it all wrong, brother," David announced, stepping into the nursery from where he had been standing outside in the corridor. The small room was suddenly crowded, but he was soon kneeling in front of Nancy. "*Mia donna* Nancy, may I have the honor of becoming your big brother?" he asked in Italian.

Nancy grinned and wrapped her arms around his neck. "*Sì*," she said, grinning.

David chuckled as he patted her back. "I'll teach you how to play whist," he said. "And I promise to fend off all those suitors who are going to be breaking down the doors at Devonville House to court you."

"Let's not get ahead of ourselves," Will warned gently. "She might not be ours to simply... take."

The words had everyone sobering until Antony reached

for Nancy's hand and announced they were going to play a game of Morra.

"I think that's our cue to take our leave," Will said.

Barbara sighed but leaned over and kissed the girl's cheek as well as Antony's. "Enjoy your game," she murmured.

Antony bowed as Nancy curtsied, and the two went into the adjacent room.

Will's gaze fell on the nurse, who was still watching them from the adjacent doorway. Her eyes were bright with unshed tears, and he realized right away she was frightened for her future. "You will stay on as her nurse, will you not? Come to England with us if we're allowed to take her?"

After a quick round of translations between the girl and Nicoletta, the nurse nodded enthusiastically.

"She has no family in Roma," Nicoletta said. "Because like Nancy, she is an orphan," she added.

"Then let us hope this works out, or I fear my countess will be heartbroken," he replied, his words loud enough for only Nicoletta to hear.

*S*till out in the corridor, Vittoria pressed her back to the wall and wiped a tear from the top of one cheek. She had surreptitiously followed the rest of the family up the stairs when she realized something had happened, but until she had overheard David's query to the young girl, she hadn't sorted what that might be.

Poor *Donna* Nancy. Although Vittoria had lost her mother when she wasn't yet seventeen—and still missed her terribly—she was now old enough to become a mother herself. Nancy was far too young to lose both of her parents.

That David would be the one to put the girl at ease—to

ask her if he might be her brother—was so unexpected. So gallant.

I promise to fend off all those suitors who are going to be breaking down the doors at Devonville House to court you.

Had she misjudged him? Assumed the worst because she had been so stubborn when Nicoletta insisted she would like him? Maybe even enough to consider courtship should he wish it?

Tomorrow was another day. The viscount would no doubt show his true colors with her—if he hadn't already.

CHAPTER 26
HUNGER PREVAILS

*M*eanwhile, back at Villa D'Avalos

The last vestiges of her orgasm leaving her drowsy, Armenia angled her head so she could regard the man who had passed out atop her, essentially trapping her beneath him.

This certainly wasn't the afternoon she had imagined when she had awoken that morning. She had thought to discover Mr. McAdams' true intentions—a quick tumble and a remark about seeing her sometime in the future—and lead him on until they were about to do the deed before unceremoniously ordering him out of her house and her life.

She'd had enough of entitled—and titled—men expecting her to be at their beck and call years ago. Expecting her to jump into bed and provide relief for arousals they claimed she had caused.

Conte Mancino had been the last. Their annual escape to Taormina had been a trip she looked forward to every spring. A couple of months in a villa perched on a hill overlooking the Bay of Giardini Naxos provided respite from dealing with her brother and his machinations. Their last liaison had ended badly, though, when she learned he had several lovers in Naples—all younger than her.

The experience had been both a startling reminder of her fading beauty and the fickleness of men. Coupled with the announcement that Nicoletta would be marrying the Marchese Montblanc instead of Donald Slater made something snap inside her.

She was done with men. Done with their schemes and done with their lies.

Then along came Patrick McAdams to reawaken something inside her she had long ago stuffed away.

Desire.

Not because he was handsome, or because he was at least as tall as she was, or because he seemed to listen to what she said when she spoke.

He was so damned *earnest*. So open about his regard for her. If she wasn't careful, he would break the shell around her hardened heart and have her agreeing with whatever he wanted to do.

She speared Patrick's hair with her fingers, scraping his scalp. Feeling him shiver, she grinned. "You needn't have been concerned about humiliating yourself," she murmured.

He chuckled and lifted his head. Despite his stare, Armenia continued watching him from where she had angled her head on the pillow. "You as well," he whispered, sighing with satisfaction as he moved his hands to the sides of breasts to lift them until they were pressed to the sides of his head. He barely had the strength to raise his head so that he could kiss each nipple. "What have you done to me, my Venus?"

She tittered, the response causing her entire body to vibrate beneath him. "I might ask the same of you." Her legs gave up her hold on him, straightening so her feet rested on either side of his knees.

He chuckled in response, rolling off of her but winding an arm behind her shoulders so she ended up half atop him when he landed on his back at the edge of the bed. He turned his head and kissed the side of her face. "*Grazie*," he whispered.

She grinned before glancing over at him. "*Prego*."

"Are you hungry?" he asked.

"I am famished," she said, reminded there was food out in the sitting room.

"Would you be amenable to eating in bed?" he asked.

"I do most mornings," she replied. At seeing his curious expression, she added, "DeLuca brings me a cup of chocolate and toast, sometimes fruit."

"I'll be right back," he said, stepping off the bed to make his way to the sitting room.

Armenia watched as he opened the door, inhaling softly at seeing his nakedness, the shape of his muscular legs and angular buttocks evident despite the gloom. Light from the sitting room briefly cast him in silhouette before he disappeared.

Tempted to pull on a dressing robe, she was about to rise from the bed when he returned with a tray. Two plates were piled with a variety of meats and cheeses, cut fruits, and two cups of coffee.

He joined her on the bed, balancing the tray so its sides straddled his thighs as he leaned against the headboard. "May I feed you?"

Armenia scoffed, but joined him at the head of the bed, pulling a blanket up to cover her chest. "Depends on what you're offering," she teased.

A huge grin split his face. "A better double entendre I've not heard," he said, offering her a section of an orange. She took it between her lips, but before she could reach up to take hold of it, a drop of juice escaped and began running down her chin.

"I'll get it," he said, leaning over to lick it with his tongue. He managed to kiss her lips in the process, surprising her.

"The oranges here never disappoint," he commented, before helping himself to a slice of rolled ham. He handed her one. "In fact, I have found nothing here about which to complain," he remarked.

"That's because you haven't been here long enough," she said, before finishing off the ham.

"Perhaps," he said between bites of an apricot. "This is so good," he added, holding up the fruit.

"There are apricot and cherry trees on the D'Avalos property outside of town," she said, helping herself to another section of orange.

"The farm with the sheep?"

Her mouth full, she nodded.

"How is it you're not married? I would have guessed you were a widow, except I distinctly remember you saying you never married."

Armenia nearly choked on the last of her orange. She contemplated telling him it was none of his business, but his curiosity seemed so sincere. "I refused the man my father arranged for me to marry," she stated. "He was old enough to be my father and possessed the worst manners when it came to eating."

Patrick was in the middle of chewing another piece of meat but stopped, his eyes widening with worry.

"*You* needn't be concerned," she said. "He chewed with his mouth open and made the most annoying noises. He ate much like pigs do."

"What happened to him?"

She rolled her eyes. "He choked to death at his wedding

banquet a few months later. *Donna* Rossi was never more relieved."

Blinking, Patrick appeared not to believe her. "You are... joking with me?" he guessed.

She shook her head before popping a cherry into her mouth. "I am not. She ended up marrying his son from his first marriage. He was a widower," she quickly added.

"Well, I suppose that's one way to keep the family fortune," he murmured. "You must have had other offers," he prompted.

She sighed before clearing her throat. "Two, neither one very serious," she replied. "When my brother's wife died in the childbed, he required a hostess and never pursued a match for me, which I appreciated more than he could know." She saw Patrick wince. "That doesn't mean..." She stopped when she saw his expression suddenly change. "What?" she whispered.

"Will you marry me?"

She inhaled softly. "You haven't even known me an entire day," she countered.

"I want to learn everything there is to know about you," he claimed. "I promise to honor you. I promise fidelity," he added, apparently knowing that last vow would have her considering his proposal with more seriousness.

"Why?" she asked gently.

He inhaled deeply and let the breath out in a *whoosh*. "Something happened last night. I was minding my own business—literally—and then I saw you watching me, and it was as if my eyes were opened for the first time in years," he explained. "As if I've been going through life blind and you made me see everything so clearly. Then you made me want you."

Armenia swallowed, remembering her earlier thoughts

on their meeting. "Want?" she repeated. "Like... like a possession?"

His shoulders noticeably dropping, he said, "I know it sounds like that, because part of it is."

Shocked at his admission, she said, "Oh? And the other part?" She swallowed the other words she nearly blurted out. Never in her life had she wanted to accept a man's attentions as much as she did Patrick's.

Whatever was wrong with her?

"Armenia, I cannot abide the thought of another man with you," he claimed. "I don't think it's only jealousy, either. I feel I have a duty to protect you. To make you happy. To make love to you whenever you're of a mind to be worshipped." He leaned down and placed a kiss on her bare shoulder. "Be my Venus, will you?"

Armenia inhaled softly, murmuring when he suckled her earlobe. "Might I think on it for a day or two?"

He nodded. "I'm not going anywhere." He closed his eyes and made an odd sound in his throat. "I mean to say, I will go back to my lodgings when you've had enough of me today. But I hope you'll allow me to continue paying calls on you, and not just for this," he added, waving to the bed and the tray of food. "I enjoy your company. Especially your candor. It will take the rest of our lifetimes for you to show me all the Italian art in this town." He kissed her cheek. "And I adore making love to you."

Even before he had finished his litany of reasons he wanted to marry her, Armenia was already experiencing a renewal of the arousal she had felt earlier that day. The throbbing at the top of her thighs matched the beat of her heart, and her nipples hardened behind the blanket she still clutched to her chest.

"Put the tray on the floor," she ordered.

Patrick jerked at hearing the command in her voice, but he quickly did her bidding.

"Now lie back," she said. She saw him swallow but he was quick to shift his body farther down onto the bed and settle his head into the pillow. His semi-rigid cock suddenly stood at attention, as if it knew more than he did what was about to happen.

Armenia tossed the blanket from her body and straddled him, happy to see his reaction of surprise when she clasped her hands over both of his and raised them so they were on either side of his head. "Don't touch me," she whispered.

His eyes darkened, but his hands went slack beneath her hold. As she moved her hips so her wet quim slid along his velvety length, she lowered her breasts until her nipples skimmed through the sprinkling of crisp graying curls on his chest. They were joined by a lock of hair that had escaped its pins, the raven mass sliding down the side of his chest.

He bucked beneath her, his face displaying humor. "That tickles," he claimed.

She grinned and then lifted her hips. His manhood seemed to know exactly where her opening was, for she was able to keep her hands clasped on his as she lowered her hips and took in his entire length during her slow descent. Her core throbbed with need, as did his cock. She ground herself against his groin, felt his sac tighten. She gave up her hold on one of his hands so she could reach back and lift it with three fingers.

His reaction beneath her was immediate as his hips jerked up. She was reminded of riding a young horse attempting to unseat its rider, but she knew he didn't want to buck her off of him. Not if the sounds he was making were any indication.

"I *have* to touch you," he said in a hoarse whisper.

Before she could put voice to a response, he had his free hand where their bodies met, his thumb pressing against her swollen womanhood. Combined with how she moved atop him, his ministrations helped to set off her impending release. She was caught off-guard when the sudden and sharp orgasm gripped her and sent her over the edge of oblivion.

"*Coglione*," she whispered, her spine arching as she threw her head back. She was lost in the increasing waves of pleasure that rolled through her, barely aware when his release had him spilling his seed into her, and only then because she heard his growls and murmurs that sounded as if he was praying to a god of love.

When her body seemed to lose all its strength along with all its bones, she crumpled down onto him, the last few inches happening as if in a dream as he captured her torso and slowed her descent until she landed on him.

She felt an arm wrap around her back while one of his hands cupped her head to place it in the small of his shoulder. Straightening her legs, she felt him kiss her forehead before she allowed sleep to take her.

CHAPTER 27
A BATH BEFORE DINNER

Meanwhile, back at Villa Montblanc

Prior to the start of their Grand Tour, the practice of afternoon napping had been a foreign concept to the Slaters and Forsters. After their long walking tour of Rome and the excitement of meeting Nancy, most in their party were happy to retreat to their guest bedchambers in Villa Montblanc.

Not all of them did so to sleep. Vittoria took the opportunity to take a bath prior to that night's dinner in the hopes her feet could recover. She winced as she pulled her feet from the black leather half-boots that had been delivered to Palazzo D'Avalos only the week before. Her toes were red, and blood oozed from an older wound that had reopened whilst on that day's walk.

At least the slippers her lady's maid had packed for that night's dinner were her most comfortable pair. She feared she would be limping otherwise.

Once she was in the tub, she dismissed her lady's maid with instructions she be left alone until it was time to dress for dinner.

She wanted time to think. Time to sort the events of the prior evening at the ball and to review the conversations she'd had with David during their walk that day.

David.

How could a man be so exasperating? So self-confident? So damned amiable? So handsome despite a clear lack of Italian heritage?

Surely such a beast was a rogue. Ready to pounce on the first young lady with whom he thought he could take advantage.

And yet he hadn't. Not even the night before when they were alone in the library.

Damn him.

She wasn't even sure why she accused him of being a rogue when they were in the company of his family.

That wasn't exactly true. She knew why.

The thought that he had slighted her by not attempting to ruin her hurt more than she realized. After being raised to believe she was a beautiful young lady and that every young man—and old—would want to have their way with her had left her with the impression every man would misbehave in her company. Every man would forfeit his good breeding in order to have his way with her.

That David, Viscount Penton, didn't make a move in that regard should have felt like a breath of fresh air. Instead, it felt as if she had been doused with a bucket of cold water.

Wasn't she worthy of his attentions—good or bad? Beautiful enough to incite his worst behavior? Alluring enough to have him bowing at her feet.

She lifted one of her wounded feet above the level of the water and winced. *No one would bow to these feet*, she thought sourly, noting how they were still red and swollen in several places.

Not once had David attempted to trap her in a dark

alcove or take liberties whilst they were alone in the barouche. There had only been a moment in the Pantheon when she thought certain he intended to kiss her.

If the priest hadn't interrupted them, would he have kissed her? She couldn't deny the excitement she had felt at the thought that he might bestow a kiss on her lips. It would be her first—she refused to count any of the sloppy kisses *Don* Luciano had landed on her neck before his near demise in the alcove the night before. Thank the gods his lips hadn't managed to find hers in the dark. She might have bit off one of them. Had he tried to insert his tongue in her mouth, she would have bit his tongue.

After her mother's death, Vittoria took her instruction for how to deal with men from Aunt Armenia. Her great aunt had listed all the possible ways in which to deny a rogue's attempts to ruin a young lady, her instructions obviously gained from experience.

Vittoria had listened intently, determined she be prepared for a come-out she had been taught would include an attempt at ruination by *Don* Luciano and any number of other inappropriate overtures by the young bucks expected to attend the ball.

Don Luciano behaved as expected and suffered for his behavior. However, no other man tried anything untoward. None of her dance partners tried to kiss her, or to "accidentally" cup a breast, or trap her against a column or a wall. They were all on their very best behavior.

Including Viscount Penton.

Damn him.

Perhaps she would discover more during dinner that evening. Aunt Armenia would be joining them, and with any luck, she might discover if her expectations were realistic.

CHAPTER 28
DIMPLES DELIGHT

eanwhile, in the master bedchamber at Villa D'Avalos

Not sure what had him awakening with a start, Patrick glanced around Armenia's bedchamber expecting to see her up and about.

She wasn't, though. Although he remembered her falling asleep atop him, she had slid off and was lying on her stomach, a bed linen barely covering her backside.

He lifted himself onto an elbow, and with his free hand, he traced the bumps of her spine down to the fabric. Just above the edge were two slight indentations directly above the globes of her derriere. Grinning, he used a fingertip to circle each one, delighting in how her body shivered beneath his touch.

"Whatever are you doing?" she asked, her voice thick with sleep.

"Apologies. I didn't mean to wake you," he whispered.

"Liar."

He chuckled softly as he continued to tease her warm skin with his fingertips. From her soft gasps and the way her skin reacted, he knew she was either experiencing a tickle or a frisson of pleasure. "You have the most adorable dimples on your backside," he murmured.

Now wide awake, Armenia lifted herself onto her elbows and glanced back over her shoulder, her face half-hidden by a lock of hair that had escaped its pins. "What dimples?"

To prevent her from moving away from him or turning over, he flattened his hand over the small of her back as he moved down the bed. "These dimples," he replied, right before he reached out with his tongue to lick each one in turn.

She inhaled sharply and whispered something in Italian as she attempted to lift her hips from the mattress.

He slid his hand over the curve of one globe, drawing the bed linen off her body until it was well past her bottom. He kissed each dimple in turn before touching them with the tip of his nose.

Inhaling the scent of her feminine musk, he chuckled softly. "These dimples," he repeated.

Free of the bed linen, he watched as Armenia drew up her knees, further lifting her backside from the bed as he continued to run his palm over her warm skin. Desire once again had his cock hardening, the tip already dripping in anticipation of another round of lovemaking.

"Well?"

He gave a start when he realized she was once again attempting to look back at him from over her shoulder. For a moment, Patrick didn't realize her intentions. He didn't understand she was inviting him to enter her right then and there.

He moved his hand around her derriere and then between her spread thighs to discover she was already wet with desire.

She jerked against his palm, and he felt her swollen

womanhood rub against his middle finger. She moved again, her inhalations of breath the only sound she made as she rocked her quim against his hand.

Settling onto his haunches, Patrick gripped one of her hips and drew her closer to his body as he continued to rub her swollen sex, soon replacing his hand with his engorged manhood.

He groaned when he felt one of her hands cover his to press it harder against her womanhood, her cries of pleasure muffled in the mattress as she guided his cock into her throbbing channel.

He wasn't prepared for how much pleasure he would experience with the first tentative thrust. He wasn't expecting her to lift herself onto her arms, using one hand to grip a rung of the iron headboard as if to brace herself. Wasn't ready when she pushed her bum into his groin, ensuring he was buried as deep as he would go. He wasn't expecting her to cover his hand with one of her own and move it to grasp a breast, the pebbled nipple settling between two of his fingers.

When he sensed he was about to break apart into a million pieces—there could be no other way to describe what he experienced when his orgasm took him from the here and now—he had only enough strength to pull her up so her back was pressed against the front of his body, her head tossed back over one of his shoulders as he settled on his haunches and gave into the pleasure.

Her orgasm followed as he tightened his hold on her, and he knew from how her body quaked that she, too, was lost to the pleasure.

This time, he didn't pass out. He didn't allow sleep to take him. He simply remained where he was. He did take advantage of Armenia's exposed neck to place a kiss there, which seemed to arouse her from her post-coital stupor.

"Those dimples," he whispered.

Despite her drowsy demeanor, she tittered. "Next time I'm going to discover if *you* have them," she warned.

Patrick inhaled and grinned. Her comment implied they would be doing this again. "Next time," he agreed.

half-hour later

"When may I call on you again?" Patrick asked, grasping her hand to kiss the back of it. She wore only a dressing gown, her hair completely free of its pins so it hung well below her shoulders. A few streaks of gray interrupted the otherwise raven color, but he thought it suited her age and bearing.

From her heightened color, it was apparent she had been tumbled and was happy about it.

"If I didn't have to attend a family dinner at the Villa Montblanc this evening, I would ask you to stay," she murmured. "Come for dinner on the morrow," she added. "Seven o'clock."

He nodded. "I shall be here," he promised. He leaned forward and kissed her cheek before barely brushing them over her lips. "*Buonsera*, my Venus."

"Good night, Patrick," she whispered.

Making his way out of the courtyard and into the street, Patrick experienced a moment of regret. Armenia hadn't invited him to spend the night, but then she had mentioned the family dinner.

About to turn around, he remembered he hadn't been in his office since that morning. Duty called, and although he found walking more difficult than usual, he made it across the Piazza Navona and into his building as the sun was setting beyond the river.

CHAPTER 29
A DINNER BORDERS
ON DISASTER

wo hours later

The parlor in Villa Montblanc was buzzing when Armenia entered, her great niece Vittoria following behind. She wondered what she had missed in not joining their party for their walking tour of Rome, even if she was secretly glad she had instead opted to spend her day in the company of Patrick McAdams.

How could she not? The businessman had been a perfect gentleman for their walking tour of four fountains, and then he had continued to impress her with his insistence that he actually felt affection for her. Enough that he had insisted they be married.

Time would tell on that account.

She had invited him for dinner the following evening. Part of her expected that after a night of retrospection, he would send his regrets. The rest of her hoped beyond all reason he would show up at Villa D'Avalos clutching a dozen red roses and a ring featuring an enormous gemstone.

A girl could dream, couldn't she? Even if she was nearly old enough to be his mother?

As for how she would reply to his marriage proposal—should he offer another one—she still wasn't sure. She probably should accept on the basis of his bed sport alone, but was she really willing to give up her life as a fairly happy and rather well-to-do spinster in exchange for becoming a textiles matriarch?

He would have to be willing to move into her villa, for there was no way she would give up her home for any man —no matter how good he was in bed.

Nor would she move to America. At some point, she expected he would wish to rejoin his son in Boston. What then?

"*Zia* Armenia!"

The greeting from her niece, Nicoletta, pulled her from her reverie, and she quickly displayed a huge grin for the benefit of her hostess and the members of her husband's family that filled the Montblanc Villa parlor. She paused to allow Vittoria to join her at her side, and the two curtsied in unison once the gentlemen in the room had stood and bowed.

"Thank you so much for the invitation, *mia donna*. This is a perfect ending to a rather pleasant day," she said as she grasped Nicoletta's hands and allowed her niece to kiss her on both cheeks.

She watched as Vittoria followed suit, and the two took the only remaining seats in the parlor.

Everyone else settled back into their chairs or settees, although she noted that David, Viscount Penton, was left leaning against the fireplace mantel. From his expression, she thought he might be experiencing a bout of indigestion, which given the fact that they hadn't yet eaten anything, seemed rather odd.

"I see the marchese is once again in the company of *Donna* Nancy," Armenia murmured, her gaze going to the youngsters. The two were seated at the gaming table at the back of the parlor.

"The Russos were in a terrible accident last night. They did not survive," Nicoletta said in a quiet voice. "We're keeping Nancy until we learn what might become of her."

Armenia's eyes widened briefly before she said, "Whatever happens, do not allow her to go to the family in Naples."

"I am in agreement," Nicoletta replied. "Donald has already sent a letter of inquiry asking if Nancy might remain with us." She nodded in the direction of Barbara. "Or become a ward."

Armenia nodded her understanding before she directed a smile at Barbara. "You must tell me all about your walking tour," she said.

"Most invigorating, so interesting, and immensely satisfying," the countess said, her attention darting to the door.

Armenia followed her line of sight to discover the butler waiting for an opening in their conversation.

"*Viene servita la cena,*" he announced. *Dinner is served.*

"*Grazie,*" Donald replied. He stood and offered his arm to Nicoletta at the same time Antony did the same for Nancy. The two children made their way to the door followed by the others who had paired off and followed in order of their rank.

"Might you two join me?" David asked, directing his query to Armenia and Vittoria. He held out both arms, bent at the elbows.

Armenia was quick to accept his offer, giving him a nod as she placed an arm on his. Although she was a statuesque woman and only a couple of inches shorter than he was, she did nothing to compensate for her height. Instead, she noticed David straightening as much as he could by pulling back his shoulders.

Visibly limping, Vittoria fell in at the back of the procession.

An odd sound emanated from David's throat, and the conte's daughter was suddenly pulled up next to him. "Why are you limping?" he asked in a whisper.

"Because my feet are quite sore from our walk today," she hissed in reply.

Armenia furrowed her brows at hearing the obvious disdain in her niece's voice. "The discomfort you are experiencing is not *Don* Penton's fault," she whispered.

Vittoria dipped her head. "Apologies," she replied.

Once they were in the dining room, Nicoletta was seated at one end with Donald taking the carver. The others couples took chairs across the table from one another so that Armenia was left next to David and Vittoria was opposite them.

Footmen appeared with the wine and first course, and a lively discussion about that day's sights ensued. Armenia displayed a pleasant expression in between bites of food. Although she usually ate very little at dinner, she was famished.

"It is unfortunate you did not join us for our walk today," Barbara said from the other end of the table.

Armenia set down her glass of wine. "Indeed. I do believe our paths nearly crossed in the Piazza del Rotunda, though," she commented. "I was there with a new acquaintance to admire the interior of the Pantheon."

"The interior?" Diana repeated. "What pray tell was your interest, my lady?"

Despite her plan to simply keep quiet during dinner, Armenia was forced to participate. "The perfect number involved in its construction," she replied, the memory of her kiss with Patrick McAdams beneath the oculus sending a frisson through her entire body. "At least, from a Greek's perspective."

"Six?" David said from her right.

"Eight-and-twenty," Randy said. "But..." He paused, his brows furrowing in concentration.

"Originally there were eight-and-twenty red porphyry columns in the Pantheon. They have since been replaced with granite copies," Armenia explained. "There are also eight-and-twenty coffers in each row of the ceiling."

"Fascinating," Diana murmured. "I do wish you had been with us. Pray tell, what else did you see today?"

Armenia felt heat color her face as several eyes turned to regard her with anticipation. For a moment, she thought to shock them with a comment about Patrick's physique, but reason had her saying, "Four fountains is all. I live very close to Piazza Navona, you see, where there are three."

"We'll have to go there on one of our walks," Helen said.

"After the Forum and the Colosseum, my love," Tom said with a chuckle.

"Is that tomorrow's itinerary?" Armenia asked.

"Indeed. Will you join us, *Zia* Armenia?" Nicoletta asked. "We'll be taking the coaches, of course. I can send one for you," she offered.

When everyone's eyes were on her, Armenia realized she could hardly decline. The outing would certainly help the day go by faster. "I should like that very much, although I must be back at Villa D'Avalos by five o'clock." Before anyone could ask, she added, "I am hosting a friend for dinner." She knew Vittoria was staring at her even before her gaze swept to the young lady.

"I'll send the coach so it arrives around eleven o'clock," Nicoletta said, grinning in delight.

"I shall look forward to being your escort on the

morrow," David said, directing his comment to Armenia. He drained his glass of wine in two gulps.

She blinked. "Why, *grazie*. I don't believe I've had the benefit of such a handsome young man on my arm for a couple of decades."

He chuckled, but when his gaze settled on Vittoria, the humor quickly dissipated from his face.

Vittoria was staring daggers at him.

Armenia was sure he was about to mention he would also see to escorting Vittoria, but a footman stopped to refill their wine glasses and to set the next course before them.

By the time they had resumed eating, the conversation had turned to something they had learned at one of the other piazzas that day, and Armenia was relieved to simply eat in silence.

Nicoletta caught her attention once, though, a pleading look that had her noticing how Vittoria and David were both sulking. The two were taking turns staring at one another. When one realized the other's attention was on them, they quickly took a drink of wine or pretended interest in something on their plate.

Armenia might have felt amusement at seeing what could possibly be a lovers' tiff in progress—didn't they realize that life was too short for such pettiness?—but at no point had she thought the two felt affection for one another.

Just the opposite given how they had behaved with one another in the parlor.

She glanced over at Nicoletta, a brow arched in silent query. The young matron's look of defeat had her scoffing softly. "Affection cannot be forced," she whispered.

"I understand," the marchesa replied sadly.

At no point did either David or Vittoria seem to notice they were the topic of the other women's quiet conversation.

Given how many glasses of wine the two consumed, it shouldn't have been a surprise. By the time dessert was served, they were obviously inebriated, and neither were happy drunks.

CHAPTER 30
BROTHERS COME TO
AN UNDERSTANDING

*L*ater *that evening, at the same dining table*

The faint strains of a *piano-forte* faded to silence as Donald finished the last of his grappa. He glanced over at his father and arched a brow.

"I think that must be our ladies letting us know they are ready for us in the parlor," Will said, a grin lighting his face.

"Not a moment too soon," Randy murmured, a quelling glance directed across and down the table at David. His cousin had imbibed entirely too much liquor at the end of the extravagant meal, his usual amiable manner and sparkling dinner conversation entirely missing that evening. In its place was a bitterness aimed at the young lady who had been sitting across from him. He didn't seem to realize she had been absent from the table ever since all the women took their leave the hour prior.

To her credit, Lady Vittoria had pretended to ignore him during the entire seven-course meal.

"Apologies," David whispered. "I know I have not been myself this day," he admitted.

Seated adjacent to Donald at the mahogany table, Will

pushed back and stood. "Apology accepted, but know this, young man. Your manner will be most improved by breakfast, or you shall be remaining behind when we tour the Roman Forum on the morrow."

David's glassy eyes widened in alarm. "Uh, yes, sir," he replied sheepishly.

Randy and Tom stood and followed their uncle out the door, both silent as a lively tune once again sounded from the parlor. Donald and David remained at the table, however.

"Do you wish to talk about whatever it is that has you vexed?" Donald asked his younger brother.

The viscount furrowed his brows. Despite the nearly eight years difference in their ages, the expression made the two appear as if they might be twins. "I did *nothing* wrong last night," he stated.

Surprised at the odd response, Donald leaned back in his chair and crossed his arms. "Has someone claimed you did?"

David stared at his brother for a moment as if he might be mad. "Didn't you hear Lady Vittoria? She... she called me a... a *rogue*," he claimed. "And try as I might all day whilst we walked about all those fountains, I could not convince her otherwise."

One of Donald's eyebrows arched. "Were you?"

David blinked. "No. I... I tried to *help*. I followed her and that *Don* Diavala or... Luciano... whoever he was," he stammered while waving a hand dismissively. "How was I to know Vittoria could look after herself?"

Donald stared at his brother a moment, his face displaying confusion. "What *are* you talking about?" he finally asked, as if he thought David's words were said from a drunken stupor.

"That damned *Don* Luciano."

Obviously not expecting the response, Donald nodded. "Now, he *is* a rake," he stated.

"Exactly! As soon as Lady Vittoria had been announced and was at the bottom of the stairs, he offered her his arm and escorted her right out of the ballroom and into an alcove," David explained. "The one with the statue of Apollo."

"Go on," Donald urged, his look of alarm apparent as he leaned forward.

"I was about to offer my assistance to the lady, but she ... well, let us just say she must have realized what Luciano intended, for I think she might have damaged the Tucci family jewels with her fist," he said. "I managed to do some harm when he suddenly bent over and his face collided with *my* knee. I think it might have broken his nose."

"Oh," Donald whispered in awe.

"And then Apollo delivered the final blow by tumbling off his caryatid. His arrow might have... *impaled* the conte heir's crotch."

Wincing despite the obvious moment of humor he experienced, Donald suddenly barked a laugh. "Now *that* is a sight I would have paid good money to see," he claimed. "*Don* Luciano is a well-known libertine, but I've never known him to pursue virgins. Especially at their come-out balls," he added thoughtfully.

David screwed his face into a grimace, unaware the libertine had such a reputation. "Do you suppose he had something else in mind?"

Although he seemed about to respond, Donald leaned back, his gaze going up to the chandelier above the dining table. "Perhaps," he whispered.

"What are you thinking?"

Pulled from his brief reverie, Donald glanced towards the door as if to ensure no one else was listening to their conversation. He turned his attention back to David. "There is talk that the Tucci *contea* is in some trouble. Financial trouble," he explained.

"Aren't they all?" David asked before downing the rest of what was in his glass of grappa.

"Surprisingly, no," Donald replied. "Edoardo is doing rather well despite his father's mismanagement of the D'Avalos *contea*," he added. "And there are others who do well from their vineyards and farms."

Despite his eyes still appearing glassy from too much drink that evening, David seemed to understand his brother's hint. "You think Luciano *wanted* to be caught with Lady Vittoria? So he would be forced to marry her?" he guessed.

Donald nodded. "For her dowry," he whispered. "I have to reason to believe Edoardo has set aside a rather generous settlement for his only daughter."

David jerked back as if he had been slapped across the face. "Damnation," he murmured.

"Damnation is right," Donald agreed. "But you being there last night—in that alcove—means you were in just as much danger of a false accusation as *Don* Luciano."

"From the lady herself," David groused. "She is convinced my intentions were not honorable when I was merely trying to... to help," he claimed.

"And if you had been caught with her?"

David blinked. "What are you asking?"

Donald chuckled softly. "Would you do the honorable thing? Take her to wife to save her from ruination?"

His brother's scoff was loud. "Not *now* I wouldn't," he replied. When he noted how Donald continued to stare at him, as if challenging him, he sighed loudly. "Well, she's a rather unpleasant creature, in case you haven't noticed," he added in a quiet voice.

"I hadn't," Donald stated.

David's responding scoff was quieter. "She's a *shrew*, Donald. A spoiled rotten brat, and far too beautiful for her age," he said as he leaned forward, his arms resting on the tabletop. "Argh."

"Vittoria cannot help that she is beautiful," Donald replied. "You need only look at *Donna* Armenia and Nicoletta and her cousin, Elizabeth Bennett-Jones, to know that exquisite beauty runs in that family." He paused before adding, "As for being spoiled, I suppose Edoardo has indulged her. She is his only daughter, after all, and it's been hard for him since the death of his wife."

Screwing his face into a grimace, David sighed. "That doesn't give her the right to be a shrew."

Donald covered his mouth with a hand, the crinkling at the edges of his eyes giving away his humor.

"What?" David challenged.

"She is the first, isn't she?" Donald asked, rubbing his hand over the side of his face as he grinned in delight.

"What are you talking about?"

Donald chuckled. "She is the first woman who hasn't fallen at your feet and claimed undying love for you," he said, grinning. "The amiable and lovable Viscount Penton humbled by an Italian aristocrat's daughter."

David's eyes rounded. "Take that back," he demanded.

Donald sobered, but he shook his head. "You have never been challenged by a woman before, have you?"

A growl sounded from his brother. "In case you're not aware, and despite my brief betrothal to Lady Jane Fitzsimmons, I've not exactly had a lot of opportunities when it comes to women," David stated.

"I am aware, as I shared that same problem prior to meeting Nicoletta," Donald countered.

"I intended to use this Grand Tour as a means to... to—"

"Sow your wild oats. To meet lots of young ladies all

over Europe and have your way with them," Donald finished for him.

David furrowed his brows. "Well, not like *that*," he responded. "I would have... woo'd them," he added, before his eyes suddenly rounded. "Is that what you did?"

Donald dipped his head. "I fear our Father instilled in me the need to be extra honorable. Remember, I am the bastard in the family."

Wincing, David shook his head. "He's done the same with me. And since he's been chaperoning our cousins and me during this entire trip—instead of you, I might add—I haven't exactly had the opportunity to spend time in the company of the other sex," he complained.

"If you had, would you?" Donald challenged.

Blinking several times, David allowed a long sigh. "I might have spent time at a brothel," he whispered.

"Probably best for your prick that you didn't."

David rolled his eyes and made an odd sound in his throat. "Probably."

"So...?"

David stared at his brother for a moment. "So... what?"

"Do you love her?"

The query was so unexpected, David straightened in his chair as if he had been struck. "Love who?"

Donald grunted his disbelief. "Vittoria."

"*What?!*"

"Do you think you could at least... *like* her?" he pressed.

"From where *is* this coming?" David asked in confusion.

Glancing back toward the door, Donald lowered his voice and said, "I would be remiss if I didn't tell you that there has been some... *hope* that you and Vittoria might consider... courtship," he stammered.

David blinked several times, his mouth opening and closing as if he couldn't believe what he was hearing. "If I were a female, I would be down there on the floor having just fainted after hearing such a... such a ridiculous suggestion," he claimed, pointing down to the Turkish carpeting with a forefinger for emphasis. "In fact, I might yet do so."

"Which, given what you've told me, means *she* is probably about to pass out on the parlor room floor," Donald said absently.

"What?"

Donald once again glanced in the direction of the door. "I have reason to believe Nikky is discussing the same possibility of courtship with her niece right about now. I was... unaware the two of you were... incompatible." He rolled his eyes.

David dropped his head to the dining room table and began banging it on the cloth-covered surface. "If I wasn't so damned amiable, and agreeable, I could still be betrothed to Lady Jane Fitzsimmons," he murmured. "I could be looking forward to a life—"

"Of extreme boredom," Donald interrupted.

Straightening in his chair, David appeared a bit unsteady for a moment, his forehead red where it had struck the table. "What?"

It was Donald's turn to scoff. "Lady Jane Fitzsimmons is perfectly pretty and proper, but you know damned well you would have grown bored if you were ever wed to her. Far better she ended up with Marcus Henley."

Staring at his brother as if he had grown horns, David shook his head. "So instead of a perfectly proper and pretty young English girl, I'm supposed to marry a *shrew*?" he countered with disgust.

Donald cleared his throat and leaned forward. "I once thought Nikky a spoiled rotten brat," he said in a whisper. He arched a brow. "But now I am very happily married to her," he added, waggling both his brows.

Before David could reply, Donald got to his feet and headed for the door.

"Where are you going?"

"To the parlor to collect my gorgeous wife so she can have her way with me in our bedchamber."

David watched as his brother disappeared, his brows furrowing in confusion as he replayed his brother's parting words in his head. He finally chuckled softly. "Damnation," he whispered softly.

CHAPTER 31
A DISCUSSION
WITH A VALET

*M*eanwhile...

Patrick McAdams stood still as his valet undid the knot of his cravat and wondered if Giovanni would realize it wasn't finished exactly the same as when he had tied it earlier that morning.

When he had finally left Armenia's bed late that afternoon, it had taken some time for him to dress himself. Despite his post-coital euphoria, his limbs had felt rubbery, his movements made as if in slow motion.

Apparently Armenia had noticed, for she had seen to wrapping the length of silk around his neck, careful to pleat the fabric the same as it had been before she had stripped it away. However, Patrick hadn't paid any mind to the finishing knot she used.

That moment when she stood before him, dressed only in a silk robe, the fabric hugging her luscious curves, her hair completely free of its pins, and her face still flushed from their last round of lovemaking, had reminded him of Signora Ricci's assessment of Armenia D'Avalos.

Whore.

Hiding his wince from Armenia's brown-eyed gaze had been difficult. Pulling her into his arms and kissing her with one last open-mouthed kiss had only made him wonder once again as to why Signora Ricci would make such a claim.

What did the woman know?

To his credit, Giovanni didn't comment on the cravat, but from his furrowed brow, Patrick knew the young man had noticed it was different from how he had knotted it that morning.

"How long has your mother been a widow?" Patrick asked, curious as to how Giovanni would respond.

The valet pulled the silk cloth from around his neck. "My father died five… six years ago, *signore*."

"I am sorry for your loss. What did he do for his living?" Patrick asked, pulling his shirt over his head. Rather than tossing the garment onto the bed, he gave it to the valet.

Giovanni froze, his eyes downcast. "Nothing."

Patrick gave a start. "Was he… unable to work?" He couldn't think of another word to describe someone too injured or addled to perform labor.

"I do not know," he replied. "We did not live with him." He busied himself with folding the cravat and shirt.

Nodding, Patrick moved to the bed and sat down on the edge of it. "But you knew who he was?"

Giovanni dipped his head. "*Sì*."

"Did he know you?" He visibly winced asking the question—he knew it was far too personal, and he wouldn't have been surprised if the manservant refused to answer.

A shrug preceded the servant's response. "I do not think so."

Patrick swallowed as Giovanni pulled the boots from his feet. "I apologize. I did not mean to pry," he murmured. "But I do like to know more about those I employ."

Giovanni lifted a shoulder as if he didn't mind the questions. "May I ask you a question, *signore*?" He set aside the boots and went to work on removing Patrick's stockings.

"Of course." Patrick steeled himself in anticipation of an uncomfortable query.

"Do you have a son?"

Patrick nearly chuckled. "I do. He lives in Boston and runs our office there," he replied.

"Does he live with his mother?"

Shaking his head, Patrick said, "We both did until she died last year, and I have not remarried." *Yet*, he almost added.

"So... he... he *knows* you?"

Patrick gave a start and briefly wondered if he misunderstood Giovanni's English. "He does. My move to Rome has meant this is the first time we have not lived under the same roof since his birth."

Giovanni seemed to think on his response for a time before he said, "I am a bastard. It is why my name is my mother's and not...*his*," he added.

"If it had been his, what would your name be?"

Lifting his chin, Giovanni replied, "D'Avalos."

His suspicions confirmed, Patrick remembered the name Armenia had used for her older brother. "Enrico?" he guessed. He had no idea how many other men might have been part of the D'Avalos line living in the palazzo.

Giovanni's eyes briefly rounded. "*Sì*. How did you...?" He glanced towards the door, as if he worried their conversation might not be private.

"*Donna* Armenia D'Avalos... uh, your aunt, implied it was a possibility." Patrick watched as the manservant rose from his knees and stood staring at something in his mind's eye. "It is my intention to take her to wife," he added, curious to see how the young man would react.

"Marry her?" Giovanni repeated.

"Yes. I... uh, find myself quite in love with her." He cleared his throat. "Which is why your mother's comment about her this morning has me... rather concerned."

Taking a step backwards, the stockings still hanging from one hand, Giovanni shook his head. "My mother is a... a *busybody*," he said, as if he struggled for the English word. "A gossip. Do not heed her slander."

Narrowing his eyes, Patrick regarded his servant for a time before he finally nodded. "All right. But usually, where there is smoke, there is fire," he murmured, hoping Giovanni would understand his point.

For a moment, the servant glanced about the room, his manner becoming that of a caged animal. "I will tell you what I know, but..."

"But... what?" Patrick prompted.

"I should not."

"Because you are a loyal servant?"

Giovanni nodded vigorously.

"But you are employed by me now. Who was your employer before I hired you?" Although there had been a character provided to him by the service registry he had used to hire the Riccis, he hadn't read it. At the time, he didn't think he could understand the derivation of Latin used in the document.

Now he knew better.

"I heard things. Overheard things when I worked at his lordship's residence."

Patrick inhaled sharply. "You worked for the Conte Enrico D'Avalos?" he asked in surprise. "I thought your mother had been dismissed—"

"*Sì.* She worked in another household," Giovanni said. "When I was old enough, I went to the butler at Villa D'Avalos and was hired as a footman. I worked there until..."

He lifted a shoulder. "Until I was mistaken for his lordship's son."

Patrick sighed. "Having met the current conte last evening, I can say there is definitely a family resemblance," he murmured. "And these conversations you overheard? Were they injurious to *Donna* Armenia?"

Giovanni once again glanced towards the closed door. "Not because of anything *she* did," he whispered. "Of her own accord, I mean to say," he quickly added. "The conte, though, he..." Here Giovanni swallowed. "He allowed his friends to court her even though they had no intention of ever marrying her." The way he said the word 'court' implied an entirely different meaning. "I once saw him accept a purse full of lira so a visiting aristocrat could spend the night with her."

Bile rose in Patrick's throat before he could swallow it, the bitter aftertaste a perfect companion for the rage that swept through him. "It is fortunate for the late conte that he is already dead, or I would see to it by my own hands," he said in a hoarse whisper. "He was supposed to be her protector. Not her... her *pimp*."

"*Sì*," Giovanni agreed. "I do not believe the current conte—"

"Your brother," Patrick interrupted.

"—is like his... *our* father."

"He had better not be." Patrick was briefly reminded that the ball he had attended the night before had been in honor of Edoardo's daughter's come-out. Until the girl was married, Armenia would be assisting with her attendance at various entertainments. She had invited him to dinner, which meant there either wasn't something already scheduled or it was due to start later that night. "I have been invited to dinner at Villa D'Avalos tomorrow evening," he added. "If you could be sure my dinner clothes are brushed out, I would appreciate it."

"*Sì*," Giovanni replied. "Do you require anything else, *signore*?"

Patrick shook his head. "That will be all until morning." Before the servant could reach the door, he asked, "Did you ever tell your mother what you discovered about *Donna* Armenia?"

Giovanni turned around, his head dropping so his chin nearly touched his chest. "I did not."

Patrick winced, realizing it was the gossip among the household servants that had led to Signora Ricci's assessment of Armenia.

She might have been no better than a prostitute—a courtesan—in the eyes of the aristocrats who bedded her with her brother's permission, but that didn't make her a whore in his eyes.

The proof would be his proposal. At some point during his appointments on the morrow, he would have to pay a call at a jeweler.

He needed a betrothal ring. And roses. Lots of roses.

CHAPTER 32
A RAKE, A ROGUE,
A LIBERTINO

Near midnight at Villa Montblanc

Instead of retiring to the parlor with the rest of his family, David made his way to the library and settled into an overstuffed velvet chair.

Only a single sconce lit the corridor outside the room, which suited him as he considered his brother's earlier words.

I would be remiss if I didn't tell you that there has been some hope that you and Vittoria might consider courtship.

The mere thought of courting Vittoria had him girding his loins, until he remembered how she had looked when she was descending the stairs the night before.

She had appeared positively regal. Confident. Gorgeous. Knowing what he did about her now, the silver gown she had worn might have been armor, her dove gray gloves gauntlets, the diamond-encrusted comb decorating her elaborate coiffure a weapon capable of wounding an adversary.

But it was her questing gaze that had caught his attention. She had been looking for someone, and from the way she had placed her arm on *Don* Luciano's proffered arm when she reached the bottom of the stairs, it was apparent she had found the subject of her search.

Don Diavala.

Of all the people in the ballroom for her come-out, why ever in the world would she be looking for him?

A rake. A libertine. A predator of young ladies.

Or her prey.

David sat up straight in the chair and blinked in the darkness.

Vittoria hadn't been seeking out the conte's son with the intention of joining him for a tryst. She had *wanted* him to lure her into an alcove. Wanted the opportunity to grasp his nut sac in her hand and squeeze the life out of it—and perhaps out of him.

From what David had learned from his brother, he now realized Luciano Nicholas Michael Tucci, heir to a *contea*, had been determined they be caught so Vittoria would be forced to marry him. He would gain her dowry in the process.

If her gown's skirts had allowed it, her knee might have done the damage David's knee accomplished. He had interrupted her assault on the conte's heir, though, and taken away a victory that should have been hers and hers alone.

Vittoria!

Stunned at how his body responded to his memory of the night before—to the memory of *her*—his cock hardened and his heart raced with excitement—David took a steadying breath.

No wonder she was so angry with him. Accusing him of being a rogue, a rake, and a libertine were probably the only insults she knew would hurt him.

I would be remiss if I didn't tell you that there has been some hope that you and Vittoria might consider courtship.

David banged the back of his head against the chair, the stuffing far too forgiving to cause any damage or any pain, for that matter. Nicoletta and Donald had probably told her to consider a courtship with him. She might have even been amenable to it if he hadn't interrupted her assault on the libertine.

I owe her an apology. Right now.

Without giving a thought to the time or to the impropriety of visiting a young lady's bedchamber in the middle of the night, David was up and out of the chair far too fast. He had to steady himself and, once he was out in the corridor, consider exactly which bedchamber might be hers.

Like his family, she was a guest at Villa Montblanc, Nicoletta having encouraged her to spend the night so she could join them on their planned outing to the Roman Forum on the morrow.

With all the bedchambers located on the second floor, David stood at the top of the stairs and glanced left and right. He knew their host's and his parent's apartments were at the ends of the corridor. That left three bedchambers on either side. He was fairly sure he knew where his cousins and their wives were staying—in the rooms on either side of his. That left the three bedchambers on the other side of the corridor.

He paused before the first and pressed his ear against the wood door. Not hearing anything, he moved to the second and was about to continue down the corridor when he thought he heard a soft sob. Lifting a knuckle, he was about to knock but feared it might be heard by others. Instead, he pushed down on the door handle. It easily gave way, and he opened it enough to poke his head through the opening.

A gasp was followed by, "*Chi c'è?*"

"It's only me, *mia donna*," David whispered, his relief at

opening the correct door quickly replaced by concern at hearing the familiar sounds of a woman crying. "What's wrong?" He carefully closed the door behind him and remained where he was, allowing his eyes to adjust to the soft candlelight from a bedside lamp.

Dressed in a nightrail, Vittoria was sitting on the edge of a bed with a linen handkerchief pressed to her cheek. Her bare feet, the toes red from being stuffed into her uncomfortable half-boots earlier that day, peeked out from beneath the hem of her gown.

At the sight of him, she quickly stood. With the flame from the candle lamp behind her, the silhouette of her naked body was evident. Her long raven hair had been caught in a braid that hung over one shoulder.

David swallowed, well aware his manhood was reacting in a most undignified manner. He bowed. "Apologies, *mia donna.*"

"I didn't mean to wake anyone," she whispered.

"You didn't," he replied, realizing too late he could have used her sobbing as his excuse for being there. "May I... may I join you?"

For a moment, she seemed uncertain of how to respond, and then it looked as if she might deny him. Instead, she waved toward the end of the bed, and David was quick to settle next to the corner post, leaving a good deal of space between them.

Meanwhile, she sat near the head of the bed with her arms crossed beneath her bosom. The position merely enhanced the shape of her breasts, her nipples apparent behind the thin cotton fabric.

"Pray tell, why are you crying?"

She sniffled and held out one of her feet.

Despite the dim lighting, David could see the red splotches where her half-boots had been too tight or where they had nearly rubbed the skin raw. He motioned with a hand. "Give me your foot," he ordered.

"Why?"

"So I can... rub it," he stammered. "It's a courtesy some men do for their wives, I'm told. Then I believe they see to it a shoemaker is employed to make custom slippers and boots so they fit their lady's feet better than those simply bought off the shelf." He paused and furrowed a brow. "Although I think the men still rub their feet."

She blinked several times, but finally did his bidding, jerking her foot when he took it in both hands.

"I wish to apologize, *mia donna*," he whispered, cradling her heel in one palm as he massaged the top of her foot between his thumb and fingers.

Vittoria inhaled sharply and sniffled. From the way her brows furrowed, he knew he had doubly surprised her. "For... for what?"

"Last night I thought I was... *saving* you from *Don* Luciano, but I realized tonight that you *wanted* to defend yourself. By yourself. That my intervention was unwanted. Probably unnecessary," he explained, changing his hold on her foot to rub the instep. Despite her slight inhalation of breath, he continued. "Mayhap unneeded, although I am glad I was there since I do not believe your gown would have allowed you to deliver the killing blow, so to speak."

She made an odd sound in her throat. "That's what the statue was for," she whispered, her eyes closing when she seemed to be enjoying his ministrations.

He chuckled softly. "Apollo was rather effective there at the end," he agreed. "You never did say if you were... injured."

Shaking her head, she sniffled again. "I was not."

"You were quite formidable," he said. "You looked as if

you were wearing armor, given all the silver of your gown and gloves." He lifted a hand to his head. "Your diamonds."

For a moment, she didn't seem to understand his meaning. "I didn't wish to be his wife, and I thought it best I make it clear at the very beginning of the ball."

"Ah. Mission accomplished," he said, allowing a wan grin after his initial wince. "Here. Give me your other foot."

This time she didn't hesitate, shifting on the bed so she could lift her other leg onto the counterpane all while gripping the hem of her nightrail to keep her knees covered. She used the handkerchief to wipe her nose as David went to work on the foot. "If the statue hadn't fallen on him, I would have stabbed him with the comb," she said, her voice too calm for speaking of such violence.

"Oh," he responded, not bothering to ask which body part she intended to stab. David nearly moved a hand to cover his crotch, but he continued massaging her foot. "Do you believe all men to be like *Don* Luciano?"

Vittoria's eyes rounded again. "Of course not."

Perplexed, David furrowed his brows. "Then why did you think the worst of *me*? Why did you accuse *me* of being a rogue?" he asked.

She lifted a shoulder. "Other than your name, I did not know anything about you."

"But even after you learned I was Donald's brother, you continued to accuse me," he countered.

"I didn't want you to like me," she stated.

David recoiled as if she had slapped him across the face, and he stilled his hands. "Why ever not?"

For a moment, her gaze remained directed at the canopy above their heads. "Nikky told me you might wish to court me."

Blinking, David made an odd sound in his throat. "My brother said something about it after dinner this evening," he murmured. His eyes suddenly widened when the delayed sense of offense settled over him. "What would be so bad about me wanting to court you?" he asked in dismay.

"You are English," she stated, the simple words said without censure.

He blinked. "So?"

"You live in England." Before he had a chance to respond, she added, "You're an aristocrat. An heir to a *marchesato*."

Furrowing a brow, he said, "You must know, *mia donna*, there are many young ladies who find that rather desirable in a man."

"Then you should court one of them."

David blinked again. "Well, I plan to," he replied.

"Good," she stated.

Although he knew he should have felt relief at how they seemed to have settled their differences, David didn't take his leave. Instead, he regarded her with a look of hurt. "Is there some reason you don't wish to do as your *Prozia* Adeline did? Become a marchioness and move to England, I mean?" he asked. "She seems to like it."

Vittoria shook her head. "I suppose I should welcome the opportunity, but..." She once again shrugged. "Roma is my home."

David finally nodded his understanding. "Very well." He took a breath and let it out. "Well, I suppose that's that," he murmured, standing. He turned to bow, but paused when he saw her staring at him with a look of disbelief. "What is it?"

She pulled her shoulders back and bent her knees until she could wrap her arms around her shins, leaving her bare feet still on display. She *huffed*. "You certainly give up easily."

Narrowing his eyes, David regarded her with confusion for a moment. "You... you little minx," he whispered.

Her eyes rounded as he approached her, and she quickly unfolded her body and got to her feet as if she might attempt to escape. He stood before her, his gaze taking in her features before he used a hand to lift the braid from her shoulder. He allowed the silken mass to slide over his palm, his gaze following it until the last of the strands fell from his hand.

To her credit, she didn't look away, nor attempt to move from where she stood. "Are you going to prove you're a rogue now?" she asked in a breathless whisper.

Torn between taking his leave or leaving her wanting more, he reached out with his hands to pull her face towards his. His lips captured hers before she could put voice to a protest, and he reveled in the quiet whimper he heard before she finally returned the kiss.

He continued to kiss her for an entire minute, his fingers not moving beyond her jaw and neck and his body never touching hers.

If he had pulled her closer—if their bodies had collided and remained pressed against one another—he knew he wouldn't be leaving her bedchamber that evening. He would accept her challenge, see to her ruination, and be forever known as a rogue.

They would be forced to marry one another.

She obviously didn't want that. He wasn't sure he did, either, so it was with a good deal of satisfaction when he was able to end the kiss, lift her hand to his lips to kiss the back of it, and then bow before taking his leave of her bedchamber without so much as a *"buona notte."*

As for sleeping, it would be hours before he even tried to close his eyes.

CHAPTER 33
CONTEMPLATING
IN THE DARK

Meanwhile, back in Vittoria's bedchamber

Unsteady on her feet, Vittoria practically fell back on the bed, her fingers clutching the counterpane for support.

She lifted one of her hands to her lips, her forefinger and middle finger brushing over the plumped pillows made more so by David's scorching kiss.

Had that really happened? Had she really *allowed* it to happen? Not once had she thought to bring up a knee or lift a hand with the intention of slapping him across the face.

She'd had no hint of his intentions.

She'd had no warning he would do such a thing.

He didn't even like her.

Or did he?

She supposed the moment she gave in and offered her feet to his therapeutic hands had emboldened him. Closing her eyes, she remembered how good his fingers had felt rubbing the balls of her feet, pressing against her arches, massaging her sore toes. The sensations had been positively blissful.

This was something he claimed husbands did for their wives? Not that she had ever heard, but she had lived a fairly sheltered life, her parents not allowing her in mixed company other than during dinners or *soirées*. No one talked about foot massages during such entertainments.

Pity.

She could imagine how the men might boast of their skillful hands instead of the other skills they hinted at with their double entendres and waggling eyebrows.

And hadn't he made some mention of seeing to it his wife would have a shoemaker create half-boots and slippers better suited to her actual feet and not some antiquated idea of fashionable footwear?

The thought of having her own shoemaker brought a smile to her lips, and she once again remembered the kiss.

She supposed he had merely proven her assessment he was a rogue. Yes, that was it. Take liberties by invading her bedchamber in the middle of the night, massage her feet, and kiss her senseless.

A rather effective strategy, she had to admit. She certainly enjoyed it.

All of it.

There had been that moment before he touched his lips to her when his fingers had slid over her cheeks and down to her neck, leaving tingles in their wake. That moment when their lips touched and his eyes had closed, and she could make out his long, dark lashes resting on the tops of his cheekbones.

There had been a stab of jealousy thinking his lashes were more lush than her own before their lips suddenly locked and she was forced to close her own eyes and concentrate on exactly what it was she was supposed to do during a kiss.

Apparently, a slight suckling was the only effort required

to satisfy him, for she was sure she heard his moan of contentment after only a few seconds.

Or was that hers?

That he could continue the kiss without inserting more than the tip of his tongue past her lips was a testament to his skill—or perhaps lack of it. He hadn't tried to invade her mouth with his entire tongue, nor had he touched hers in an effort to engage it in some sort of duel. Armenia had warned her only a few nights ago that men tended to kiss with their tongues in the manner of the French.

The idea of it had disgusted her.

So when David hadn't done anything more than touch his tongue to her teeth, she had been pleasantly surprised. Pleasantly pleased, for the sensation had been a tickle of sorts.

And he hadn't slobbered like some Alpenmastiff happy to discover his master.

She lifted her hands to her face, surprised to discover there were still tears on her cheeks. Glancing about, she realized she had dropped her handkerchief on the nightstand. Retrieving it, she wiped her face and sniffled one last time.

Pulling back the bed linens, she regarded the expanse of white and wondered what it would be like to climb into bed with a man.

With David.

An odd sensation fluttered through her abdomen, and she inhaled softly. Placing a hand over her belly, she grinned as she settled onto the bed and stretched.

Her feet no longer hurt. Her lips seemed to buzz with excitement. Her breasts felt heavy, the nipples hard enough to poke against the fabric of her nightrail. If she wasn't so tired, she might have left the bed and gone in search of David's bedchamber.

Make him finish what he had started, whatever that might be.

The thought had her eyes widening in shock.

What?

Give a rogue what he wants? Willingly?

Never.

CHAPTER 34
WITH THESE RINGS

The following morning

Rising to the sound of a soft rain, Patrick stood from his bed and chuckled softly as he attempted to stretch. Although he was sore in several places, his memories of what had caused the minor aches and pains made it all worth it.

He rang for Giovanni and was pleasantly surprised when the valet appeared only a few minutes later. "You're awake early," he said to the younger man.

"My mother insists I wake before dawn," Giovanni replied. "I have to help her with moving pots of water to the stove." At his employer's look of confusion, he added, "Today she does the laundry."

"Oh, of course," Patrick replied. "Tell me, what time are jewelry shops usually open here in Rome? Or perhaps I need to see a goldsmith," he considered.

Pulling a top coat and waistcoat from the wardrobe, the valet paused to stare at him a moment. "Most have already opened, *signore*."

Patrick gave a start. "Open until sundown, I suppose?"

he guessed. "Closed during the midday?" He remembered how few people were out whilst he and Armenia had been touring the last fountain the day before.

Giovanni nodded. "As are most of the shops," he agreed.

"Might you know of a nearby florist?"

His cheeks reddening, the valet said, "Around the corner." He pointed to the south. "For your special lady?"

"Indeed. I know I mentioned it last night, but I do plan to be married soon."

Shaking his head as he retrieved a cravat from a drawer, Giovanni said, "*Sì, signore.*" His brows furrowed. "Would your wife be moving in with you here?"

Patrick inhaled to answer and realized he hadn't considered living arrangements. Armenia had a villa. One that she had lived in nearly her entire life, or at least when her family was in Rome. All he could offer were rooms in a building he happened to own, staffed by a housekeeper who possessed a poor opinion of her. "Whatever we decide, I plan to keep you on," he said by way of assurance.

"And my mother?"

Lifting a shoulder, Patrick said, "I'll still require a house-keeper here."

"Very good, sir."

Patrick couldn't help but notice the sound of relief in the young man's voice.

*W*hen he finished his breakfast, Patrick followed the verbal directions Giovanni had supplied regarding a nearby jewelry district. He headed southwest on foot until he reached Via del Pellegrino, managing to avoid the puddles left behind by that morning's brief rain.

Tiny shops were lined up on either side of the thin

street, matching arches above each entry on one side while the shop with the number he sought—14—was on the opposite side. His attention went to the stone blocks set in a decorative pattern above the door's transom where the words *Gioielleria Herzel* were emblazoned. Above the main floor were another three stories of a building that included not only the jewel shop but several others. Shutters hung on either side of the windows, some open while others were shut against the morning sun.

The window adjacent to the door featured various pieces of jewelry on display, all set in gold. He admired a sapphire and diamond parure before ducking into the shop.

Once his eyes adjusted to the darker interior, he spotted a goldsmith in the back already at work. Shoulders hunched and an optical device strapped around his head, the man nodded in his direction and called out a welcome.

Patrick returned the greeting before he turned his attention to a glass-fronted display case. A black velvet tray behind the glass caught his eye.

A number of rings, all of them set in gold, were lined up from small to large. Some sported a gemstone while others were simply bands of metal. A few included engravings of leaves and flowers or a series of tiny letters.

Dumbfounded, Patrick stood and stared at the selection. Although he had come with the intention of simply choosing a wedding band, he realized he hadn't considered there would be options.

"Difficult to decide, isn't it?"

The words, said in English with a British accent, had Patrick giving a start. He glanced over to discover a young man staring at the same tray of rings, his arms crossed despite the brim of a top hat clutched in one hand.

"It is," he agreed. He stepped back, his brows furrowing

when he realized he recognized the man. "You were at the D'Avalos ball two nights ago," he said.

"As were you. David Slater, Viscount Penton," David said by way of introduction, holding out his right hand.

"Patrick McAdams. McAdams Textiles," he replied, shaking the proffered hand. "Pray tell, what is a British viscount doing here in Rome?"

"I'm on my Grand Tour with my cousins," David replied, his gaze going back to the rings. "They and my brother have all succumbed to the parson's mousetrap over the course of the past two years."

"And now it's your turn?" Patrick guessed, a smirk lifting the corners of his lips.

"Eventually," David hedged. "I found from past experience it's best to be ready."

Patrick regarded the young aristocrat with an arched brow. "Past experience?" he repeated. "So… did someone get away?" He winced at the thought the viscount could already be a widower, and he regretted having put voice to the flippant query.

David inhaled and let the air out in a *whoosh*. "Something like that. She liked the betrothal ring, so I let her keep it," he explained. "Her husband is now a rather good friend, and come to think of it, he's also a relative of sorts. Brother to my cousin's wife."

Obviously surprised by the young man's cavalier attitude regarding a jewel, Patrick said, "Rather sporting of you."

Shrugging, David continued to examine the rings. "It wasn't an heirloom, of course. I wouldn't bestow such a treasure on a woman until the actual wedding."

"*Posso aiutarla*?" *May I help you?*

The two turned to discover a young lady standing on the other side of the display. Engrossed in their discussion, neither had seen her approach from the back of the shop.

"*Possiamo vedere gli anelli?*" David asked. *May we see the rings?*

"*Sì*," she replied, pulling the tray from the cabinet to place it atop the display. She moved a candle lamp closer so the rings were better lit.

"How do you decide?" Patrick asked, aiming his query at David.

"Have you a lady in mind?"

"I do. I almost proposed yesterday, but, uh..."

"Thought better of it?" David guessed.

"I was interrupted. By a priest."

David chuckled softly and then suddenly sobered. "Did he... did he catch you kissing your lady, by chance?" he asked.

Patrick arched a brow in surprise. "He did, actually. It was most inconvenient."

David barked a laugh. "In the Pantheon?"

Glancing around the small shop, Patrick felt his cheeks grow hot. He lowered his voice. "How do you know about that?" he asked. "Were... were you there?"

"A few minutes after you, apparently," David replied. "I... I was escorting a young lady. We were with my brother and my cousins on a walking tour," he explained. "I wasn't going to kiss the girl, but the priest obviously thought that was my intention."

"Because?" Patrick prompted, once again displaying his teasing smirk.

David seemed to consider the query before he dipped his head. "Despite my protestations and behavior to the contrary, *Donna* Vittoria believes I am a rogue. But why the priest would think I am, I've no idea."

Patrick gave a start. "*Donna* Vittoria? D'Avalos?" he guessed.

Apparently not surprised Patrick would make the

connection—he had been at her come-out ball—David merely nodded.

"Huh," Patrick responded. "You think a ring will change her mind?"

David gave a start. "I have absolutely no idea," he replied. "I'm not even sure I like the girl."

"What?"

"Had you asked me my opinion of her yesterday morning, I would have told you she's a shrew. A spoiled rotten brat."

Chuckling, Patrick said, "Well, she is the daughter of a conte. But a shrew?" He suddenly sobered.

"What is it?" David asked, his dark brows furrowing at seeing the change in Patrick.

"Prior to her come-out ball, Vittoria was apparently only seen in the company of her parents and her aunts," he explained, remembering what Armenia had told him. "She's probably lived a rather sheltered life as an aristocrat's daughter, but she has been raised to be a proper young lady. Although she's not yet betrothed, she knows what's expected of her, especially if she ends up the wife of an aristocrat," he continued. "She's *Donna* Armenia's niece," he added.

"Great niece," David corrected him. "She is my sister-in-law's niece."

Realization dawned as Patrick stared at the young man. "Your sister-in-law is the Marchesa Montblanc?" he asked in awe.

"Indeed. My brother, Donald, married her a couple of years ago."

Patrick scoffed. "How is it a Brit would even know *Donna* Montblanc?"

David seemed to consider how to respond before he said, "Well, they met eight years ago in Catania…" He shrugged. "Donald was near the end of his Grand Tour at the time. When her father promised her to another, they pledged their undying love, and Donald returned to England, heartbroken, of course," he said dramatically. He rolled his eyes. "He didn't tell any of us what had happened until a fortnight before we set off on our Grand Tour—when he learned Montblanc had died and insisted he hurry to be with Nicoletta," he explained.

"That's quite a tale of young love." Patrick narrowed his eyes. "So... if you don't intend to propose to *Donna* Vittoria, pray tell, why are *you* here? In a jewelry shop?" he asked, waving to the tray of rings. He had to suppress a grin at seeing how the shopkeeper was staring at them. She probably couldn't understand everything they had been saying, but from her widened eyes, she obviously recognized the names they had mentioned.

David reached out and lifted a gold band topped with a sapphire. "I like to be prepared," he replied, examining the jewel in the light from the candle lamp. "And you? Who will be wearing *your* ring, if you don't mind me asking?" He turned his attention on Patrick. "The woman you were kissing in the Pantheon?"

Patrick cleared his throat. "That is the hope," he replied. "*Donna* Armenia, in fact."

"D'Avalos?" David asked in surprise.

"She is the one," he acknowledged.

The gasp that sounded in reply didn't come from David, and both he and Patrick turned to stare at the shopgirl.

"*Mi scusi*," she said, her face reddening with embarrassment.

"Why did you react so?" Patrick asked. From her blank expression, he realized she didn't understand his query. David repeated his words in Italian, and she dipped her head.

"*Abbiamo sempre pensato che Donna Armenia fosse una zitella.*" *We have always thought Lady Armenia a spinster.* She aimed the rest of her comment to Patrick. "*Lei merita un brav'uomo.*" *She deserves a good man.*

Although he didn't understand her every word, he nodded when he sorted the sentiment. "*Grazie.*" He pointed to the tray of rings. "*Hai qualche consiglio?*" *Do you have a recommendation?*

Without pausing, she lifted an oval ruby-topped gold band from the tray. "*Rossa,*" she stated. "*Il suo colore.*" *Red, her color.*

Patrick reached for the ring and examined the setting.

"Those are diamonds," David remarked, pointing to the gems set on either side of a rather large oval ruby. "And that ruby is... remarkable," he added in awe. He replaced the sapphire ring he had been holding and plucked another ruby-topped ring from the tray.

The cushion-cut gemstone wasn't nearly as large, and its setting lacked the diamonds on either side, but its color was exquisite. It would make an exceptional betrothal ring.

"I'll take it," Patrick stated, offering the larger ruby ring to the shopgirl. "Uh... *quanto?*"

"Don't pay more than two-thousand," David whispered, his attention still on the smaller ruby ring he held.

The girl pulled a tiny tag from the tray and held it out. Patrick and David both leaned over, but Patrick pulled out a pair of reading spectacles and settled them on his nose before he studied the tag.

1750.

He nodded.

David watched as Patrick pulled a purse from his waistcoat, his eyes widening as the older man dumped out the necessary *scudi romani* coins. "Do you always carry that amount of blunt on your person?" he asked in surprise.

"Not usually, no," Patrick replied with a chuckle. He nodded toward the ring David still clutched between a thumb and forefinger. "Is that for *Donna* Vittoria?"

David scoffed. "I haven't yet decided."

"Liar," Patrick teased, grinning. While the shopgirl counted his payment, he continued to regard David with amusement. "So, if not in the Pantheon, did you ever have the chance to kiss her?"

David nodded. "I did. Right after I massaged her feet," he murmured absently. "We walked a good deal yesterday."

A whimper sounded from the shopgirl, and they both glanced in her direction to see her busily securing the ruby ring in a hinged box.

"She was in a good deal of pain due to poor-fitting half-boots," David added, his gaze on the girl.

Patrick arched a brow. The shopgirl obviously understood more English than they had assumed, and he realized she would probably spread word of what she had overheard to everyone she knew. "Might you know of any *calzolai* near here, signora?" he asked.

She nodded. "*Signore* Rossetti." She pointed toward the front of the shop. "Across and up three," she said, holding up three fingers.

"What are you about, Mr. McAdams?" David asked, his suspicion evident. He handed over the ring he had been holding to the shopgirl. "I'd like to buy this one."

Pulling the tag from the tray, she held it out to him. He nodded and retrieved his purse from his waistcoat pocket.

"You might start your courtship on the right foot with a pair of half-boots made to fit your lady perfectly," Patrick suggested.

"No pun intended, I'm sure," David countered dryly.

"None at all," Patrick replied, accepting the hinged box from the shopgirl. He tucked it into a pocket. "Over in

America, they've begun making shoes specifically for left and right feet. Makes for much more comfortable footwear."

David finished counting out his payment and considered Patrick's comment. "I believe we have a shoemaker or two doing the same in London. In fact..." He stopped speaking, his eyes suddenly rounding. "McAdams, you're a genius," he stated, his gaze on his mind's eye.

Patrick gave a start. "Hardly, but..." He took the box the shopgirl was trying to give to David and handed it to him. "I'll take it," he said. "What has you so dumbfounded?"

"My great aunt Adele. She told us about her husband's cousin... uh, cousin's son," he stammered. "He fell in love with a woman who had a crushed foot—from some sort of accident with a horse—and he hired a shoemaker to make all sorts of shoes for her. Boots, slippers, dance shoes," he murmured. "All made specifically for each foot so they fit perfectly."

"Did she marry him?"

David grinned in delight. "Yes. Apparently she even loves him more than her horses," he added, stuffing the ring box into his waistcoat pocket. "*Grazie*," he said to the shopgirl.

Patrick screwed his face into a grimace. "Here I was thinking only of a ring and flowers," he whispered.

"Oh, those should work fine," David commented. They took their leave of the jewelry shop and made their way to the shoemaker's workshop. "Your *Donna* Armenia joined us for dinner last night," he commented.

"She mentioned she was due at the Villa Montblanc for dinner," he replied, curious if the viscount would provide any more information about her.

"She didn't say much, but given how many there were at the table, she probably couldn't get a word in if she had wanted to," David said.

"Did she seem... happy?" Patrick asked.

David furrowed his brows as if he was trying to remember. "Secretly so, now that you ask," he replied. "That must have been some kiss in the Pantheon."

Patrick resisted the urge to mention there was far more than a kiss exchanged the afternoon prior. "I'm rather surprised myself," he said. "As a widower, I never thought I would find another woman I would want as my wife."

"Love at first sight?" David guessed.

"Indeed. Despite my graying hair, I feel as if I'm twenty years younger," he claimed. He didn't mention that morning's soreness. The short walk had alleviated most of his aches and pains.

David chuckled and then sobered. "What if I really don't like her?"

Patrick halted and turned to stare at the viscount. "Then you wouldn't have massaged her feet, kissed her senseless—you did kiss her senseless, did you not?"

"I... I did," David acknowledged.

"Then spent four-hundred lira on a betrothal ring, and..." He motioned to the Rossetti *calzolai* shop. "We wouldn't be going in there to order specially made half-boots."

David nodded. "You're right," he said. He reached out to open the door when he noticed Patrick's sudden hesitance. "What?"

"How will you know what size to have him make the boots?" Patrick asked, preceding David into the workshop. The odor of leather and polish filled their nostrils.

"I held her feet in my hands," David replied, pantomiming his moves from the night before.

"You obviously liked her feet," Patrick teased, waggling his brows. His attention was caught by a few pairs of boots and slippers on a nearby shelf.

Although it took several minutes to make the shoemaker understand what he wanted, David was soon holding wooden carvings of various sized feet. He finally settled on one of a particular length but explained that it wasn't wide enough where the toes should go.

Another round of negotiations ensued, and soon the shoemaker had a drawing of a foot that suited David. Before he had a chance to pay the man, a young woman took the drawing and began transferring the measurements to a piece of leather she had stretched out on a workbench. Her brother was already working on the soles, a set of one-inch heels set off to one side.

"Color?"

"Uh... black."

"Three o'clock," the shoemaker said.

"Three o'clock," David repeated. "Please, keep the pattern. If this works, there will be orders for more," he said.

Nodding his understanding, the *calzolai* joined his children in the construction of Vittoria's half-boots.

Meanwhile, Patrick and David made their way out of the workshop and to the nearby intersection. "How did you get here?" David asked, not seeing another town coach.

"I walked. My apartment and office are near Piazza Navona."

"Would you like a ride? I borrowed a town coach to get here," David offered.

"Thank you, but I will walk."

"Might I ask when you'll propose?" David asked as the tiger opened the coach door for him.

Patrick nodded. "She has invited me to dinner this evening."

"So... during the dessert course?" David guessed.

"I doubt I'll make it to the first course," Patrick replied, his grin broad.

"Good luck, Mr. McAdams."

"To you, too. If this works, we'll be part of the same family."

He watched the town coach as the wheels clattered on the black brick street, glad for the serendipitous meeting. Although he remembered Armenia's list of places best suited for marriage proposals, he had already decided he preferred the privacy of her home.

Heading north, he found the florist Giovanni had mentioned and placed an order for red roses to be delivered to Villa D'Avalos as soon as they could. Seeing they had a dozen more, he ordered those be delivered at noon. He wrote notes for both with instructions on which ones were to be used for each delivery.

His hand gripping the ring box through his top coat pocket, he made his way to his office, wondering the entire time how he would manage to get any work done that day.

CHAPTER 35
A TOUR OF THE COLOSSEUM

An hour later

Despite the light rain shower that had awakened her earlier that morning, Armenia was pleasantly surprised to discover the marble tiles making up the courtyard of Villa D'Avalos were dry when she stepped out to meet the Montblanc town coach at eleven o'clock.

Nicoletta's servants were punctual.

Armenia pressed a gloved hand into the one offered by the tiger and stepped up into the coach, wincing at the slight discomfort she felt at the top of her thighs. The delicious soreness had her grinning, though. She felt at least ten years younger, and the mirror seemed to have agreed with her that morning.

She chuckled softly at realizing Nicoletta had sent the newest Montblanc equipage, the blue velvet interior not yet showing signs of wear. The *marchesato's* crest emblazoned in gold on the door reflected the mid-morning light.

She was barely seated when the coach lurched into motion and passed through the arched wrought iron doors to the street beyond. Settling back into the squabs, she hoped she hadn't overlooked any of the arrangements for that evening's dinner. If everything went as planned, she intended to invite Patrick to spend the night.

A frisson shot through her at the memory of their afternoon together. Would he have awakened sore from their time together? Had he put voice to a curse? Or had he smiled as she had, happy to know she would be seeing him again soon?

Given the light traffic, it didn't take long to get to Villa Montblanc. Most of Nicoletta's extended family was already in the front court choosing coaches for the trip to the Roman Forum and the Colosseum. Once the one in which she rode stopped, the tiger opened the door. Donald leaned in and greeted her.

"Pardon the delay. It seems we are missing Vittoria and my brother," he said. "And one of the coaches."

Armenia arched a brow. "Do you suppose they have settled their differences?" Try as she might to imagine the two of them having departed Villa Montblanc in the same coach, she thought it rather unlikely.

Donald guffawed. "Neither were at breakfast this morning. I may have blistered his ears last night," he added, rolling his eyes in frustration.

"So that is why you didn't join us in the parlor?" she guessed.

"Indeed."

"I will have a word with her," she replied. "I am sure it is merely a misunderstanding betwixt them."

He straightened and glanced back toward the house. "Well, here is Vittoria," he murmured. "She looks... happy?" he added, uncertainty sounding in his voice.

"She does indeed, and she is positively gorgeous on this fine morning."

Donald whirled to his left to discover his brother

approaching the coach from another that had just pulled into the courtyard. "Where have *you* been?"

"Seeing to a possible future," David replied, "and a guide book," he added, lifting the tome from beneath his arm. He nodded to Vittoria, who still displayed a flush of color at hearing his compliment about her appearance. He offered his hand. She placed her gloved hand into it and joined her great aunt so she was seated in the direction of travel.

"*Buongiorno, zia,*" she said brightly.

"*Buongiorno.* Feeling better? You're not limping."

"Not yet," Vittoria replied.

Nicoletta followed her niece into the coach and ended up seated between Donald and David. She inhaled deeply and let out a long sigh. "I almost insisted the children join us today, but I think it's best Antony spend time with his tutor."

"How is *Donna* Nancy fairing?" Armenia asked.

"She misses her mother, but she seems resigned to what has happened," Nicoletta replied. "She insisted on joining Antony when his tutor arrived. Claims she wants to learn how to read."

"Good," Armenia replied. "And Amalia?"

"Amalia is about to become even more spoiled than she already is, given how Mother and my new cousins insist on holding her," David said. He was grinning, though. A year ago, he wouldn't have so much as held a babe, but having spent a good deal of time in the company of Helen's younger brother whilst they were in Egypt, he discovered he had a special rapport with toddlers.

"You're the one who's spoiling her," Donald accused. "I saw you giving her a biscuit before dinner."

"So she would agree to play cards with me. I'm teaching her how to play whist," David said in all seriousness.

"She's only a year old," Donald countered.

"She's more clever than you think."

"You're a fool if you think you're going to teach a babe how to play cards."

Seated across from Vittoria, David ignored the accusation and said, "After we've seen the Forum, might we take a detour to Via del Pellegrino? I have an order I need to pick up after three o'clock."

Donald's eyes rounded, but he said, "I think that can be arranged."

Armenia displayed a similar expression for a moment, her gaze going to David. Their eyes briefly met, and despite the tight confines of the coach, he lifted one of his shoulders in a shrug.

Nicoletta inhaled softly. "Isn't that the jewel—?"

"I've ordered a pair of boots from a *calzolai*," David interrupted.

Nicoletta glanced down at his riding boots. "Oh, yes, yours do look a bit worn," she said.

David gave a start, but he didn't put voice to a reply.

*T*he trip to the Forum didn't take long, and despite the earlier rain, there were a number of other *turistas* admiring the ruins spread out below Palatine Hill. The coaches pulled up and parked in a long line outside the Colosseum.

"Where do we even *start*?" Barbara asked in awe, her gaze going to the ruins off in the distance to the east and north.

"Here at the Colosseum," Will said, waving toward the circular, four-story structure. "It's not completely intact, but then it is quite old," he said.

Diana stepped out of the coach and grinned.

"This isn't your first time here, is it?" Randy asked.

She shook her head. "Father brought us several years ago. Before Michael left for university," she replied, referring to her younger brother. Pulling her sketchbook from her satchel, she paged through it until a partially-completed drawing of the Colosseum appeared. She pointed out where she had drawn in a small olive tree that was now much larger. "I plan to finish this right now," she stated.

Randy chuckled, and once the rest of their party were out of the coaches and barouche, the group set off to climb a set of stairs that were still in good condition so they could wander through the structure.

"The south side was damaged in an earthquake," David said. He had the guidebook opened and was comparing a drawing in it to what they were seeing. "The original marble facing is missing, and many of the decorations have been stolen."

"It's so overgrown with vines and such," Helen remarked, her gaze going up to where arched corridors circled the amphitheater seating.

"The seats used to be marble, but it's long since been carted away for use in other buildings," Will commented. He was careful in where he stepped over the eroded stone making up the first level, pointing out places where Barbara needed to be careful.

"Can we continue to go up?" Tom asked, his gaze following the concourse.

"If you can find stairs that haven't crumbled to bits," Randy said, joining them.

"Where is Diana?"

"Out by the Meta Sudans. She's completing a drawing she started the last time she was here."

"You left her alone?" Barbara asked in shock.

"Lady Armenia is with her, as is Lady Vittoria. They have both been here and opted not to come in."

"Oh," Barbara said with relief. "What, pray tell, is the Meta Sudans?"

"It's another fountain," David replied. "The conical shape we saw inside that circle near the Arch of Constantine. Although..." He scoffed. "It says here that although there used to be a pool of water around it, it was given its name because it means 'sweating turning post'. Apparently the water didn't gush out as it does in most fountains but rather oozed out," he explained.

"I'm going to see if I can climb up and look for the women through those arched openings," Randy said.

"I'll join you," David offered.

They had made it to a set of eroded stairs and begun to climb when Randy said, "I couldn't help but notice that Lady Vittoria seems to have overcome her derision of you. What the hell happened betwixt you two?"

David made an odd sound in this throat. "I made the mistake of trying to save her from an overzealous would-be suitor at the beginning of the ball. As it happens, she is her own best protector."

A guffaw escaped Randy. "You're saying she bested a rake?"

"He was a rather handsome bloke, but now he has a broken nose, and his family jewels are probably no longer."

Randy's look of amusement changed to a grimace. "What did he do to her? And what did you do to him?"

David held up a hand as they made it to the next level concourse. "She did most of the damage. I only broke his nose with my knee, and Apollo delivered the death blow, so to speak."

"So... why was she angry with *you*? She called you a rogue." His brows suddenly rose. "Did you take advantage?"

"No!" David replied, stepping over a chunk of rock in order to make his way it into a belvedere. The arched opening looked out to the east, and he quickly spotted the three ladies. They were seated on a blanket one of the coachmen had seen to spreading out on the lawn. "As I said, I tried to help. She... took offense, though. Which is why she's been behaving as such a shrew towards me. But..." He lifted a shoulder and sighed.

"But?" Randy prompted.

"I, uh, talked with her. Last night. Made my case and cleared the air betwixt us."

Waving in the hope Diana might see him, Randy turned his attention back to his cousin. "You weren't in the parlor last night," he stated.

David dipped his head. "I went to her bedchamber."

"You *what*?" Randy glanced around, as if he feared they might have been overheard. "Were you *mad*?"

"Probably," David admitted. "But I don't regret it, and I don't believe she does, either."

"What did you do?"

"Well, she was limping into dinner last night, so I... I might have massaged her feet." He took a steadying breath. "Her naked feet," he added in a whisper. "I particularly liked her toes. The one next to her big toe is longer and—"

"Oh, my God!" Randy interrupted. "Who are you, and what have you done with my cousin?"

David gave a start. "Don't you massage Diana's feet?"

Randy blinked. Twice. "On occasion, but... we are *married*." His brows suddenly furrowed. "Wait. Does this mean...?" He let the query trail off when he noticed Diana waving at him. He forced a grin and waved back, blowing her a kiss.

"I am considering it. I arranged for a pair of half-boots to be made for her. To better fit her feet," David explained. "After I bought a betrothal ring. Which reminds me..."

"You're going to propose?" The look of disbelief Randy displayed was almost comical.

David sighed. "I... I haven't yet decided, but I wanted to replace the ring I allowed Lady Jane to keep."

"You do know she cannot accept the shoes," Randy said, not making it a question.

"No one has to know from where she got them," David argued. He nodded in the direction of the three ladies still ensconced on the blanket. "But I don't want her suffering because her aunts insist she join us on all these tours."

Crossing his arms over his chest, Randy regarded his cousin with a critical eye. "I'm not sure if you know this, but I remember thinking at the start of this Grand Tour that *you* were going to be in trouble all the time."

David blinked. "Oh. Because I'm amiable and handsome and all the ladies fall prostrate at my feet?"

Randy chuckled. "Something like that," he admitted. He sobered. "You realize she may not wish to leave her home. To leave..." He waved a hand to indicate Rome. "All this for a life in Oxfordshire?"

"London," David stated. "I won't be living in Oxfordshire any longer. I told Father I was going to see to learning the business of the marquessate when we return."

Nodding his understanding, Randy said, "I may be joining you there in a few years," he said.

"I'm counting on it," David replied. He glanced around the interior of the Colosseum. "Are you up for another level?"

"I am if you are."

The two set off in search of another set of stairs.

"What were you about to say earlier?" Randy asked. When David directed a questioning look at him, he added, "'Which reminds me...'"

Nearly breathless, they made their way to another

belvedere terrace and glanced out. "I met Lady Armenia's beau this morning at the jewelry shop."

"I didn't know she had one."

"He's an American. Owns a textiles firm."

Randy furrowed his brows. "The gentleman with whom she was dancing at the ball? I think she only danced the one time," he said. "Do you think he's after her fortune?"

David shook his head. "No," he whispered, his gaze on his mind's eye. "He reminded me of Father, when he talks about Mother," he murmured. "Bought her a gold band with a huge ruby and some diamonds."

Whistling softly, Randy chuckled. "That must have cost a fortune."

"Indeed. Two fortunes. I hope she says 'yes', for his sake."

"When will you propose?"

David chuckled softly. "I've only just decided I like her," he said on a sigh.

"You wouldn't have massaged her feet if you didn't, you dolt," Randy countered happily.

They moved away from the arched opening and stared down at the oval below. The floor was long gone, and the evidence of the underground tunnels and passageways supporting gladiatorial combat were visible despite having been partially filled in with dirt over the centuries.

"Um..." Randy said, stepping backwards until his back was pressed against the stone wall of the top tier.

"What is it?" David asked.

"I, uh, might be, uh..."

David noted how pale his cousin suddenly appeared. "Scared of heights?" he guessed.

Randy nodded.

"Oh. Well, do you think you could turn around and face the stairs as you go down?"

"That worked for the Red Pyramid," Randy replied in a quiet voice.

"*You* climbed the Red Pyramid?" David asked in surprise.

Randy nodded. "With Diana. We only went up fifty feet, but..." He gingerly set a booted foot down on the top step and turned to face David. "Could you go first? Maybe... provide some direction?"

Chuckling softly, David did his cousin's bidding for the top two concourses. Once they reached the first level, Randy faced the interior and easily skipped down the last set of stairs to join the rest of their party out on the lawn.

Diana held up her completed sketch, and he leaned over and kissed her on the forehead.

"I thought you were scared of heights," she said in a quiet voice.

"I am," he acknowledged. "But I wanted to see you."

She grinned and allowed him to help her to her feet.

"Bounder," she accused, tucking her sketchbook back into her satchel. "What's next?"

Will waved a hand to indicate the Forum. "All the rest of it," he said. He led the way as everyone followed.

At the end of the procession, David, who had passed off the guidebook to Tom, stood between Armenia and Vittoria. It took all his self-control not to inform the two of what he knew was in their futures.

Marriage proposals.

CHAPTER 36
A STROLL THROUGH
THE FORUM

few minutes later
"Do we go left or right?" Will asked over his shoulder. There were clear pathways in the lawn around the ruins of the Roman Forum as well as a pavement that appeared rather straight.

"Stay to the right and we'll loop around when we reach the other end," David called out.

They had already reached the Arch of Titus, where Randy attempted to read the inscription at the top.

SENATVS POPVLVSQVE ROMANVS DIVO TITO DIVI VESPASIANI F(ILIO) VESPASIANO AVGVSTO

"The Senate and People of Rome dedicate this to the Divine Titus Vespasian Augustus, son of the Divine Vespasian," he called out, his voice far more dramatic than necessary.

"Divine?" Barbara repeated.

"Titus was deified after his death," Will explained, "So, yes, he was divine."

Randy passed under the arch and read the inscription on the other side. "This monument, remarkable in terms of both religion and art, had weakened from age: Pius the Seventh, Supreme Pontiff, by new works on the model of the ancient exemplar ordered it reinforced and preserved. In the twenty-fourth year of his sacred rulership."

Will followed him and looked up, shaking his head slightly. "That wasn't there when I was last here, but then, this arch was in rather poor condition at the time. The restoration work has been well done."

"Says here it was done in eighteen-twenty-one," Tom said, the guidebook opened over one arm.

"What was that building there?" Helen asked, pointing north to what appeared to be mostly rubble atop a flat area. She had seen it from the Colosseum, where the foundations holding up the platform had been more apparent.

"The Temple of Venus and Roma," Tom replied. "Supposedly the largest temple in Ancient Rome."

"Felled by an earthquake?" David guessed.

"Indeed. It collapsed sometime in the early eighthundreds. Then a church was built there." Tom furrowed a brow. "It says here that Hadrian was rather clever regarding the choice of goddesses to honor with such a large temple."

"Venus, the goddess of love. Amor," David offered. "Reverse the spelling of 'amor' and you have 'Roma'," he added, his gaze darting to Vittoria. "The symmetry was perfect."

Vittoria's eyes rounded slightly, but she didn't put voice to a reply.

"That must have been a rather large building," Barbara remarked, pointing to one with arches on the front as well as multi-storied arches at the back.

"The Basilica of Maxentius," Tom announced. "This is about the highest point in the Forum and one of the last structures to be built here, sometime in the fourth century." He glanced around. "Maxentius built it, but when Constantine defeated him, he replaced Maxentius' statue with a colossal bronze statue of himself."

"He wanted anyone who visited this basilica to feel his power simply by stepping inside," Diana remarked. "The temple was an immense structure, and so was the statue—it was said to be forty feet high. Parts of it were discovered when the basilica was excavated in the late fourteen-hundreds."

"Where are they now?" Helen asked, her gaze directed to the interior of the ruin. "Surely something that large would still be here."

"Nine fragments of it were uncovered during the original excavation of the basilica, and they were moved to Capitoline Hill, in the courtyard of the Palazzo dei Conservatori," Diana explained, pointing to the hill at the eastern end of the Forum. "They are part of what they call the Capitoline Collection and were arranged by Michelangelo," she added. "Although the visible parts of his body were made of acrolith, a sort of composite material, the draped clothing was formed in gilt bronze, which was looted, of course," she added in disgust. She pulled out her sketchbook and turned to a page showing a drawing she had done of what the original statue might have looked like.

David scoffed. "He's posed exactly like Jupiter used to be shown sitting on his throne," he said. "Holding a staff in one hand and an orb in the other."

"It is possible the statue *was* originally of Jupiter," Diana replied. "There is some evidence the face was reworked to remove a beard and to change the shape of the forehead to better match Constantine's face and curly hair."

"Rather egotistical of him," Armenia remarked.

Vittoria tittered. "Men," she whispered.

"We're not *all* like that," David argued. When Vittoria

glanced over at him, he winked at her. A blush colored her face before she could break eye contact.

"Let's move on," Tom said, after clearing his throat. He didn't notice Helen's smirk, her amusement due to the conversation of the three that followed them.

"What is now the entrance to the Church of Saints Cosma and Damiano..." Tom pointed to a round building with a large bronze door and a couple of columns in front, "was originally The Temple of Divus Romulus."

"*The* Romulus? How is it in such good condition?" Randy asked in awe.

"No, not for the founder of Roma," Diana replied. "It was named for the son of Maxentius. He died at a very young age," she explained.

"The entrance is higher than I would expect," Barbara remarked.

"Indeed, but that bronze door is the original, and it says here, the ancient key mechanism still works," Tom said with excitement, his finger pointing to a page in the guidebook. He turned and faced east again. "Now *this* is considered the entrance to the Forum," he announced. "We're actually walking on what used to be the via Sacra," he claimed. "The road the victorious generals would have walked when they returned from battle."

"Rode in a golden chariot, you mean," Diana interjected.

"Pulled by four white horses," Tom read from the book.

"But they only did the processionals if a general killed at least five-thousand of the enemy and brought their lands under Roman control," Diana explained. "The procession would go all the way to the Temple of Jove on Capitoline Hill." She pointed straight ahead to indicate the hill.

Armenia glanced over at David. "She is quite the historian," she whispered.

David nodded. "Indeed. She remembers everything she's ever heard or read or seen," he explained.

"Which means she has to have read about it," Armenia pressed. Before David could agree, he saw Vittoria's expression of delight and nearly tripped.

"I suppose that comes in rather handy when she's in the midst of an argument," Vittoria commented.

"Oh, we know better than to argue with her," David assured her, which earned him a demure smile.

"What about *Don* Forster?"

David chuckled. "He knows better than all of us."

"I heard that," Randy said, but when he turned around, he was grinning. "I happen to like having my own encyclopedia at my side. She's an immense time-saver," he added, leaning over to buss Diana on the cheek.

Obviously stunned by his public display of affection, Diana blushed.

Unaware of what was happening behind him, Tom announced, "To the north is the Temple of Antoninus and Faustina."

"Those Corinthian columns are still in remarkable condition," Helen murmured. "All ten of them."

"That's because it's a church now. The Church of San Lorenzo degli Speziali," Tom said, his attention once again on the guidebook.

"The Temple of the Divine Julius would have been located here," he said, pointing to a platform and an altar, "and over there should be the Basilica of Aemilia." He waved to a few columns, but the rest was buried under layers of dirt and debris.

"Well, I know what *that* is," Will said, turning to face a rectangular brick building to the north. "The Curia Julia."

When Helen aimed a blank expression at Diana, her

sister-in-law said, "The Roman Senate. A rather tall structure given it didn't have any upper stories."

"Why such a high building?" Barbara asked, turning her query to Diana.

"It was a means to express its importance. Its grandeur, but I think it was also for the acoustics. With three hundred senators, it would have been necessary for them to clearly hear the speeches." Her attention went to a number of standing columns to the south, and she broke away from the group, pulling her sketchbook from her satchel as she hurried off.

"Can we go inside?" Helen asked.

"It's a church now," Tom said, silently reading from the guidebook. "This area out in front of the Senate was known as the Comitium, and this area out here would have been the Central Piazza," he stated, glancing around the flat area that surrounded them. "Apparently this was where they held gladiatorial competitions before the Colosseum was built, and there was a slave market here. Now it's called the *Campo Vaccino*."

"What did you say?" Will asked.

Tom pointed to some livestock that were grazing off to the south. "We're probably standing atop ruins, but..." He shrugged. "It's literally named 'cow field'," he said with a shrug.

"It appears to be a good pasture land," Randy remarked.

Will guffawed, his attention going to the Arch of Septimus Severus. "Ah, the arch celebrating the victory against the Parti," he said.

"The Parti?" Barbara repeated.

"A sworn enemy of Rome. Septimus Severus and his sons, Caracalla and Geta, were the victors," Will explained. "This arch marks the beginning of the rise of the Capitoline Hill and..." He pointed up to a ruin. "The Temple of

Jove, where they would make a sacrifice to thank the gods."

Randy was reading the inscription at the top of the arch, but he frowned suddenly. "There is no mention of Geta," he said. "In fact, it appears his name was here but it's been removed. Etched out."

"That's because Caracalla didn't wish to share the imperial power when Septimus died," David said, earning him a look of awe from Vittoria. "He ordered his brother's name be removed from the arch as well as from all historical documents after he killed his brother."

"No surprise there. Caracalla was one of the cruelest of all the emperors," Will commented. He waved to the large building at the end of the Forum. "Now that building appears to be part ancient and part Middle Ages," he said.

"The Tabularium," Tom replied. "The base is made of peperino and travertine blocks, and it has vaulted corridors and arched windows. Above that is the Palazzo Senatorio where all the offices and records of the Senate were kept." He read some more from the guidebook before adding, "Michelangelo remodeled it in the sixteenth century."

The group continued on to the next visible ruin, the Temple of Saturn. Only the temple's portico, entablature, and eight columns remained standing. Seated on a nearby marble block, Diana was continuing a sketch she had obviously started the last time she had been in the Forum.

Randy joined her, crossing his arms as he leaned against the block to watch her work. "Has anything changed?" he asked.

"The height of the weeds," she replied, grinning. "I merely wished to draw the capitals. I didn't have time to complete them when I was last here, nor did I have a chance to sketch the Temple of Castor and Pollux."

David, Vittoria, and Armenia sauntered by, and when

Vittoria overheard Diana, she said, "There are only the three columns left standing." She pointed to the west. Beyond the rubble of the Julia Basilica, another ruined temple, the three Corinthian columns could be seen against the backdrop of the Colosseum.

"Castor and Pollux?" David said in confusion. "They were Greek gods. Wasn't it against the Roman religious laws to have any temples of foreign gods inside the city walls?"

"Indeed," Diana replied. "However, an exception was made because the temple was built after one of the first victories of the Romans over the Latins," she explained.

The others in their group joined them, Tom still studying the guidebook and comparing what he was seeing against what was written. "It says here the Romans were so desperate, they invoked the gods, and the twins of Jove, Castor and Pollux, appeared on white horses and led the Romans to victory. At the very same time, they both appeared in Rome to announce the battle had been won."

"That temple was so important, it's said the Senate met there," Vittoria added. "It included the office of..." Here she seemed to struggle for a translation. "Weights and measures."

"But most importantly, it was where fathers gave their children their official names," Diana said. She stood from the block and announced her drawing complete. Randy offered his arm and they headed to the area below the three columns.

The rest of the party followed, their steps slowing when it was apparent there was only one more artifact visible. The women were happy to take seats on some marble blocks to rest while Diana worked on her drawing. Meanwhile, the men admired the remains of palazzos on Palantine Hill. "We'll have to tour those on another day," Will commented to Tom.

"Agreed. I don't know about you, but I am hungry."

"You're always hungry," Will replied, giving his nephew a punch on the shoulder.

When Diana completed her sketch, the group gathered near the last remaining arch before reaching the Colosseum.

"The Arch of Constantine," Will stated, his hand waving to the most imposing of all the triumphal arches in Rome.

Randy glanced up at the inscription. Although the original bronze letters were missing, the recesses left behind displayed the text so it was easy to read. "To the Emperor Caesar Flavius Constantine the Greatest, pious and fortunate, the Senate and People of Rome, because by divine inspiration and his own greatness of spirit, with his army and just force of arms, on both the tyrant and all of his faction at the same time, he avenged the State. We dedicate this arch decorated with triumphal insignia."

"Who was the tyrant?" David asked.

"Maxentius at the Battle of the Milvian Bridge. Around three-hundred AD," Diana replied. "As you can see, it's completely covered with scenes exalting Constantine and depicting the more glorious episodes of the Roman Empire."

"Well, I think Rome has conquered me," Barbara said wearily. "I apologize, but I do think I've seen enough for one day."

Murmurs of agreement had Donald waving to the coachmen. The equipage joined them near the base of the Colosseum, and they climbed into the coaches and barouche to head for Villa Montblanc and a late luncheon.

CHAPTER 37
A DETOUR
PROVIDES PRIVACY

few minutes later
  Once the coaches and barouche merged into the midday traffic of Rome, David surreptitiously glanced at his pocket watch.

Sitting opposite him in the barouche, Armenia asked, "Might you know the time, *mio don*?"

"Half past two o'clock, *mia donna*," he replied.

Armenia's eyes widened. "Oh, dear. Would you two mind very much if I had the coachman take me home directly? I have an appointment soon, and I really must change clothes."

Vittoria glanced over at her great aunt, her eyes widening. "Shall we have the coachman wave down one of the other coaches?"

"Whatever for?" Armenia asked.

"If we take you home straight away..." She directed a pointed glance at David. "I won't have a chaperone."

Armenia lifted a shoulder, but she turned her attention to David and said, "May I trust you'll be on your very best behavior with my niece, young man?"

David was about to turn around to tap the coachman's arm when he noticed her wink at him. He hesitated with his response, uncertain if she had done so deliberately or if she merely had something in her eye. "Of course, *mia donna. Donna* Vittoria rode with me yesterday after our walking tour. She can vouch for me." He didn't wait for Vittoria to say anything, turning on the bench to capture the coachman's attention. "Villa D'Avalos, *signore.*"

The coachman acknowledged the change of destination, and David turned around to discover Armenia and Vittoria whispering behind an open fan.

Pretending he didn't notice, David simply aimed his gaze at the passing scenery, eventually recognizing buildings they had passed the day before. "Do you live close to Piazza Navona, *mia donna?*"

"I do," she replied.

"*Zia* Armenia lives in a villa the family has owned for many generations," Vittoria claimed. "We worry about her, though," she said, as if Armenia wasn't sitting right next to her. "Living there all by herself."

The barouche slowed, and the tiger jumped down to open the wrought iron gate leading into the courtyard.

David studied what he could see of the house. From his brief perusal, he knew the property was well-maintained despite its age.

A reminder of that morning's encounter with the American Patrick McAdams had him grinning. "I rather doubt she's going to be living there by herself much longer," he replied.

"Whatever are you talking about?" Armenia asked, her dark brows furrowed in confusion.

"Oh, apologies, *mia donna*. I was merely remembering how *Signore* McAdams regarded you during the ball the other night," David explained. "I do believe he's in love with you."

Vittoria gasped, her eyes rounding as she regarded her aunt with surprise. Armenia appeared momentarily stunned. "Who is *Signore* McAdams?" Vittoria asked, her query directed at her aunt.

"An American," Armenia replied, lifting a shoulder in a shrug. "His business is textiles," she added.

"In fact, I wouldn't be surprised if he paid a call on you this evening bearing..." David paused, realizing he really shouldn't give away Mr. McAdams' intentions. "*Gifts*," he finished lamely.

Armenia blinked, her face displaying a blush. "You said that as if you are privy to his plans, *mio don*," she accused. "Rather cheeky of you."

"I suppose so. My apologies," David replied. "Still..." He clamped his mouth shut, struggling with how much he should say. He wanted to help the American in his pursuit of Lady Armenia, and he knew Patrick wasn't certain as to how she would react to his proposal, but he didn't want to undermine the man's attempts at courtship before he even had a chance to make a good impression on the spinster.

The coachman opened the door and held out a hand with the intention of assisting Armenia from the barouche. David scrambled out of the equipage first, though, and he turned and offered his hand instead.

Armenia placed her gloved hand in his and accompanied him to the front door of the villa. Before the butler had the door opened, David whispered, "He wants to spend the rest of his life with you, *mia donna*."

Reacting as if he had slapped her across the face, Armenia blinked several times. "And you?"

Confused, David gave his head a shake. "Me?"

"Are you going to spend the rest of your life with *her*?" Armenia nodded in the direction of Vittoria.

It was David's turn to react, and he chuckled softly. "That all depends, *mia donna*."

"On what?" she challenged.

David glanced in the direction of the barouche, not surprised to see Vittoria watching them with curiosity. "Well, first I have to make her *like* me," he said. "I would really prefer a match based on mutual affection, you see." He dipped his head. "Tell me, is it entirely inappropriate for a man to arrange for a pair of half-boots to be made for a young lady?"

Armenia once again blinked. "Have you already ordered them?"

He nodded. "I'm going to fetch them now."

She displayed a grin of delight. "I won't tell if you won't, and might I suggest you sit next to her in the barouche?"

David nodded. "*Grazie, mia donna*."

He lifted her hand to his lips and kissed the back of it. "I hope you'll give Mr. McAdams a chance to make you happy."

Her eyes widening at hearing David's comment, Armenia didn't have a chance to put voice to an answer when he bowed and rushed back to the barouche.

When David reached the barouche, he murmured the address of the shoemaker to the coachman. Climbing into the equipage, he took Armenia's seat next to Vittoria as the coachman closed the door.

"*Donna* Armenia told me I should sit next to you," he said, before Vittoria could put voice to a protest.

"She told me I was to allow you to do whatever you wished," she countered.

David blinked. "Uh... really?"

"Almost as if she *wants* you to ruin me." Despite hearing David's scoff of disbelief, she allowed a *huff*. "I cannot blame her. She agreed to help with my come-out and to see to it I was successful at landing a husband," Vittoria said sadly. "The sooner that's accomplished, the better for her."

David shifted on the bench when the horses pulled the barouche out of the courtyard and into the street. "I don't believe that's her motivation," he argued. "In fact, she has your very best interests at heart, *mia donna*."

"How do you mean?" she challenged.

David pulled one of her hands into his and gave it a gentle squeeze. "If I give you the answer, I'll sound like a braggart. I am a gentleman, and so you will have to ask her directly for her reasoning."

Vittoria inhaled softly. "She is not wrong, *mio don*. You will one day be a marquess—"

"Probably when I am well past fifty years old—"

"—Your family is wealthy—"

"Probably, but I intend to learn for certain when I take over as the man of business for the marquessate."

"Marrying you would be a sort of prize."

He turned to regard Vittoria with a look of confusion. "I've never thought of myself as a prize, but I suppose in a transactional sort of arrangement, I would be." He said this last on a sigh of disappointment and followed it with a rude sound from his throat.

"I am only a prize because of my dowry," she replied.

David scoffed loudly. "Hardly. You're gorgeous. You are far wiser than most girls your age. Able to defend yourself against the worst of our sex." He paused before adding, "And you've grown up in an aristocratic household, so you already know what's expected of you when it comes to being a... a helpmate and a mother."

Vittoria stared at him in wonder for a moment and seemed about to reply when she suddenly straightened on the bench, her gaze darting about. "Where are we going?" she asked in alarm.

"Oh, uh... I asked the coachman to stop at a particular shop so that I might collect an order I placed this morning."

She slowly settled back against the squabs. "What sort of order?"

David shifted on the bench, turning his body so he was at an angle to better face her. "Before I answer that, might I ask about the half-boots you're wearing today?"

She blinked at the sudden change of topic. "What about them?"

"I couldn't help but notice you weren't limping today," he replied.

She straightened one leg so the hem of her hunter green walking gown fell onto the top of her ankle, exposing the half-foot. The brown leather was well worn and far softer than the leather of the black half-boots she had worn the day before. "Different boots," she stated. "I would have worn these yesterday, but my lady's maid insisted I wear the black because the color of my gown required it." She didn't own any other color that would have worked with the azure blue walking gown she had worn the day before..

"Good," he replied.

"Good?" she repeated. The barouche stopped in an area where several streets intersected. She glanced around as David stood from his seat.

"*Sì*," he said. "Would you like to come along? I'll only be a moment, but I'd rather not leave you here by yourself."

She stood and followed him out of the barouche, gripping his hand as she took the two steps down to the pavement and glanced around. "Where are we?"

"Via Pellegrino," he replied. He offered his arm, and she

took it. Still glancing about in an effort to determine if she had ever been to this part of Rome, Vittoria finally gave up and simply followed him along a thin street. At the fourth shop on the right, he opened the door for her, and the unmistakeable scents of leather and polish assaulted her nostrils. "You ordered boots?" she guessed.

"I did," he replied, grinning. A dimple appeared in the base of one cheek, and she had to resist the urge to poke a finger into it.

The *calzolai* recognized David immediately and bowed to Vittoria. "*Benvenuti*," he said before calling out to one of his children. The daughter appeared with the half-boots, her eyes widening in delight at seeing Vittoria. "*Per Lei*," she said, holding out the footwear. *For you.*

Vittoria inhaled softly and glanced over at David. "I think these may be too small for you, *mio don*," she said.

"Oh, they are," he agreed. "But they should fit you perfectly."

Blinking several times, Vittoria stared at the half-boots and then at David. "For me?"

"*Per Lei*," he affirmed. "Would you like to try them on?"

The *calzolai's* daughter was already indicating a chair for Vittoria to use. Once she was settled, the girl knelt to undo the laces and remove the pair of brown half-boots.

Vittoria let out a sigh of relief. Despite their better fit, the brown ones had grown more uncomfortable with all the walking they had done that day. She watched as the girl slid the new ones onto her feet and quickly laced them. After tying a bow, she straightened and stood aside.

David was quick to offer his hand. "Do they fit?" he asked, worry evident in his voice.

Gingerly taking first one step and then another, Vittoria allowed a tentative grin. "They feel so different. As if they are made for each foot."

"That's because they are." He watched as she continued walking in a circle, her steps quickening as her smile broadened.

"But... how did you know what size to have them made?" she asked in awe.

He pantomimed holding a foot and massaging it before lifting a shoulder. "Am I to understand I got it right?" he murmured.

She nodded, tears pricking the corners of her eyes.

"Well, don't cry," he said, his eyes widening with alarm. "Are they giving you pain? Do they pinch? Do they..."

She didn't allow him to continue his query, lifting herself onto tiptoes to kiss his lips, her gloved hands gripping his arms for support.

Although someone gasped to her right and someone said, "*Oh, mio*," to her left, Vittoria was determined she be allowed to finish the kiss before she finally pulled away. It was then she realized his hands had gone to her waist, his palms pressed against her as if he, too, needed something to hold onto.

She stared up at David, relieved when she didn't see any sign of censure in his eyes. If anything, he seemed to be waging an internal war with himself, his brows furrowing with his questioning stare.

"*Grazie*," she whispered.

David's mouth opened and closed several times before he remembered they had an audience. "*Prego*." He motioned to the *calzolai*. "Be sure to keep the pattern, *signore*," he said. "In fact, make another pair in..." He turned to Vittoria. "What color would you like? Blue, for the gown you wore yesterday?"

Vittoria inhaled softly, stunned he would remember the color of her walking gown. She held out the skirts of the hunter green gown she wore. "Or green?" she replied.

"A pair in hunter green and a pair in blue," he ordered. "No hurry, though."

The *calzolai* nodded vigorously, a grin of delight lighting his face. "*Molto bene,*" he said.

"*Molto bene*, indeed," David replied. He accepted the package the girl offered, realizing they were the brown half-boots Vittoria had been wearing. He offered his arm and Vittoria took it, but before he headed for the door, he turned to face her. "Does this mean... you *like* me now?" he asked. "Or do you still think me a rogue?"

Vittoria arched a teasing brow. "Can it not be a bit of both?"

His mouth dropped open, but he apparently saw the glint in her eye. "You minx," he accused.

Her grin of delight lit up the entire workshop. "Finally," she whispered happily. She quickly sobered, though, glancing at the *calzolai* before she turned her attention back on David. "Does this mean you like *me*? Or do you still think I'm a shrew?"

She watched as David struggled to hide his sudden humor. "Can it not be a bit of both?"

Although she should have expected his response—he could tease her as readily as she had done to him—Vittoria couldn't help the moment of hurt she felt.

Perhaps it showed on her face, for he was quick with an amendment. "Actually, you have proven you're not a shrew, *mia donna*," he said.

Vittoria let out the breath she didn't realize she had been holding. "*Bene*," she murmured

"Mayhap a bit spoiled..." he adding, grinning before he leaned forward and bussed her on the forehead.

She inhaled softly, remembering how many times she had seen Donald do the same with Nicoletta. How she had seen their father do the same with their mother only that morning.

A form of apology. An acknowledgment of error.

A gesture of affection.

She watched as David turned and reached for the young girl's hand and kissed the back of it. The girl giggled, her grin wide as she blushed a bright red.

"*Grazie, signora, signore,*" David said to the girl and to the *calzolai* before he opened the door for Vittoria. The two took their leave of the shop, Vittoria happily stutter-stepping in her new half-boots as they made their way back to the barouche.

From the doorway of the jewelry shop across the thin street, a young woman watched the couple exiting the *calzolai*'s shop, and she grinned. "*Povero uomo,*" she murmured on a chuckle.

Poor man.

CHAPTER 38
ROSES, MORE ROSES, AND
A BATH INTERRUPTED

*M*eanwhile, *back at Villa D'Avalos*

Armenia watched as David bounded back into the barouche, struck by how much he looked like his older brother. How much he behaved like Donald had all those years ago when he was on his Grand Tour and had courted her niece, Nicoletta, in good faith.

At first, she had merely thought Donald was placating her niece. Doing her bidding because he was able to bed her—what young man would turn down the opportunity to experience sexual congress whilst on his Grand Tour? But she soon realized Donald had done so because he truly wished to make Nicoletta his wife.

How wrong she had been about Donald back then! The memory of the heartsick man's last night in Catania came back to her in a flash. The anger she had felt at what her brother had done. The rage she experienced when she learned Nicoletta would be marrying the much older Marchese Montblanc. How stunned she had been when Nicoletta later explained the motivation behind it all.

As her natural father, Montblanc saw their "marriage-in-name-only" as the means of ensuring he had an heir, and it gave Nicoletta the opportunity to live with her real father, a man far more caring than Enrico D'Avalos had been.

The cur.

As a result of machinations, Montblanc had his heir—his very own grandson—because of Donald. Nicoletta was left a titled lady with a fortune. And now they were happily married with another child.

Not only was he a doting father, Donald had proved his ability to manage multiple properties as well as the Montblanc fortune. He wasn't a spendthrift, even if he did tend to spoil his wife. Armenia was fairly sure he would spoil Amalia even more.

She was quite sure David would be much like his older brother in that regard. That is, if he did decide to court and marry Vittoria.

When Nicoletta had confided in her the week prior—to inform Armenia of her in-laws' impending arrival and her plans to act as a matchmaker for her niece, Armenia had been hesitant.

David was terribly young to be considering marriage, but then Donald had been about the same age when he first courted Nicoletta.

The crack of the coachman's whip brought Armenia out of her brief reverie, and she lifted a gloved hand to wave as the horses took the barouche from her courtyard. One of her own footmen saw to closing the wrought-iron gate, and before she could turn to go up the marble step to her front door, DeLuca had the door open for her.

Before she had even crossed the threshold, the scent of roses assaulted her nostrils.

"Roses?" she said, her attention going to a huge bouquet in a vase in the middle of the round table in the entry.

"*Si.* They were delivered earlier this afternoon," he replied in Italian, taking her parasol from her grasp.

Armenia stepped up to the bouquet, her gaze darting about the red blooms and surrounding greenery in search of a card. She plucked the tiny white envelope and quickly unfolded it.

I thought of you all night long. I look forward to our dinner this evening. ~ Patrick

Clutching the note in her gloved hand, Armenia inhaled softly.

"They are not the only ones, *mia donna*," DeLuca said.

She turned to stare at the servant. "What's this?"

"I put the second delivery in the vase in the dining room—"

"The second delivery?" she repeated.

He nodded. "They came at noon. Then the next bouquet arrived a short time ago. I put those in the vase in your sitting room."

Armenia blinked, finally allowing a tentative smile. "I shall have to discover who those might be from," she said, moving to the stairs. "Has cook everything she needs for this evening's dinner?"

He nodded. "All is in readiness, signora. I was about to go down to the cellars for the wine."

"Very good. Send Marcella to my apartment. I need to bathe and dress for dinner," she said.

"*Si, signora.*" He hurried off towards the servants' quarters.

Armenia followed the scent of roses up the curved stairs to the first floor corridor. The cloisonné vase in the dining room featured another bouquet of red roses, the note resting against the base. She quickly unfolded it, a gloved hand going to her mouth when she read the masculine scrawl.

> *I thought of you all morning. I look forward to our*
> *dinner this evening. All my love. ~ Patrick*

Collecting the notes, she rushed up the stairs and into her apartment, stopping at seeing the even larger bouquet of red roses on the low table in front of the settee.

The note poked out from between the blooms, and she pulled it out, half expecting to discover Patrick had changed his mind and had sent his regrets.

For this note, she opened it more slowly, tears pricking her eyes when she read his familiar words.

> *I am still thinking of you. I look forward to our dinner*
> *this evening. All my love and kisses. ~Patrick*
> *P.S. I plan to arrive with more roses, but first I must find*
> *some.*

Armenia tittered as tears streamed down her face, and she remembered what David had said only a few minutes ago.

"*He loves you.*"

How had he known?

"*Donna?*"

Armenia whirled to see her lady's maid standing at the door. "Oh, Marcella. I must bathe and change for dinner. I expect my guest to arrive in a few hours."

The servant dipped a curtsy. "I will see to it the water is brought up."

A half-hour later, Armenia stepped into the copper tub and groaned in relief once she was surrounded by the warm water. Her feet hurt from the earlier walk in the Colosseum and the Forum, and she wasn't looking forward to stuffing them into the slippers that matched her red dinner gown.

Sighing, she settled her head against the back of the tub and closed her eyes. Although she was aware of movement nearby, she knew Marcella would be preparing her gown and underthings, perhaps setting aside the bath linens for when she was finished soaking away the aches from the day.

The scent of roses had her grinning. Patrick's generosity meant several rooms would continue to smell good for at least a week.

"You're even more gorgeous than when I left you yesterday."

The words sounded as if they were said from far away, or perhaps because she imagined them in her semi-dream state. She inhaled deeply. "The roses are beautiful," she murmured.

The brush of a kiss on her cheek had her slowly opening her eyes to discover Patrick leaning over her, a bouquet of red roses clutched in one of his hands. He wasn't dressed for dinner but appeared to be wearing business attire. "You're here," she whispered in awe.

He chuckled. "Gladly so, but I merely stopped to drop off some more roses. DeLuca sent me up, I think because he didn't know where to take these," he said, indicating the flowers. "I'll return in a couple of hours for dinner," he added.

Blinking several times, Armenia gave a start and sat up in the tub. "I must have fallen asleep," she said. "I spent the day on a tour with Nicoletta's family. In the Forum," she explained.

"I didn't mean to wake you, but I... I had to kiss you," he said, grinning as he attempted to keep his gaze from sweeping over the surface of the bathwater. It was evident she wasn't wearing her shift, and his manhood reacted by hardening in anticipation.

He lifted one of her hands from the edge of the tub and kissed the back of it before he turned it over to kiss her palm.

She inhaled softly and then gasped when she saw how wrinkled her fingertips were. "Oh, dear. I didn't realize how long I've been in here."

"Would you like help getting out?" He set the roses aside.

"I'm not sure I want you to see me in all my glory by the light of day," she said, covering her breasts with one arm.

"Trust me when I tell you, it will be a treat for me."

Before Armenia could reply, he reached down and grasped both her hands in his and pulled her up. Water sluiced down her body, some splashing onto Patrick, but he merely gazed at her.

Once she was standing, he reached over and grabbed a bath linen from a nearby chair. He shook it out and quickly wrapped it around her. "Do you require another?" he asked.

"This will be enough," she replied, ensuring she was mostly covered. "*Grazie.*"

He dipped his head. "I should leave. Let you finish. I need to dress as well," he said.

She glanced over at the roses. "Are there any roses left in all of Rome?"

He chuckled. "Not anywhere near here," he acknowledged. "But I've certainly made friends with a number of florists."

"No doubt," she replied dryly.

He pried one of her hands from the towel and kissed the back of it. "I'll return soon."

Nodding, she leaned forward and kissed him on the

cheek. "Thank you for the roses. For the notes," she whispered.

"I wonder what you'll think when you read that one," he teased, nodding to where he had left the bouquet. He bowed and took his leave.

Armenia waited, listening until the sounds of his boot heels faded down the marble stairs. Once she was sure he was gone, she carefully lifted the roses. Glad the florist had wrapped their stems with a linen—she didn't wish to be impaled by a thorn—she found the note and pulled it out.

Marcella appeared in the doorway, a look of confusion on her face. "I thought I heard a man's voice," she said, hurrying to pluck another bath linen from the stack on the chair. She unfurled it and wrapped it around Armenia's shoulders.

"You did. My dinner guest," Armenia replied. "Could you see to putting these into water for me? I'd like them on the dressing table."

Marcella nodded, taking the bouquet from her mistress. "*Sì, signora.*"

Once her lady's maid was gone, Armenia unfolded the note and tittered.

> *I do not believe I can wait any longer to see you today. I look forward to our dinner this evening and to every other dinner we share for the rest of our lives.*
> *All my love and kisses and my heart. ~Patrick*

Inhaling a shaky breath Armenia, knew she would be hosting Patrick for far longer than just dinner that evening. She might require him to stay with her the following day as well.

Now she had to decide if she would be willing to host him for the rest of their lives.

A most pleasurable sensation rolled through her abdomen at the thought, and she moved a hand to her belly. "Perhaps I should stop thinking of reasons to deny him," she whispered.

Refolding the note, she hurried to her bedchamber so Marcella could do her hair. For the entire time the lady's maid spent on her coiffure, they were surrounded by the scent of roses.

CHAPTER 39
ROGUES AND
KNIGHTS AND SHEEP

*M*eanwhile, in a barouche David glanced over at Vittoria at the same time she turned her head in his direction. The two grinned as if they had been caught sneaking candy from the kitchens.

"What are you thinking?" he asked.

She dipped her head. "That I want you to like me."

Chuckling, David said, "I would have thought the half-boots might have proved it."

"Oh, they did what you intended. But I cannot help but think you feel..." She paused a moment, as if she was struggling to come up with the correct word in English. "*Obbligato*," she finally said. "Because you no doubt have learned the plans my aunt had for you, and I can imagine you would not wish to disappoint her. She is your sister."

David blinked. "Pardon?" He stared at her until the barouche jerked at a sudden turn. "What are you talking about?" A memory of the conversation he'd had with his brother the night before came to mind, but the details were lost in the haze of the alcohol he had consumed.

"Aunt Armenia might have agreed to see to my come-out, but it is Aunt Nicoletta who has decided to play match-maker on my behalf," she replied.

David stiffened. "Has she... found someone for you?"

Vittoria swallowed. "I believe she thinks..." She huffed. "I think she has *you* in mind."

Nodding thoughtfully, David said, "Well, I must admit I am rather honored she would hold me in such high regard."

Gasping, she stared at him. "You are?"

"Well, of course. Surely there must be someone here in Rome that you think would suit you better," he said, managing to hide a wince at the thought she might end up married to someone else. Especially when he had already decided he was going to propose.

He had the ring. He had her to himself for at least another few minutes. What the hell was he doing suggesting other candidates?

"I danced with several of them two nights ago," she replied. "None were men with whom I wished to spend my entire life," she said.

David stared her. "Not a single one?" *Not even me?*

She shook her head. "At least three enjoy the beds of... *mistresses*," she said in a whisper. "Two are in desperate straits and in need of a dowry to pay their creditors. One prefers the company of men," she added sadly. "Perhaps I really do believe every man is a rogue," she said sadly.

"Not all of us, no," he replied defensively. "I will admit, it is good that you were not raised to expect all men to be..." He waved his hands in frustration. "Knights in shining armor, but to suspect they are all libertines is not fair to those of us who are not."

Her look of confusion cleared after she interpreted his meaning. "Aunt Nikky was very lucky," she said.

David finally nodded. "My brother is a good man," he

acknowledged. "We were both raised by the same parents. The same aunt and uncle."

The barouche suddenly stopped, and the two glanced around to discover they were back at Villa Montblanc. "That was fast," he murmured.

Once the tiger had the door opened, David jumped down and turned to help Vittoria from the carriage. Before he could offer his arm to her, he realized they were being watched.

His father stood leaning against the front door, his expression suggesting he was not a happy man.

"Father, what's happened?" he asked as they approached him.

Will held up his pocket watch. "The other two coaches arrived here over an hour ago. Where have you been?"

"We had to drop Armenia at her villa," Vittoria replied, cradling the package containing her old half-boots in her arms. "She is hosting a guest for dinner this evening."

His expression softening, Will seemed to accept her explanation. He motioned to her package. "Did you take another detour?" he asked, his query directed to David.

"Yes, Father. I... I saw to it *Donna* Vittoria has a more comfortable pair of half-boots," he admitted. "Her feet were damaged from yesterday's walking tour."

Will's brows shot up. "Did you... did you *buy* them for her?" he asked, his voice lowered as if he only wished for David to hear the query.

"I did, Father. I know it was inappropriate—"

"But it was very appreciated," Vittoria said, positioning one foot so it appeared from beneath the hem of her gown. "They fit to perfection, so he has arranged for two more pairs to be made for me."

Glancing down at her foot, Will made an odd sound in his

throat. His censure was apparent, but before he could scold his son, David said, "It worked for one of your cousins, Father. I was told he found a shoemaker in London who could make bespoke footwear for his lady who had a crushed foot. He ordered a dozen pairs of slippers and boots for his bride-to-be."

Will gave a start. "I suppose your Grandmother Cherise told you about that?" he guessed.

David shook his head. "Great Aunt Adele did."

Unable to hide the sudden humor he felt, Will said, "Whatever you do, don't tell your mother."

"Oh, she was there when Adele told us about it," David replied.

Will crossed his arms and regarded the couple for a moment before his eyes widened. "Are you two...?"

Vittoria turned, stood on tiptoes, and kissed David on his cheek. "I'm very lucky to have met him, *mio don*," she said.

"... getting married?"

David cleared his throat. "She hasn't yet asked me, Father," he teased, a grin appearing when Vittoria gasped. "I, uh, should probably have a word with Conte D'Avalos and continue the conversation *Donna* Vittoria and I were having before our arrival."

Vittoria inhaled softly, her cheeks coloring with her sudden blush. "Perhaps after dinner?" she prompted. "I must go and change clothes."

David nodded, and Will opened the door for her. When she was out of earshot, Will turned to David and shook his head. "I thought you didn't like her?"

"Because I thought she was a shrew. She is not," he replied.

"I thought she didn't like you," Will pressed.

"Because she thought I was a rogue, because... well, she

has been raised to believe there are no honorable men," David replied.

Will gave a start. "And you've proved otherwise?"

David considered the query for a moment. "I am trying very hard, sir."

Will once again glanced at his pocket watch. "If you leave now for Palazzo D'Avalos, you can probably secure an appointment with the conte for the next day or so," he suggested.

Glancing back at the barouche, David realized the coachman was waiting for orders. "That's an excellent idea," he said.

He didn't bother saying a farewell but rather jogged back to the barouche, told the coachmen his new destination, and climbed into the equipage.

Will watched from where he stood and chuckled softly.

A half-hour later, Palazzo D'Avalos

Reviewing what he intended to say to the conte in his head—in English—David was about to translate it into Italian when the butler approached him.

He hadn't expected to gain an audience with the aristocrat on this day. He had merely thought to secure an appointment. Learning from the butler that the conte was not only in residence but in his study had David asking if he might be allowed to meet with him. He had watched as the servant crossed the large space David recognized had been used as a ballroom only two nights prior.

Two nights?

Now the space was barely recognizable, a number of settees, chairs, and end tables set up on Turkish rugs to emphasize the placement of the huge, carved marble fireplace that dominated one wall.

For a moment, David wondered why he hadn't noticed it during the ball and realized it had been hidden behind a mirrored panel. Farther back, he recognized the corridor into which *Don* Luciano had taken Vittoria. Around the corner from there was the alcove featuring the statue of Apollo.

He hoped Apollo had survived his tumble from the caryatid.

Before the butler could say anything, Conte Edoardo D'Avalos emerged from the corridor opposite the one that had David's attention.

"*Don* Penton, it is an honor to host you once again," Edoardo called out in accented English.

"*Mio don*, it is I who is honored to be received with no appointment," David replied, bowing to the conte.

"You are the second on this day."

"Oh?"

"Do you recall meeting an American gentleman during the ball?"

David nodded. "Patrick McAdams," he stated.

"That's the one."

"By chance, was he here to ask your permission for him to marry *Donna* Armenia?"

Edoardo gave a start. "Seems you know *Signore* McAdams better than I do."

"I might have crossed paths with him this morning. At a jewelry shop."

"Jewelry?" Edoardo repeated with appreciation.

"He, uh, he said he was going to ask *Donna* Armenia for her hand in marriage," David murmured, hoping the coincidence would work in his favor—two gentlemen asking for permission to marry the conte's relatives on the same day. "May I ask if you gave your permission?"

Edoardo chucked softly. "I will tell you what I told him.

Aunt Armenia will make her own decision as to whether or not she marries and to whom," he said with a sigh. "I have no say in the matter."

"Then I hope she agrees to his marriage proposal," David replied. "He loves her, and he's already bought the ring. A ruby ring."

Edoardo's eyes widened. "That man has wasted no time. He only met Armenia during the ball." He angled his head to one side. "And you? Did you happen to buy anything?"

"I bought a betrothal ring." David reached into his waist-coat pocket and pulled out the ring box. Opening it, he held it out for the conte's perusal. "I wish to ask permission to court your daughter."

"Vittoria?" Edoardo asked, his manner suggesting he was surprised. He bent down to look at the ring more closely.

David experienced a moment of hesitation. "Have you another?"

Edoardo shook his head. "Gods, no," he replied, grin-ning. "One daughter is quite enough." He suddenly sobered. "Have you ruined her?"

"No, *mio don*," David replied, closing the box with a *snap*. He tucked it back into his waistcoat pocket. "I believe I saved her from ruination the night of her come-out, though." He dipped his head. "Whether she wanted my help or not."

For a moment, Edoardo regarded him with a blank expression. "Oh, that nasty business with *Don* Libertino? Or *Don* Diavala—whatever they're calling the *merda* these days?" He made a dismissive motion with a hand. "I do hope your help was appreciated?"

David was still trying to hide his reaction to hearing the conte's assessment of Vittoria's attacker when he realized he was expected to provide a response. "Not at first, no," he said on a sigh. "But, uh, I have spent the last two days in her company —on our walking tours of the city—and I have managed to clear up any misunderstandings we had about each other."

Edoardo blinked. "She didn't spend the time complaining?"

David shook his head. "No, *mio don*."

"She didn't cry about her feet hurting? Her gown not fitting? Her hair giving her pain?"

Stiffening, David furrowed his brows. "She did not."

Obviously expecting a different answer, Edoardo seemed momentarily dumbfounded. "We are speaking of my daughter, Vittoria?"

"We are, *mio don*."

"Huh. Well, why, pray tell, do you wish to marry her?"

David thought the query odd, but he remembered the reason Don Luciano wanted Vittoria and thought to make it clear he wasn't after the young lady's dowry. "I have come to feel affection for her, *mio don*. I would not even have considered marriage for myself at my age—I am only twenty-three —but my brother reminded me he fell in love with your sister at that age."

Edoardo nodded slowly. "He did. Pray tell, where will you live?"

"In London. I will be seeing to the business of the Devonville marquessate. There is a townhouse there in which we can live, and *Donna* Vittoria will not be far from your *Zia* Adeline."

Edoardo displayed a look of appreciation for a moment. "Will you bring her back to Rome on occasion?"

"That is my intention, *mio don*."

"Are you quite sure she hasn't complained about anything?"

David suppressed the urge to chuckle. "Last night I

heard her crying and learned her boots had caused her great pain—"

"Now *this* sounds like my Vittoria," he said, rolling his eyes.

"I... I arranged for a pair of bespoke half-boots to be made for her this morning. Right after I bought the ring. We fetched them only an hour or so ago, and she is quite pleased with their fit."

Edoardo seemed impressed. "What will you do if she... does it again? Cries or complains?"

Sensing a trap, David allowed a grunt. "The same thing my father does to my mother."

Edoardo's eyes rounded. "And what might that be?"

"He kisses her."

Blinking, the conte stepped back. "He kisses her," he repeated. "Hmm."

"What say you, *mio don*? Am I allowed to court your daughter?"

Edoardo nodded. "Marry her in a fortnight, and I'll not only pay you her dowry, I'll give you the sheep."

David blinked. "The *sheep*, *mio don*?" he asked in confusion.

Already turning to lead them back to his office, the conte said, "You're not going to believe this, but the American who wishes to wed Armenia has the exclusive contract for the wool from my sheep. For his textiles business," he added, stepping behind his huge desk.

"Oh. Are they pastured on your land, *mio don*?" David took the proffered chair opposite but made sure to sit on the front edge of it.

"Indeed. And they can stay there for all I care."

Furrowing his brows in confusion, David asked, "Why would you give me sheep for which you have already secured a contract for their wool? Isn't that guaranteed income for you?"

"Because I didn't ask Vittoria if she approved," he replied in a quiet voice. "They're actually *her* sheep. I bought them for her when she turned nine or ten years of age."

David blinked again. "Might I ask... why?"

"Because she insisted she wanted sheep. I bought them for her to teach her a lesson, but I'm not sure if she has learned it yet or not."

For a moment, David simply stared at the conte. "Something about the *having* not being nearly as satisfying as the *wanting*?" he guessed.

Edoardo held up his forefinger. "That is the one."

"Ah." David sighed. "Well, I do expect I'll be doing some spoiling," he murmured. "Because I wish to."

"But not too much," Edoardo warned. He pulled a sheet from a drawer and held it up to the light from a candle lamp. "Here it is. I'll be sure it's included with the contract for the dowry," he said.

"So, I have your permission, *mio don*?"

The conte nodded. "You do. I'll send a footman with the contract when I have it drawn up." He chuckled softly. "And I'll send a note to my *zia*. She'll be pleased she won't have to chaperone Vittoria at future entertainments."

"*Grazie, mio don.* If you'll allow it, I will tell my brother and *Donna* Montblanc."

"Nikky will be pleased," Edoardo said, grinning. "Her *nipote* will also be her *sorella*."

Not having thought that far ahead, David nodded. "She will," he agreed.

When David took his leave of Palazzo D'Avalos, he let out a huge sigh of relief before climbing into the barouche.

He could hardly wait to tell Vittoria he had been given her sheep.

CHAPTER 40
NEWS ARRIVES

The missive Donald had been waiting for arrived only moments before the family returned from their outing to the Roman Forum. As the rest of the family headed up the stairs, the butler quietly handed it to him, saying only that a courier from Conte Russo's *procuratore* had delivered it. "He was instructed to wait for a reply," he whispered.

Donald broke the wax seal and unfolded the parchment, frowning when he was forced to decipher a masculine scrawl that seemed to have been written in an ancient form of Latin.

He let out a sigh when he reached the end. "Where is the courier?" he asked.

"In the kitchens," the butler replied. At Donald's look of surprise, he added, "He wishes to court the scullery maid."

Donald arched a brow. "Wait ten minutes and bring him to my study."

"*Sì, signore.*"

"And ask my father to join me there."

"*Sì, signore.*" The servant hurried up the stairs as Donald headed for his study. He wasn't even seated behind his desk when his father appeared at the door.

"You've had word of the girl? Already?"

Donald lifted a shoulder. "I may have employed a bribe to expedite the issue," he admitted. "Otherwise it may have been weeks before we learned anything."

"And?" Will prompted.

"Russo and I share the same *procuratore* here in Roma," Donald explained. "Essentially a solicitor. Yesterday I sent a footman with an inquiry as to Russo's estate, specifically the terms of his will as it relates to *Donna* Nancy and our intention to take her on as a ward should there be no close relatives." He held out the parchment. "If I've interpreted the language correctly, and I'm not sure I have, I think *Donna* Nancy is set to become your ward," he replied.

Will's eyes widened before he turned his attention to the legal document. "So soon?"

"No close heirs, so no one to contest the issue. Russo's last will and testament merely stipulates the amount of the girl's dowry to be set aside for when she marries."

"It appears the conte was in debt?" Will asked, his brows furrowing as he struggled to read the document.

"Not a surprise. Most aristocrats are, at least for part of the year," Donald acknowledged. "Russo was better off than most. There are unentailed vineyards on Sicily and his villa here in Rome that should cover the debt when they're sold. Beyond that, everything else belongs to the *contea*, which would go to the equivalent of the Crown if his cousin cannot be located."

Will nodded and turned his attention back to the document. "There is a reference to Latium?" he questioned.

"The region which includes Roma," Donald replied. "The laws vary somewhat from those of the Kingdom of the

Two Sicilies, of course. Latium is a papal state, but his only property here is the villa."

"Montblanc's estate is covered under Sicily, isn't it?" Will guessed.

Donald nodded. "For now."

Will grunted when he finished perusing the parchment. "Am I mad to take on the orphaned daughter of someone I've never even met?" he asked rhetorically.

Donald chuckled softly. "You would be mad not to, given Mother's position on the matter, and you'd be doing me a huge favor."

A knock at the door had Will turning around. The courier stood on the threshold, directing a curious gaze first at him and then seemed relieved upon seeing Donald.

"Tell the *procuratore* William Slater, Earl of Bellingham, has agreed to become the legal ward for *Donna* Nancy."

Will pulled a calling card from his waistcoat pocket and handed it to the courier. "My address in England is here," he murmured.

"Also inform the *procuratore* that her dowry is to be delivered here when the estate is settled," Donald went on.

"Delivered to you?" the courier asked, his surprise evident.

"To me. *Donna* Nancy is to become the Marchesa Montblanc no later than her nineteenth birthday."

His eyes wide, the courier nodded. "*Si, signore.* I will tell him." He bowed and backed out of the study.

Will whirled around and stared at his oldest son. "The Marchesa Montblanc?" he repeated. "He's only eight years old. A bit young to be choosing a bride, is he not?"

"He's the Marquess Montblanc, and he's quite adamant on the matter," Donald countered. "It may never actually happen, and I would never be that father so presumptuous as to arrange a marriage for his titled son—nor the ward you've just agreed to take on, but..." He sighed as he shook his head. "Antony has claimed she is to be his wife since he could first talk."

Will chuckled. "Saves me the cost of the girl's come-out," he said, grinning.

"I'll let you be the one to tell Mother that," Donald warned, a smirk forcing his dimple to appear. "Do you wish to do the honors with *Donna* Nancy?"

Inhaling deeply, Will said, 'I think I shall let Barbara be the one. Antony can translate for her."

"Although I've already agreed to annual trips to England, perhaps you can bring her to Rome or to Catania on occasion," Donald suggested.

His father lifted a shoulder. "I've already been informed we'll be returning on occasion," he said. "Especially since you keep giving us grandchildren."

Donald cleared his throat. "Shall we go up and tell our wives the good news?"

"Indeed," Will replied, although he gave his son a curious glance as they made their way up the stairs.

A few minutes later, shouts of excitement filled the second floor of Villa Montblanc. Tears of joy soon followed. While their husbands welcomed the news and seemed glad for Barbara and Will, Diana and Helen were especially happy to learn they would have a new cousin.

Only one person seemed perplexed by the news, although he had to wait for David's return before he put voice to his query.

"If Nancy becomes your sister, does that mean she will be my *zia*?" Antony asked of David, his voice quiet in the general ruckus that had erupted around them.

The viscount knelt down on one knee and considered

the query for a moment. "I will think of her as my sister, and your father might do the same, but she will never truly be your aunt," he said. "Is that all right?"

Antony allowed a sigh of relief. "This is good, because I could not marry my *zia*," he said in all seriousness.

David chuckled. "You already know you are going to marry *Donna* Nancy?" he asked in surprise.

His dark brows furrowing as if he thought his uncle was teasing him, Antony said, "*Sì*. Don't you know who *you* are going to marry?"

Opening his mouth to give a vague response, David quickly swallowed his answer. "Do I?" he asked rhetorically.

Antony fisted one hand and punched him on the shoulder. "You will marry *Cugina* Vittoria."

Allowing his foot to go out from beneath his knee, David tumbled to the floor of the corridor and stared up at the ceiling. "From the mouth of babes," he murmured with a chuckle.

CHAPTER 41

A BETROTHAL IS
BETTER IN PRIVATE

*M*eanwhile, at Villa D'Avalos

When DeLuca appeared at the door to her apartment with word that Patrick had arrived with yet another bouquet of red roses, Armenia couldn't help but titter. "I must be in possession of every rose in all of Roma," she commented, glancing at the clock on the fireplace mantel to see that it was two minutes past the hour.

The American was punctual.

"Indeed, *mia donna*. What should I do with *Signore* McAdams?"

"Escort him to the parlor. The roses can go in a vase in there," she instructed. "I will be there momentarily."

She had already dismissed Marcella for the evening, deciding that even if Patrick didn't spend the night with her, she wouldn't require the lady's maid's services.

Wondering at the sense of dread she had felt most of that day, Armenia decided she needed to come to terms with what was happening.

A man she had met two nights ago was either in lust with her, a situation she found curious since she was of the same mind about him, or he had decided she would make the perfect mark.

An older spinster in possession of her own villa and a modest fortune would appear to be a catch for any man in need of a home and blunt.

There was another possibility, of course. Dare she believe what David had said earlier that afternoon? That Patrick McAdams was in love with her?

He loves you.

Was it truly "love at first sight" that had him enriching every florist in town so he could fill her villa with red roses?

The way he had gazed at her when he had found her in the tub that afternoon—not with revulsion over seeing her obviously older body, but rather with an appreciative glance, as if his mere gaze had gently caressed her body beneath the water. There had been a hint of lust, enough so she thought he might attempt to take her to the bed for a tumble. But he hadn't.

Shivering at the reminder, Armenia stood from her dressing table and made her way to the parlor. Perhaps a kiss would alleviate her worry. Food and wine would certainly help dispel the uncertainty. A night in bed would seal the deal—whatever it might be.

*P*atrick took a steadying breath and then another. If he wasn't careful, he would pass out from having taken in too much air. He was already feeling light-headed.

He couldn't decide if the scent of roses helped or not. They were certainly potent, the velvety blooms casting off their heavy aroma with every step he had taken from his apartment to her villa.

DeLuca had seen to taking the bouquet from him when

they arrived in the parlor, and with practiced expertise, he had used a knife to cut off the ends of all the stems before placing them into a large ceramic vase.

From the blue and golden yellow design displayed on its surface, Patrick decided the pottery was probably Sicilian. Somehow, the colors didn't clash with the deep red of the rose petals but seemed to enhance them.

DeLuca filled the vase with water from a pitcher he had brought with him, and then, with a nod, he had taken his leave of the parlor along with the cuttings neatly wrapped in a linen.

"*Donna* Armenia will join you in a moment," were his last words.

How long ago had that been?

About to pull out his pocket watch, he paused when he realized he was being watched.

"Armenia," he breathed, coming to his feet. Unsteady on his feet at first—he really had been breathing too much while he waited—he paused before rushing up to take her into his arms.

"Patrick," she replied, the moment before he engulfed her in an embrace.

"I've missed you," he said, placing his forehead against hers.

She tittered. "You saw me—all of me—only two hours ago," she chided, inhaling the scent of his cologne. After breathing in rose-scented air for so long, the citrus and amber was a refreshing change. "You poor thing," she added.

"Don't you dare disparage your gorgeous body," he whispered, one of his hands moving down her side to rest on her hip. His gaze dropped down, although he could see nothing beyond her generous bosom. "Which looks especially fetching in red, I might add. My very own red rose."

Before she could reply, he lifted a hand to her chin and lifted it so he could kiss her on the lips.

Not a quick kiss of greeting. Not one so long as to become awkward. When their lips parted, they simply stared at one another until Patrick swallowed.

"I know we spoke of logical locations where marriage proposals should take place, but after careful consideration, I thought it best I simply ask you in your own home," he said, lowering before her until he was on one knee. "In the place you feel most comfortable. In the place where I have fallen in love with you even more than I already was. Armenia D'Avalos, will you marry me?"

She stared at him for several seconds. Despite suspecting they might use that evening to discuss marriage, she hadn't given a thought to him actually proposing. To seeing him kneel down on one knee as he pulled a hinged box from his top coat pocket. To seeing him opening it to reveal a huge ruby ring.

The light from the chandelier reflected off the stone, casting a shower of red glitter about the parlor. Or perhaps the effect was due to the tears that had collected in her eyes.

She blinked several times, and a barely there, "Oh," sounded as one hand went to her chest. "Patrick. It's gorgeous."

His face suddenly screwed into a grimace. "Apologies, my love."

"What's wrong?" she asked in alarm, thinking he had changed his mind. Pity, too, since she was about to give him her answer.

"Kneeling seemed appropriate when I rehearsed this in my head early today, but I didn't give a thought to what would happen once I was down here, and now I fear if I... if I don't stand up now, I might not be able to."

The comment struck Armenia with a combination of

relief and humor. She tittered. "Oh, dear. Let's get you up," she said, gripping his free hand with her own to pull on it.

Patrick straightened, still holding onto the ring box with his other hand as he stared into her eyes. When he was finally standing, he allowed a tentative grin. "May I put it on your finger?"

A tear escaped one of her eyes and made its way down her cheek. "*Sì*," she whispered. She waited as he plucked the ring from its velvet bed and reached for her left hand. When he slid the ring onto her fourth finger, it was as if she was watching it happen to someone else, as if her hand wasn't her own.

Until he brought it to his lips and kissed the back of it.

"I know it seems impossible—it's only been two days— but I *do* love you," he said in a quiet voice.

"Obviously," she replied, her gaze on the enormous ruby. On her slim finger, the stone seemed entirely too large despite the snug fit of the gold band. The two diamonds on either side of the ruby winked as she wiggled her finger. "When—?"

"This morning. I actually had the benefit of Viscount Penton's counsel whilst I shopped," he said.

Armenia widened her eyes at the mention of David. "Oh?"

"He was buying a betrothal ring at the same shop."

She blinked. "He... He knew you bought this?"

Patrick nodded. "He did. Gave me guidance on what to look for. He's obviously familiar with jewelry shops. With gemstones," he said, gently lifting her hand so he could once again kiss the back of it. "I'll never tire of doing this."

Another tear ran down Armenia's cheek. She had spent most of the day on David's arm, and yet he hadn't said a word about a ring purchase. "You said he was buying a *betrothal* ring?"

"He did. One with a ruby. Not as large as this one, of course, but it's quite pretty."

"For Vittoria?"

Patrick angled his head first to one side and then the other. "Probably. He seemed, uh, a bit uncertain, but by the time he had the ring and we had gone across the lane to arrange for a pair of boots to be made for her..." He shrugged. "I would make the wager there's a marriage proposal in her future."

Relief swept through Armenia, and she stepped closer to Patrick, wrapping her arms around his middle as she rested the side of her head against one shoulder. "If Vittoria agrees to marry him, my work is done," she murmured.

He embraced her, settling the side of his face onto her head. "Because you were seeing to her come-out?" he remembered.

She nodded.

"Does that make you sad or happy or—"

"Relieved," she said on a soft chuckle. She pulled her head away from his shoulder to glance up at him. "Relieved," she repeated. "It's not as if my life was in some sort of limbo, but I did feel as if I shouldn't be—"

"Seeing me?" he finished for her.

She nodded.

"And now?"

Her grin broadened into a smile. "I can marry you."

Chuckling, Patrick placed his hands at her waist, lifted her, and spun the two of them in a circle.

Armenia shrieked in delight before he set her back on her feet.

"Are you hungry?" she asked.

"Ravenously so. I've been running all over Roma in search of roses all day," he said, pointing to the vase of blooms DeLuca had left on the table next to the settee.

Armenia followed his gaze and sighed appreciatively. "I do love red roses."

"I'll see to it you always have some," he whispered, kissing the side of her head.

"With little notes in them?" She extracted herself from his hold and hurried over to the roses to search for his latest missive.

"Uh... it's not in the bouquet," he warned. At her look of disappointment, he added, "I, uh, didn't wish for it to fall out whilst I carried them here." He reached into a waistcoat pocket and offered her the note. "It's merely my proposal, I suppose. In case I passed out while I was waiting for you."

Armenia gently took the note from his hold, but she didn't open it. "Still, I wish to keep it with the others," she said in a quiet voice. "I've never received love letters before."

He scoffed softly. "As hard as I find that to believe, I am happy to hear it," he replied, kissing her forehead.

Her stomach grumbled, reminding her she hadn't eaten since that morning. "Let's go to the dining room. Dinner should be ready."

He straightened. "We're eating at a table?" he teased.

She hooked her arm into his. "Tonight we are. I don't want any crumbs in our bed."

Patrick gave a start and allowed a soft chuckle. "Our bed?" he repeated. "Does that mean—?"

"You're moving in, the sooner the better," she stated.

He allowed a chuckle. "I'm happy to hear it. I think you should know that even though I do own a building that could be renovated into a decent house... a... a villa, I would prefer not to live where I work," he replied.

"*Bene.* If you ever displease me, you'll have a place you can spend the night," she countered.

Patrick gave a start, but when he glanced over at her, he saw that she was grinning.

"Minx," he accused.

"I'll ask DeLuca to see to quarters for your manservant," she offered as they descended the stairs.

Patrick slowed his steps, and when they reached the first floor corridor, he paused to regard her with a look of worry. "Are you... are you sure?" He remembered their conversation about Giovanni from when they toured the fountains and the other they had shared whilst in her bed.

"I am," she replied. "He is my nephew, is he not?"

Reacting as if he had been slapped across the face, Patrick nodded. "I... I'm fairly sure he is. We talked about it last night. He has as much as confirmed what you said."

She dipped her head. "He has every right to be... bitter."

"He's not, though," Patrick assured her.

"Still, it's only right he be able to live here at Villa D'Avalos," she said in a quiet voice. "He may not have the name, but..." She lifted a satin-clad shoulder and sighed. "The sins of the father shouldn't reflect poorly on him."

"Or on you," Patrick murmured. He took a breath and let it out. "Thank you," he said.

When they entered the dining room, she asked, "Have you other servants you wish to bring along?"

Patrick stiffened as he held her chair for her. "There is only one other servant. My housekeeper—who is also my cook—but I have no intention of asking that *she* be accommodated here," he replied.

"Oh?" Armenia asked, her brows furrowing with her curiosity. A footman appeared and poured wine.

"She has rooms in my building. I'll keep her on as the housekeeper there," he explained, leaning to one side when another footman delivered a bowl of soup.

Armenia dipped her head. "Giovanni's mother?" she guessed, lifting her spoon.

He nodded. "If I dismiss Signora Ricci, I fear I will lose

Giovanni's services. He says she is too old to find suitable employment." About to take a bite of soup, he paused. "Is that... acceptable? For you?"

Her eyes widening in surprise, Armenia nodded. "It is kind of you to ask."

"Of course, I would ask. You're to be my wife," he countered.

Armenia inhaled softly. "So, if I were to ask you to let her go... to give her notice, you would do that?"

Patrick lifted a shoulder and sighed. "I would, of course," he replied.

"Then you will keep her on as housekeeper for your property," Armenia stated.

Blinking in surprise, Patrick allowed a slow grin. "I love you," he stated.

"I know. The sooner we finish dinner, I'll let you prove it," she teased.

Patrick lifted the soup bowl to his lips and drank it down in a few gulps.

CHAPTER 42
ANOTHER BETROTHAL IS ALMOST UNBELIEVABLE

*M*eanwhile, at Villa Montblanc

The reality of what he had agreed to when he had met with Conte D'Avalos the hour before was settling over David when the dessert course was served at dinner that evening.

Marry her in a fortnight, and I'll not only pay you her dowry, I'll give you the sheep.

Having spent the last half hour in the library researching marriage in Rome when he should have been changing for dinner, David had grown frustrated.

He was sure the D'Avalos family was Catholic. As an Englishman, he was Anglican. Would Vittoria even be allowed to marry him? Why hadn't her father asked about it?

David glanced down the table to where his brother was seated at the carver. "Brother, pray tell, how is it you and Nikky were able to marry?"

Conversation about the table suddenly ceased. Everyone turned to stare first at David and then at Donald, their expressions indicating their curiosity.

"I admit I had wondered the same thing," Will said.

Donald straightened in his chair. "Are you asking because she is Catholic, and I am not?"

"Yes," David replied.

Inhaling slowly, his gaze briefly going to his wife, Donald finally let out the breath in a *whoosh*. "You were there," he said. "We married in Catania. A priest performed the ceremony after Nicoletta received special permission from a diocesan bishop."

"So... you have converted to Catholicism?" Will asked. There was no censure in his voice, merely curiosity.

"I have," Donald admitted. "I find it's not so very different," he added. Redirecting his attention to his brother, he said, "Nicoletta's rank helped to secure the bishop's permission, of course."

David nodded his understanding. "Did it take long? More than a fortnight to gain the special permission?"

Vittoria looked up from her plate to discover several people had turned their gaze on her. "Why are you looking at me?" she asked meekly.

Diana and Helen quickly diverted their gazes to their husbands before pretending interest in their meals.

Tom and Randy exchanged curious glances, while Barbara seemed to be watching a Shrovetide football match, her head turning back and forth between David, Donald, and their father.

"Less than a week," Nicoletta said. "Might I inquire as to why you asked?"

About to pretend it didn't matter, David decided to give a truthful answer. "Although I have no intention of converting, I'm going to need permission if I'm to secure a particular flock of sheep," he said.

Everyone regarded him as if he was a candidate for Bedlam. "Why would you have to convert to Catholicism to acquire some sheep?" Randy asked. "And since when are you interested in *sheep*?"

"Because the sheep are part of a bargain," David replied, his gaze going to Vittoria. "Seems their wool is already contracted to that American who attended *Donna* Vittoria's ball the other night."

"Mr. McAdams?" Will asked.

"Him, yes."

"He's in textiles. Has quite a thriving business in Boston and is expanding his sources for wool and silk here in Europe," Will explained.

David pulled out his pocket watch. "I expect he is proposing to *Donna* Armenia at this very moment," he said.

Vittoria blinked. "How do you know this?" she whispered.

"I was with him this morning when he bought her a ring. A ruby and diamond confection that should match quite nicely with all the red roses he intended to bestow on her today."

"Oh, how romantic," Nicoletta breathed. "They make a very handsome couple."

"Is that why I couldn't find any roses at the florist today?" Tom asked in a teasing voice.

"She must not have known of his intentions," Diana said in wonder.

"She said *nothing* of being courted whilst we were in her company today," Helen remarked, completing Diana's thought.

"Mr. McAdams is quite in love with her," David stated. "And I think... well, I think she feels affection for him, too."

"That must have been some conversation you had in your equipage after we left the Forum," Will commented.

David nodded, his gaze darting to Vittoria when he realized she was staring at him. Her expression made her appear suspicious, and her next words confirmed it.

"Those are my sheep," she stated.

The dining room was suddenly quiet as everyone turned to stare first at her and then at David.

"Your sheep?" Nicoletta repeated. Her eyes suddenly rounded. "Oh! *Those* sheep," she said on a chuckle.

"However did you come to own your own sheep?" Diana asked, her curiosity genuine.

Well aware everyone was staring at her, Vittoria lifted a shoulder. "I asked for them. For my tenth birthday," she replied.

"My brother bought her ten sheep. Eight yews and two rams," Nicoletta confirmed. "Now I think there are more than seventy sheep in that flock. Edoardo always gives her whatever she asks for," she added on a sigh.

"Which is why I'm spoiled," Vittoria said matter-of-factly. "So now I wish to know why it is *my* sheep have become part of a bargain," she added, directing her gaze on David.

"I can see to it your sheep will continue to be your sheep, but in order for you to benefit from the contract your father signed with Mr. McAdams, we'll need to marry," he said. "Within a fortnight," he added, his manner rather serious.

With the sounds of gasps and scoffs surrounding him, he pulled the ring box from his waistcoat pocket and opened it. "Vittoria D'Avalos—forgive me for not knowing all your other names since you refused to tell me—"

"Amalia Sofia Martina Isabella," Nicoletta said, leaning over so she was as close as she could get to her brother-in-law.

"—Vittoria Amalia Sofia Martina Isabella D'Avalos," he repeated, rising from his chair so he could move around to where Vittoria sat on the opposite side of the table. "Would you do me the honor of becoming my wife?" He knelt down next to her chair and held up the ring.

His mother gasped. "I thought he didn't like her," she whispered.

"That was yesterday, my sweet," Will replied. "Do keep up."

Vittoria glanced around the table before she turned her attention on the ring. "Is... is that a ruby?" she asked.

"Indeed. It's merely a betrothal ring, of course. There will be another for the ceremony," he assured her. "I bought it this morning before I ordered your half-boots," he added, hoping the reminder of the footwear would convince her of his sincerity.

She sighed and her expression displayed disappointment. "How much did *Zia* Armenia pay you?"

David blinked. "What? Nothing," he insisted. "Wait. Are you saying I could have been bribed to propose to you?"

Nervous laughter erupted around the table as Vittoria took the ring from him and slid it on her fourth finger. "Well, now we will never know," she said, holding up her hand as she finally allowed a teasing grin. She wiggled her fingers before leaning over to kiss him on the forehead. "I will give you my answer later tonight," she whispered.

"Minx," he replied. He straightened and made his way back to his seat while the others at the table watched in disbelief.

Nicoletta exchanged a quick glance with Donald before she said, "Well, ladies, I think it's time we leave the gentlemen to their drinks while we have tea in the parlor."

Murmurs of disappointment followed the announcement, but the women stood and filed out of the dining room.

The men leaned back as a footman deposited glasses of

grappa before them. Once the servant had disappeared, they turned their attentions on David.

Randy held up a hand. "I wish to go first," he stated. "Best wishes, cousin, but what the hell?" he asked. "I heard you arguing with her all day yesterday. I fear you two are going to annoy one another to death."

"That could happen," David replied dryly.

"Me next," Tom said, holding up a hand. "Allow me to be the second to say best wishes and suggest that perhaps you might take her somewhere more appropriate—more romantic—for a proposal? Trevi Fountain, perhaps?"

"We would require a chaperone," David responded. "Sort of defeats the desire for privacy."

Will lifted a hand. "I would like to say I am not surprised, but I am, and I wondered if you had thought about the logistics of such a union."

David nodded. "I have. We'll live in the Devonville town-house in London. I told Conte D'Avalos I would bring her back to Rome every two years or so." He dipped his head. "Vittoria has relatives in London, and although Lady Morganfield is getting on in age, there are a number of cousins living there."

Nodding, Will said, "She may have more friends there than she does here."

"My turn," Donald announced. "First, I wish to thank you from the bottom of my heart, because Nicoletta has been hoping for this marriage for I cannot tell you how long," he said. "Yes, she gets whatever she wants—"

"Are you referring to your wife or to Vittoria?" Tom asked in a tease.

"Both, actually, but I could not have found a better wife in all of England," Donald admitted. "The fact that she came with the Montblanc fortune means our lives are far more comfortable than I could have provided on my meager earnings from my books, so there is that as well."

"You're welcome," David replied. He lifted his glass of grappa. "Here's hoping she accepts my offer."

"Here, here," they replied in unison, downing the liquor.

*M*eanwhile, in the parlor
Arranged in chairs and a settee in a semi-circle in front of the fireplace, Barbara and Nicoletta sat to Vittoria's left and Diana and Helen took the chairs to her right. Left in the settee in the middle, Vittoria held her teacup and saucer in her hands while a maid saw to completing the tea service.

Once everyone had been served and the servant had departed, a cacophony of voices sounded while Vittoria calmly took a sip of tea.

"One at a time, *mia donnas*," she said in a quiet voice. The women collectively stopped speaking all at once and then giggled at the sudden silence.

Helen tittered. "We sounded like a hen party," she said, helping herself to a lump of sugar from the sugar-pot. "Barbara, what are your thoughts? He's your son. Should she accept his offer?"

Vittoria held up a hand. "Before you say anything, know that we shall live in London."

The older matron nodded and angled her head to one side. "I have been rather happy to gain a daughter from this country, and although I never thought it could happen again, I will be very happy to welcome you as my second daughter," she said. "And hopefully Nancy as my third."

"*Grazie*," Vittoria whispered. "So you are aware, I didn't think *Don* Penton liked me, either. At least, not until today when his actions proved he more than liked me." She lifted the hem of her skirts to reveal her half-boots. "He had these made for me," she said. "And they are far more comfortable than the slippers I should be wearing with this gown. He has already ordered two more pairs in other colors."

"Oh," Diana breathed appreciatively. "So... do you like *him*? Because, truth be told, yesterday I thought you despised him."

Vittoria allowed a long sigh. "I fear I have been raised to believe the worst of men, and due to the circumstances of our original meeting—when I did not give him all my names—I thought he was like all the others."

"A rogue, you mean?" Helen asked softly.

She nodded. "Our aristocratic society here is filled with them. It is why *Zia* Armenia has not wed. But David came to rescue me from such a beast, and I did not trust his motives."

"He's not a rogue," Diana assured her.

"I know that now," Vittoria replied.

They all turned to Nicoletta, who was beaming in delight, tears pricking the corners of her eyes. "I am so happy for you," she said, the tears escaping to roll down her cheeks. "I have been planning this match for you since I met David two years ago," she said on a sob.

"Oh, Nikky," Vittoria said, leaning over to offer her aunt a handkerchief. "Don't cry."

"I may join her," Barbara said, sniffling.

Diana and Helen exchanged quick glances. "Are you going to accept his offer?" Helen asked.

Vittoria nodded. "Of course," she replied. "I told him I would speak with him tonight. That is, if we can do so without a chaperone."

"You're allowed," Nicoletta said, grinning despite the

tears that continued to stream down her face. "Mayhap the library, for the privacy," she suggested.

"*Sì*," Vittoria replied. "I'll go there now."

The other four watched her take her leave, their collective sighs of relief resulting in another round of giggles.

CHAPTER 43
A DONNA CREATES A ROGUE

ater that night
Having finished his grappa and determined there was nothing more to be said about his intent to marry Vittoria, David was about to make his way up the stairs when he heard his name spoken in an urgent whisper.

He glanced back down the corridor to discover Vittoria standing in front of the library.

"What are you doing?" he asked.

"Waiting for you. Nikky said we can use the library. For privacy," she whispered.

David's brows arched in surprise. "Does she think I'm going to—?"

"So we can talk," Vittoria interrupted.

David's look of relief was almost comical. "Of course," he said, holding out his hand to indicate she should proceed him. Once he was inside, he carefully closed the door, aware the other men were making their way out of the dining room and to the parlor to collect their ladies.

The carpet beneath his feet seemed to swallow up any

sound, and he silently thanked his sister-by-marriage for having suggested they meet here.

Although one of the sconces was lit on the front wall, the room seemed dark, especially toward the back where a set of sofas and chairs were arranged in front of the fireplace.

Vittoria took a seat on the large sofa and patted the cushion next to her.

David accepted the invitation, wrapping an arm around the back of her shoulders once he was seated.

He was surprised Vittoria settled her head against his upper arm. "Does this mean you're accepting my offer of marriage?"

She nodded. "Everyone seems very happy for us," she murmured.

David gave a start, realizing the women's reactions must have been quite different from the men's. "My brother is over the moon," he said with a chuckle.

"When I left the parlor, Nikky was crying. Tears of joy."

"Donald told me she's been planning this match for a long time."

"Two years."

He chuckled softly and leaned over to kiss the side of her head.

"I'm not going to do anything to make your life more difficult," he vowed. "I want what you want."

Vittoria lifted her head from his arm and regarded him with surprise. "What is it you think I want?"

He dipped his head. "A husband who cares for you. Who will provide protection, so you don't have to defend yourself. A place to live—we'll have a townhouse in London. You'll have blunt for the modiste and other shopping." He paused. "And apparently some sheep."

She playfully slapped his arm. "I don't need more sheep."

"Ah, but if we had them, we could sell the wool to Mr. McAdams," he said, taking one of her hands in his to kiss her palm.

She inhaled softly. "I accept."

He leaned over and captured her lips with his, kissing her until they both needed to come up for air. When her eyes darkened and her manner grew serious, David furrowed his brows. "What is it?" he asked in a whisper.

"If I wanted you to be a rogue now, would you?"

He stared at her in disbelief. "I'm not sure I know how."

She arched a brow. "Surely you know how to..." She pointed down to his crotch. "Perform sexual congress?"

His mouth rounding into an 'o', David stared at her in shock. "I... I suppose I do," he finally replied. Apparently his manhood did, because it was suddenly doing its best to escape his pantaloons. "Are you asking me to make love to you? Right now?"

She lifted a shoulder. "If we're to be married within a fortnight, then I would prefer to know what I'm to do on my wedding night," she said.

David swallowed. "Oh. So much for you being raised as a sheltered young lady," he murmured.

"Nikky said that in England, betrothed couples always make love before they are wed," she claimed.

"Did she now?" he countered. He glanced around. "You wish to do it here?"

She nodded and stood from the sofa, standing so her back was turned to him. "If it's all right with you, I would like to keep my... I'm not sure whats it's called in English... but you can take off the corset."

David furrowed a brow as he rose to his feet. "If I'm to remove your corset, then I'll be removing your gown and all your petticoats," he reasoned, undoing the buttons down her back. The mere act had his breath catching when the nape of her neck was exposed. He used the tip of a finger to push away the tiny hairs that formed a 'v', and he placed a kiss there.

She inhaled softly as her entire body shook in his hold. "That tickles," she whispered, although she was grinning when she said it.

"It's rather likely we'll create a good deal of noise," he warned.

"Noise?" she repeated, turning in his arms to face him.

He watched as her bodice seemed to free itself from her bosom and slide down. When he stepped back, the heavy gown slipped down her body to land in a puddle at his feet. He swallowed. "I have spent the past year overhearing my cousins make love to their wives," he whispered. "At night and in the mornings—"

"The mornings?" she repeated in awe.

"Yes, and they're quite... loud about it."

Her eyes rounded. "So the ladies like what their men are doing to them?"

He nodded. "Well, yes," he hedged.

"Then do that to me," she said.

David let out his breath in a *whoosh*. "You're sure?" He waved to the velvet-clad sofa. "Here?"

She nodded.

"I cannot believe this is happening," he whispered, turning her around to undo the ties of her petticoats.

"You did not expect I would wish to be bedded?" she asked, stepping out of the garments that had dropped to the floor. She bent down and gathered them into her arms before dropping them in a heap on a nearby chair.

"To be honest, I wasn't sure what to expect. Two nights ago, you were squeezing the balls of a man who wanted to perform this very same act with you." His gaze dropped to her torso, where her corset displayed a pair of rising moons that had his manhood doing the same.

"He only wanted to marry me for my dowry," she countered, reaching to undo the buttons of his top coat and waistcoat.

Deciding he may as well do her bidding, David kicked off his shoes and went to work on the knot of his cravat. "So... just so I understand, you never felt affection for him?"

For a moment, Vittoria looked as if she had been slapped across the face. "When I was younger, I imagined we would one day marry. I would have lots of babies, and he would be a doting father, and he would never share another woman's bed," she whispered. "But then I grew up, and I learned he had lots of lovers, and I realized he would always."

David shook his head as he pulled his cravat from around his neck. "I will be faithful to you and only you," he promised. "But..."

"What?" she prompted, pushing the coats from his shoulders.

"You cannot take a lover. It would be the death of me," he murmured, his gaze dropping to see her bare legs beyond the hem of her shift—her stockings ended at the top of her calves. Below them were the half-boots he had bought for her, a sight he found rather touching. She should have been wearing dainty slippers.

Her eyes rounding in surprise, Vittoria shook her head. "I would not. I will not," she assured him.

David wasn't sure if she was the first to make a move or if it was him, but soon the two were kissing with wild abandon, their hands smoothing down one another's bodies as he searched for the ties of her corset, and she pulled the shirt from his torso. Soon they were both free of the garments and falling to the sofa, their bodies pressed together as they continued to kiss.

David moved his lips from hers to her cheek and down her neck as he left a trail of kisses that had her inhaling softly. His hand cupped a breast through the fabric of her shift, and he felt her nipple pebble. He soon had his mouth over it, which had her whimpering with need. His entire body shivered when her fingers speared his hair, her fingernails scraping his scalp.

He wasn't sure how she managed to push the shift away so her breast was exposed to his ministrations, but he wasn't about to stop and ask as he suckled and licked her bare nipple. When he moved his attentions to the other, he murmured, "You have the most beautiful breasts, my love."

"I fear they will grow too large when I have babes," she whispered. "Like Nikky's."

He stopped what he was doing and glanced up at her. "You say that as if you think that is a bad thing," he commented.

"Isn't it?"

He guffawed. "No," he replied. "In case you haven't noticed, we Slaters prefer our women to have a bit of extra flesh." Sliding a hand down the front of her body, he captured the hem of her shift and lifted it to her belly. Using only a fingertip, he drew circles on her skin, which had her inhaling softly as frissons darted about under her skin.

"You have to tell me what to do," she whispered.

He slid his hand down between her thighs, his middle finger parting her folds in search of her womanhood. "Open for me," he whispered. He kissed her lips at the same moment he circled the tip of his finger around the swollen bud, gently coaxing it from its hiding place as her ambrosia coated his finger. "That's it, my love," he whispered.

He swallowed her mewl of pleasure and added two more

fingers to rub her in circles, delighting in how her hips angled up. When he inserted a finger into her wet channel, he watched in wonder at how her chest rose in response, how her eyes grew dark with desire. "You're gorgeous," he whispered.

From the way her breathing shortened, he knew she was close to her climax, and he rubbed her womanhood with the edge of his thumb as he inserted another finger into her channel.

Her reaction was immediate, her quiet cry escaping before he could cover her mouth his. When he felt her contractions slow and her body relax beneath his, he slowly pulled his fingers from her and wiped them on his hardened manhood.

"Aren't you going to... come inside me?" she asked, readjusting her position on the sofa so she could reach down to slide a finger down his erection.

David inhaled sharply and considered the width of the sofa. "Perhaps if you sit on me, it will be easier? I don't wish to cause you pain, especially since this is your first time," he murmured as he readjusted himself so he lounged against the back of the sofa. His manhood jutted up from its nest of curls, obviously aware of what was about to happen.

He watched in wonder as she quickly straddled him as he held onto her waist. "You're quite limber," he commented between pants for air. Then he nearly fainted when she suddenly pulled her shift from her body and her bare breasts were in front of his face. The wisp of fabric sailed off somewhere to his left.

"What do I do?"

"Um..."He reached for her hand and moved it to his manhood. "You'll need to guide it. But rub it on your wetness first, so it will go in easier."

He grunted when she did his bidding, stunned when she

angled her hips and the tip of his manhood was suddenly surrounded by her ambrosia.

"Oh," she breathed. "You're rather... thick."

"Take it slow. If you can't..." He growled when he was suddenly seated nearly all the way inside her. "Oh, I am not going to last long," he murmured, burying his face between her breasts.

"It doesn't hurt," she whispered. "But I feel... full inside."

He nodded. "Raise and lower yourself. I'll help," he said, gripping her hips to demonstrate what he meant. He lifted his own hips to meet hers, and soon they were engaged in a rhythmic thrusting that had both of them murmuring words of encouragement.

He moved his thumbs to where their bodies met, and when she cried out, he knew she was close. Knew she was coming, because his cock felt as if it was no longer under his control but entirely under hers.

The sensation, entirely different from when he took his manhood in hand and rubbed it, had his entire body ceasing as intense pleasure gripped him.

For a long moment, it didn't let go but simply held him suspended as if on a precipice. He wrapped his arms around Vittoria in an attempt to ground himself, and he realized he was suffocating, his mouth and nose pressed so hard against her. He finally pulled away and sucked in air at the same moment her lips captured his in a desperate kiss. His body shuddered one last time, and he growled as he went limp beneath her.

"Oh!" she gasped happily. When her eyes opened, she quickly sobered. "Are you all right?" she asked, her brows furrowing with worry.

He nodded as he stared up at her. "I'm in heaven," he replied, finally allowing a chuckle. "And very sleepy," he whispered.

She giggled and reached for her shift. She wadded it into a ball and placed it between their bodies before lifting herself off of him. When his manhood was free of her body, she stepped off the sofa. "Lie down," she said. She bent down to capture her petticoat.

"You have the most beautiful bum," he said, as he limply fell over onto his side and sighed.

She turned around, shaking out the petticoat so it settled over his body. "What is *bum*?" she asked, once again bending down to capture the other.

"Your... arse," he whispered. He lifted an arm to capture her waist and pulled her down so she had her back pressed to his chest. He slid the hand down to her hip and around the globe of her bottom to pat it before he bent his knees into the back of hers.

She wiggled her bum into his groin, and he growled with appreciation.

"What did you do with your shift?" he asked.

"It's still down there," she whispered. "Between my legs. It has the proof of my virginity."

The comment had him fully awake. He quickly lifted his head onto an elbow and leaned over her. "Are *you* all right? Apologies, my love. I should have asked sooner."

She turned her head to gaze up at him. "I am... fine," she replied happily. "It was *molto* better than I thought it would be, you rogue," she teased.

He grinned. "For me as well," he murmured. "I'll only ever be your rogue." He planted a kiss on her shoulder. "Sleep well. I want to hold you for a time before I take you to your bed."

She nodded and sighed. "*Buona notte.*"

"*Buona notte.*"

. . .

*S*everal hours later, David awoke from a dream so vivid, it took him a moment to remember where he was. Three boys had been playing near him as he held a baby girl. Next to him, Vittoria sat with her head leaning against his shoulder.

Vittoria!

He gave a start and chuckled softly when he realized she was still tucked against the front of his body.

His manhood had realized it, too, but he wasn't about to take advantage. Better he put her to bed and return to his own room.

In the morning, he would need to convince a bishop he was desperate to marry Vittoria D'Avalos. Perhaps Donald and Nicoletta could help in that regard, since they had arranged it in Catania.

David managed to rise without waking his betrothed and quickly dressed, although he left his cravat and buttons undone. He lifted Vittoria's gown from the chair and shook it out before carefully folding it. He did the same with the petticoat she used to cover him and added her corset to the pile.

Stacking her clothes atop her, he bent and lifted her into his arms, hoping the petticoat would continue to cover her lower half.

She mewled, her arms wrapping around his neck as if she understood she had to hold on to him in her sleep. He chuckled as he took one last look around the library to be sure he hadn't missed anything, and then took her up to her bedchamber.

He discovered the linens had already been turned down, making it easy for him to put her to bed and cover her. He kissed her forehead. *"Buona notte, mia donna,"* he whispered.

Making his way across the corridor to his room, he

paused before going inside when he realized he was being watched.

At the end of the hall, his brother was leaning against the door jamb, his arms crossed as he displayed a knowing grin. He shook his head. "A rogue in Roma, indeed," he said before stepping back into his apartment. Nicoletta appeared in his place, though, her smile radiant. "Welcome to the D'Avalos family," she whispered.

"*Grazie*, sister," he replied, a hand going to his chest. "Or should I call you *zia*?"

Nicoletta quickly sobered. "*Sister* will be fine," she replied before she closed the door.

David grinned and went to bed.

CHAPTER 44
EPILOGUE

Five years later

"*Buongiorno, mia donna*," Patrick murmured, stretching his arms over his head as he lay in bed. Morning light bled in from around the drapes, and he knew it was past time he rise for the day.

Armenia snuggled closer, one arm draped over her husband's chest. "Not yet," she whispered drowsily.

"I must get to the office, preferably before noon," he replied.

"Or you could retire," she murmured.

He chuckled and leaned over to place a kiss on her head. "Not yet, but soon."

She opened her eyes. "Really?"

"Probably," he hedged. "I've received word from England that McAdams' Textiles have the exclusive contract for all the wool from a huge flock of sheep somewhere in Oxfordshire."

Armenia sat up and stared down at him. "From whom?"

He lifted a shoulder. "Well, I'm not really sure. Something about an earldom—"

"Gisborn?"

Blinking, he considered the name a moment and nodded. "*Sì.* Do you know of it?"

"*Don* Randy Forster—David's cousin—is the heir to the Gisborn earldom. They were all on their Grand Tour together. Remember?"

"He was the one whose wife was an archaeologist?" he guessed.

"That's the one."

Patrick narrowed his eyes. "When Penton was here last month, he hinted he might be acquiring more sheep, but I thought he meant for the flock on your nephew's lands," he said.

Armenia tittered. "That flock is almost too large for the D'Avalos farms," she said. "Edoardo told David he'll have to buy him more land to accommodate next year's lambs."

"Will he, do you suppose?"

"He already did. Bought it in Vittoria's name since he still claims they are her sheep. The neighbor was happy to sell since he needed the money."

"*Don* Penton does spoil her," he teased.

Armenia displayed a grimace. "I don't consider buying land for sheep spoiling her," she countered.

"I was referring to all the other things he bought for her whilst they were here. And for all those children."

"They only have four," she said.

"In what? Five years?"

"Well, I'm sure Vittoria was already with child before the bishop allowed them to marry," she countered. "Who would have ever thought David would have to beg for a special dispensation? He was a viscount, and she's a D'Avalos, after all."

"If you'll recall, I had to beg as well," he reminded her.

She leaned over and bussed him on the cheek. "Only

because you insisted on us marrying in the Pantheon," she reminded him.

"Well, of course I would. It's where we shared our first kiss, under all those perfect numbers," he reminded her.

"I remember," she whispered thoughtfully. "Would you do it again?"

"Marry you?" he asked, his eyes wide. "In a heartbeat."

She sighed contentedly. "And what sort of ring would you give me?" She held up her left hand, the ruby and diamond ring glittering when it caught a beam of light from the window.

"Oh, I see what this is about," he said, chuckling. Leaning over, he opened the drawer in the nightstand and pulled out a wrapped package. "I was saving this for our anniversary, but I believe now is a better time to put it on your other hand," he said, giving her the box.

She inhaled softly, her gaze going from him to the box and back again. "You remembered," she whispered.

"Of course I remembered," he replied. "How could I forget the second best day of my life?"

"Second best?" she repeated, scoffing softly.

He saw her look of hurt and grinned. "The first was the day you accompanied me on the tour of all those fountains. The first day I kissed you. The first day I made love to you," he said. "Before that, I would have had to say it was the day my son was born."

She dipped her head, her attention on the box. "I am honored," she murmured.

"You can open it. I think you will like it," he said, motioning to the ring box.

Armenia opened the hinged box as if she thought whatever was inside might jump out at her. She gasped. "A sapphire ring," she said in awe. "It's enormous."

"With diamonds," he said, arching a brow. He grinned as

she slid it onto the fourth finger of her right hand. "I wanted you to have a gemstone that matched your ruby but in a contrasting color," he explained.

"Oh, Patrick," she said on a sigh. "It's gorgeous," she said, holding up both hands with her thumbs pressed together. She wiggled her fingers. "You do realize you're not going to the office in the next hour," she said as she climbed back onto the bed.

Patrick chuckled and settled back onto the mattress. "Do your worst, *mia donna*," he whispered.

"Oh, I intend to do my *best*, *Signore* McAdams."

It was noon before Patrick made it to the office.

*M*eanwhile, at Devonville House in Mayfair Will regarded the pile of correspondence on the silver salver his butler had set on the edge of his desk and sighed. Although he and Barbara enjoyed the entertainments available now that they were living in Mayfair, there were times he wished they could simply remain at Devonville House and enjoy a quiet evening with Nancy.

The girl had excelled at learning English and had taken a liking to her *piano-forté* lessons, the lively notes of her practice reaching him despite the music room being at the opposite end of the house.

He pulled a missive from the pile on the salver, immediately recognizing the even print of his oldest grandson. It wasn't addressed to him, though, but rather to Nancy. The thirteen-year-olds exchanged letters on such a frequent basis, he had been forced to ensure David budgeted enough to cover the postage—for the letters from Antony as well as for those Vittoria received from Nicoletta and Armenia.

About to call for the butler to have him deliver the letter, he discovered he didn't need to—Nancy was standing on the threshold to his study waiting to gain his attention. Since their initial return from Rome, she had grown at least twelve inches and wore her hair in what could only be described as a tumble of dark curls. Although Barbara frequently fussed over its inability to stay put in a coiffure, he continually reminded her the girl was only thirteen. *She doesn't need to look as if she's attending her first ball when she comes to dinner,* he would say, only to be met with sighs of frustration. *And neither do you.* If Barbara wasn't quick on her feet, he would have enough pins pulled from her graying hair so her locks would fall past her shoulders, leaving her complaining about her ruined hair even as she tittered in delight when he attempted to nibble her ear.

What came after had him grinning with self-satisfaction.

"Pardon, Papa, but is there news from Catania?"

Will chuckled and held up the letter. "Indeed. There's one for you from Antony," he said, holding it out in her direction. "I haven't even had a chance to read it," he added, implying he regularly read her correspondence before giving it to her.

She ran to his desk and plucked the missive from his hand. "Far better that you don't," she said.

Giving a start, Will asked, "Is my grandson writing impertinent notes these days?"

Nancy screwed up her face into look of confusion. "Impertinent?" she questioned, her dark brows furrowing. "I don't know what that means."

"Good," Will said. "I feared the marchese might already be sending you love notes," he added, his manner rather jovial. He pursed his lips and made kissing noises.

"Love notes?" she repeated, her manner entirely serious.

"Yes. With claims of how much he wishes to kiss you when you next see one another," he said, pulling another missive from the pile. He didn't notice her expression of guilt when he added, "Here. Give this one to *Nonna*. It's from Nikky," he said. "Probably word of another impending grandchild," he murmured, secretly glad for his oldest son. Donald enjoyed fatherhood as much as Nicoletta did being a mother.

Nancy took the note from him, dipped a curtsy, and hurried out of the study.

She would have to let Antony know to be careful in what he said in his love notes.

*M*eanwhile, at the Devonville townhouse in London

David Slater, Earl of Bellingham, sat back in one of the parlor chairs and watched as his three sons pretended to play a game of pall mall despite there being no wickets standing in the Turkish carpet. The mallets they wielded only hit the ball on occasion, sending them sailing over the parlor carpets until they either collided with the feet of furniture or hit the baseboard moldings.

In the crook of his arm, he held his week-old daughter, her face scrunched up in an expression that suggested either a wail would soon ensue or her nappy would require changing.

The memory of a vivid dream came to mind, and he inhaled softly before he allowed a chuckle.

"What are you laughing at, Father?" William asked from where he leaned on a mallet that was far too tall for his four-year-old grip.

"You," he replied. "All of you," he added, when Donald and Eduardo looked up from where they were lining up their balls.

William furrowed his dark brow, which made him appear as if he had already taken a seat in the House of

Lords and was experiencing a case of heartburn. Since he was the next heir to the Devonville marquessate, David thought it rather fitting.

"What did I do that was funny?"

David shook his head. "Nothing, my lord," he said. "I am simply amused on this day," he added.

He was imagining what Patrick McAdams might think when he learned he had the exclusive contract for wool from the flock of sheep that he had talked Randy into buying for the fallow land surrounding the Gisborn farmlands.

Although the heir to the Gisborn earldom had resisted the plan, he soon capitulated when Diana informed him it would make it easier for her to excavate the land to continue her search for Roman ruins if sheep cleared it first.

She had already unearthed a treasure trove of Roman coins and evidence there had been a Roman settlement on the lands north of the River Isis at some point in the past. The neighboring lands would no doubt yield more finds, further enriching the Gisborn coffers.

Only the day before, he had received the deed to land adjacent to the D'Avalos farmlands, a necessary purchase given Vittoria's flock of sheep had grown much larger since the couple's wedding. He had arranged for the purchase to be as if she had paid for it, so Vittoria's name was on the deed. He hadn't yet showed her the document, but thought to give it to her on their fifth wedding anniversary along with another ring as part of a sapphire parure.

He glanced down at his daughter, Barbara Armenia Nicoletta Slater, and wondered if she would ever be of a mind to ask for a flock of sheep for her tenth birthday.

He hoped not.

Lifting the bundle to his shoulder, he realized he was being watched and grinned.

"Here you all are," Vittoria said, her hands on her hips.

David couldn't help the way his manhood reacted. Despite it only being a week since the birth of Barbara, Vittoria was already slimming down, even if her breasts seemed to enlarge with every babe. "Hello, my love," he said, coming to his feet. He hurried over to take her hand to his lips. "Are you sure it's not too soon for you to be up and about?" he asked in worry.

She lifted herself onto tiptoes and kissed his cheek. "I merely gave birth," she countered. "I'm not ill."

"You're certain you don't wish to hire a nurse?" he pressed. Every other English aristocrat's wife employed a wet nurse to see to their babes, but Vittoria had insisted she see to feeding her own babes.

"I am sure," she said, taking the baby from him. "I'm surprised she's not complaining," she murmured.

"Not yet," he replied.

"She likes it when you hold her. They all do," she said quietly.

David kissed her forehead. "Your *Prozia* Adeline has sent word she wishes to meet the newest addition to the family."

"I already sent word I would pay her a call with Barbara on the morrow," Vittoria replied. "*Zia* Adeline is terribly old. I fear this may be the last time I see her."

David grunted. "You said that when you took every other one of our babes to meet her," he reminded her.

His own mother had been the first to pay a call at the townhouse, insisting—as she had with the boys—to be able to hold the babe between feedings. His father had spent far less time with the children, his duties as the Marquess of Devonville consuming most of his time despite David continuing his role as man of business for the marquessate.

Vittoria grinned. "So our babies prolong her life," she said.

Chuckling softly, David watched as she took her leave before he turned his attention back to his sons.

"Well, boys, what shall we do before you have to take your afternoon naps?" he asked.

A cacophony of responses ensued, and he glanced over at the card table. "Cards, it is," he said.

The three boys cheered and clambered up onto the chairs surrounding the green felt-covered table, and David proceeded to shuffle and deal.

Any day now, he expected he would win a hand.

AUTHOR NOTES

Fontana del Nettuno

Located at the northern end of Piazza Navona, this fountain didn't acquire its decorations of Neptune surrounded by tritons and mythological creatures until 1978.

Arch of Constantine

Besides being the most "imposing of all the triumphal arches in Rome," this arch is different from others in that it has three openings and is aligned along the street where victories were celebrated. The decorations covering it—statues and reliefs—are reused from older monuments. There are some who believe this was done to save cost or because there was a scarcity of skilled labor (many artisans were moving to the new capital of the Roman Empire, Constantinople). The other reason might have been to provide familiarity. People would have already seen the image of victories and Rome's power in other monuments, and these allowed them to easily connect Constantine's reign with those of the most beloved past emperors. Of course, all the faces on the decorations were changed so they looked like Constantine.

The Forum

Archaeological excavations hadn't been done in the area of the Forum prior to the time of this story. Covered in dirt and debris, it truly was a cow pasture. However, those on their Grand Tour were able to see what we have described in this story. The practice of reusing marble and stone blocks taken from older temples was a common practice, a form of recycling we can only lament these days.

ABOUT THE AUTHOR

A self-described nerd and lover of science, Linda Rae spent many years as a published technical writer specializing in 3D graphics workstations, software and 3D animation (her movie credits include SHREK and SHREK 2). Mythology, immortality, and ancient Greece have been lifelong interests.

A fan of action-adventure movies, she can frequently be found at the local cinema. Although she no longer has any tropical fish, she does follow the San Jose Sharks. She is a member of Novelists, Inc. and Wyoming Writers, Inc. and makes her home in Cody, Wyoming.

For more information:
www.lindaraesande.com
Sign up for Linda Rae's newsletter:
Regency Romance with a Twist
For articles on research and travels, read Linda's Rae blog:
Regency Romance with a Twist

* 9 7 8 1 9 6 8 0 1 4 0 3 2 *